WHEN LUCK RUNS OUT

BOOK THIRTEEN OF THE EMPIRE OF BONES SAGA

TERRY MIXON

YOWLING
CAT PRESS

When Luck Runs Out

Published by Yowling Cat Press ®

Digital edition date: 6/21/2023

Print ISBN: 978-1947376366

Large Print ISBN: 978-1947376373

Cover art - image copyrights as follows:

DepositPhotos|Ivankmit

Dreamstime | Philcold

Dreamstime | Marciomauro

Luca Oleastri

Donna Mixon

Cover design and composition by Donna Mixon

Print edition design and layout by Terry Mixon

Audio edition performed and produced by Veronica Giguere

Reach her at: v@voicesbyveronica.com

ALSO BY TERRY MIXON

You can always find the most up to date listing of Terry's titles on his Amazon Author Page.

Note: the links below (ebook only, obviously) redirect you to my website where you can click a button to go to Amazon. This allows me to participate in Amazon's associates program and earn a little more. Sorry for any inconvenience.

The Last Hunter

The Last Hunter

Bonds of Blood

Alpha Strike

The Enemy Revealed

Command Authority

The Grand Conspiracy

Shield of Humanity

Fog of War

Ships of the Line

Operation Liberty

The Empire of Bones Saga

Empire of Bones

Veil of Shadows

Command Decisions

Ghosts of Empire

Paying the Price

Recon in Force

Behind Enemy Lines

The Terra Gambit

Hidden Enemies

Race to Terra

Ruined Terra

Victory on Terra

When Luck Runs Out

Gunboat Diplomacy

The Imperial Marines Saga

Spoils of War

Imperial Recruit

Enemy Action

The Humanity Unlimited Saga

Liberty Station

Freedom Express

Tree of Liberty

Blood of Patriots

Single Novels

Scorched Earth

Storm Divers

The Vigilante Series with Glynn Stewart

Heart of Vengeance

Oath of Vengeance

Bound By Law

Bound By Honor

Bound By Blood

Box Sets

The Empire of Bones Saga Volume 1

The Empire of Bones Saga Volume 2

The Empire of Bones Saga Volume 3

The Empire of Bones Saga Volume 4

Humanity Unlimited Publisher's Pack 1

Humanity Unlimited Publisher's Pack 2

Want to get updates from Terry about new books and other general nonsense going on in his life? He promises there will be cats. Go to TerryMixon.com/Mailing-List and sign up.

DEDICATION

This book would not be possible without the love and support of my beautiful wife. Donna, I love you more than life itself.

ACKNOWLEDGMENTS

I want to thank the folks that support me on Patreon. You got to read this book as I was writing it and that kept me working. You have my deepest thanks.

In particular, I want to thank those patrons that supported me at the $10 level and above:

Bryan Barnes
Dave Dolan
David Goldstein
Eugene Humbert
Christian A. Michelsen
John Page
Keith Ramsey
Carl Rumbolo
Dale Thompson
Raymond Wang
Clark Williams

Finally, I want to thank my readers for putting up with me. You guys are great.

1

"Are we ready to flip?" Kelsey Bandar asked from behind *Persephone*'s command seat. There wasn't much room on the cramped bridge of the Marine Raider strike ship—which only held three control consoles—but they were all friends.

Until half a year ago, *Persephone* had been hers. Now Angela Ellis, one of her closest friends, was in command. She had to admit that Angela was far better suited to the task than she had been.

Her friend had really grown into the role since they'd escaped Terra. Any uncertainty the woman might've initially had about commanding a warship was long gone. Now she was a confident leader in charge of a well-trained crew.

Persephone wasn't working solo anymore, either. They'd linked up with Jared's fleet a month after they'd escaped from Terra. If push came to shove, they could now fight. At least they could when they weren't scouting.

They'd left that security behind and were now three flips away from support. Admittedly, they could get back to the fleet in just a few minutes because of the peculiar nature of the multiflip point network, but they'd be unable to communicate except with low-speed FTL coms.

That was something they'd only use if they had to. The gravitic pulses it used were hard to detect, but not impossible, and they dared not even hint at the technology to the AIs or their enslaved humans.

Carl Owlet turned in response to her question. As the resident scientific genius, he was still figuring out how the multiflip points worked. Thankfully, he'd made some progress as they'd crept ever closer to Twilight River, the home of the master AI that held the remains of the old Terran Empire in thrall.

"The probe we sent through the branch just popped back and reports that the other side is clear, but it picked up activity in the system. Nothing close enough to detect our arrival, though."

"Send the probe back and then take us through the flip point, Angela," Kelsey said. "You know the drill."

"Helm, make it happen," the big woman commanded. "Verify all systems are set to stealth nominal. We don't want to give the locals any indication that we've arrived."

"All systems verified, Major," Senior Lieutenant Jack Thompson responded. "Flipping the ship."

There was a brief churning inside Kelsey's gut before they vanished from one system and appeared in another, having traversed the distance between them instantly. Thankfully, her Marine Raider augmentation made the process a *lot* less disorienting than it had once been.

As they appeared in the new system, no one said a word, and the ship began launching additional probes to gather information about the system without giving away their presence.

It would take hours for the stealthed probes to determine who was in the system and what they were doing, but the location of the system itself should be easy enough to identify based on the starfield.

"Fiona," Kelsey said, glancing toward the ceiling. "Can you tell us where we are?"

"I'm working on that, Colonel," the artificial intelligence said through the ship's speakers. "I anticipate having our location dialed in within the next few minutes."

Fiona had chosen to present herself as female even though she had no biological body. Like Marcus, the AI aboard Jared's flagship

Invincible, and Harrison, the AI running the shipyards on Boxer Station at Harrison's World, she was made up of the same hardware as the AIs they were fighting.

The only difference was that Carl had scrubbed their core rules of all the homicidal nastiness that the master AI had built into its own brood. He'd also inserted a core rule that the AIs had to obey orders from herself or Jared.

She still wasn't sure that had been the best decision, but it was done and couldn't be undone without unraveling their personalities, so they'd all have to live with his choice.

Jared Mertz, her brother—technically her half brother, even though they shared no genetic link whatsoever—and the commander of this expedition, had remained with the fleet in a system that wasn't on any of the old Imperial maps.

To the best of their knowledge, humanity had never discovered the star or the pristine world that orbited dead center of its habitable zone. That was a real loss for humanity, because the world rivaled Avalon or Terra in its beauty. Her husband, Russ Talbot, was leading an exploratory mission down to its surface even now.

Kelsey returned her thoughts to the mission at hand. She was glad that they were able to get away for a little while. It really strained one's nerves to have to slip through the Rebel Empire—the AI-enslaved remnants of the old Terran Empire—with an entire fleet of ships while hoping that no one noticed your passage.

As a Marine Raider strike ship, *Persephone*'s hull was coated with materials that were difficult to detect. In addition to that, she had stealth fields that they could throw over her hull to absorb incoming scans. Unless someone was right on top of them, they'd have no idea that she was there at all.

The protection wasn't perfect, of course. The closer *Persephone* got to an actively scanning enemy, the higher the chances she'd be noticed.

Their most significant risk of discovery during this particular mission was random patrols that might inadvertently come across them once they'd flipped into a system but before they'd had a chance to get the lay of the land.

Based on what she'd seen so far, the Rebel Empire was taking nothing for granted. The AIs had destroyers in a lot of systems doing exactly that. So far as they knew, the AIs didn't suspect the existence of flip points that didn't fit the standard model, which at least made what they were doing possible.

Multiflip points occurred in roughly the same area of a system as regular flip points—which meant they were mostly spread out between the habitable zone and the innermost gas giants—but they were *much* more difficult to detect.

Far flip points sat way out in the outer system, and were as detectable as regular flip points, but no one had ever bothered searching for flip points at so great a distance from a star. They were also like regular flip points in that they could only go to a single destination, but part of their unusual nature was that the distance traversed was significantly greater than a regular flip point.

Where a standard flip point might allow a ship to go up to a couple of hundred light-years, a far flip point could reach an average of a thousand. The shortest one they'd found thus far had been over seven hundred light-years. The longest had been more than thirteen hundred.

Still, to her mind, it was the multiflip points that were the most interesting. She didn't know how they worked because Carl hadn't finalized a working theory yet, but they were devilishly difficult to detect. Also, depending on the frequency generated by the flip drive, they could potentially take you to different destinations through what he called branches, using a tree metaphor.

More interestingly, when you arrived at the destination multiflip point, it could, in turn, take you to even more destinations. Without leaving the section of space around the multiflip point, a ship that had mapped the various branches could flip three or four times in the space of a couple of minutes and visit as many systems.

One of the dangers they'd discovered was that some of those branches only allowed for a limited amount of tonnage, and it might vary depending on the direction you were traversing a branch. It might allow for a cruiser to make the trip out but limit the return to a destroyer. Or no ship at all.

That had to do with the energy distribution inside the branches of the multiflip point network and was why mapping was critical. They had to probe each branch carefully to get an idea of how much tonnage it would allow so that they wouldn't be stranded on the other side if they used it.

Another one of Carl's inventions had made the process somewhat easier. He'd created an external frequency modulator that could be installed on an existing flip drive that would allow it to take them through branches that might not otherwise be traversable.

He'd also designed a flip drive that could do the work much more precisely and even had one built at a Rebel Empire shipyard. That had taken a covert mission and acquired them some allies in the process. That specialized flip drive was now a resident aboard the Fleet carrier *Audacious*.

She and her commanding officer, Commodore Zia Anderson, were separated from the fleet because of one of those one-way branches, and Kelsey was worried about the woman and her crew. Zia was working with the resistance inside the Rebel Empire, but she didn't have any support from the fleet or the New Terran Empire.

Kelsey hoped that things were okay with them and their unplanned guest. Kelsey's mother, the former empress of the New Terran Empire, had stowed away to be with Kelsey at the start of her mission and had decided to remain with the resistance and act as an ambassador for the New Terran Empire.

What could possibly go wrong with that?

Kelsey just hoped that Justine Bandar didn't sleep with the wrong person. When it came to affairs, her mother didn't have much common sense, though Kelsey's biological sire was a powerful and canny Imperial senator, one who'd bled to prove his loyalty to the emperor and the Empire.

"I've identified this system," Fiona said. "It was never permanently occupied by humans and thus never given a colloquial name, so it's listed in the Imperial Catalog as Y-73598F-8A. The star is an unremarkable red dwarf, and there are no listed resources of note. It does, however, have one intriguing feature."

The main screen changed from a view of space to a map of the flip lines around Twilight River. One of the systems near their target began blinking.

"Y-73598F-8A is two flips away from Twilight River. This particular branch of the multiflip point network has brought us significantly closer to the master AI than any of our previous explorations. In fact, based on the signal traffic that I'm picking up inside the system, I believe that it hosts a significant defensive force."

"That's good," Angela said with a relieved smile. "The closest we'd gotten before was five systems out, and even that had a sizable picket force of destroyers. This will allow us to get an idea of how much protection the master AI has layered around itself. If it isn't too significant, the fallback plan of forcing our way into Twilight River using Admiral Mertz's fleet might work."

"I wouldn't get my hopes up if I were you," Kelsey warned. "This thing has had five centuries to build up its defenses. Each layer inside this onion is going to be tougher than the last. Whatever we find here will just be a tithe of what's in the next system, and Twilight River itself will be worse yet."

That was a grim forecast but one that she honestly believed. If it came to the point that they couldn't slip into Twilight River through a back door, she seriously doubted that they'd be able to get into it at all.

"Thank you, Debbie Downer," Carl muttered loudly enough for everyone to hear.

She smiled slightly as everyone else chuckled. The scientist was irrepressible.

"Carl, honey, use your inside voice," Angela told her husband.

Kelsey still had trouble imagining the big marine woman and the slight scientist being a couple, but she supposed it wasn't any more outlandish than her and Talbot. She was smaller than most women, much less Carl, while Talbot was bigger than Angela. Quite the visual mismatch.

The young man grinned at his wife. "I had to lighten the mood a bit. I'm starting to get a better idea of how the multiflip point network is laid out, and I think there's a good chance that we're going to find a branch that leads where we want to go.

"I've tried making a map of the various multiflip points that we've explored, but it looks like spaghetti. Honestly, I don't think a visual representation is ever going to be useful to us humans, but I've come up with an analogy that might give you a better idea of what the multiflip point network looks like.

"When I was growing up, my mom gave me a toy ball made out of hand-carved wooden dowels and wheeled hubs. Basically, each dowel led to a hub that had more dowels coming out of it that led to different hubs in turn.

"The multiflip point network doesn't form a sphere, but each individual multiflip point is like those hubs and branches in the toy. While it's possible to jump from one hub to another and even back to the one you came from via a different hub, the truth is much grander than that.

"I suspect that if you explored nothing but multiflip points, you could cross from one edge of the galaxy to the other, given enough time. It's like each multiflip point covers a small subset of the stars within range of it. I call those nodes.

"Obviously, a node is an extremely *small* subset of multiflip points, but other nodes nearby incorporate a new subset of systems. If we look at all the nodes that are within range of Twilight River, the chances that one of those multiflip points has a branch that leads to Twilight River is quite high."

Kelsey pursed her lips. "I think I understand what you're saying. If I remember right, the normal flip points only cover about one in ten stars. You're saying that the multiflip points cover a much wider and deeper zone than that. If you add the two kinds of flip points together and add in far flip points, what kind of coverage are we looking at? Are any stars unreachable?"

"You can't prove a negative," Carl said with a shake of his head. "The closest we could come to determining that is to have a lot of ships scouring a relatively small sector of space until they'd found every single flip point. Even then, you couldn't be sure that you didn't miss one.

"But, if I had to guess, I'd wager that there are some stars that are unreachable. The percentage is going to be lower than what everyone has always assumed.

"I think we've got a roughly three-in-four chance of finding a way into Twilight River. The trick will be exploring all of the potential locations without having someone see us or having events overtake us.

"With the Clans going to war against the Rebel Empire, that's going to stir the pot. Maybe it's going to help us, but I'll bet it won't be long before they strike at Twilight River as well."

Kelsey sighed. The Clans might've descended from the crews of Old Empire Fleet vessels that had escaped the Fall through what had turned out to be a multiflip point that seemed like a one-way trip, but they'd grown into a strange society that had been raiding the Rebel Empire for unwilling colonists—particularly women—to bolster their population numbers for centuries.

They were the most paranoid and aggressive group that Kelsey had ever met. After Commander Raul Castille—a now-deceased Rebel Empire security officer—had used the stolen Dresden orbital to smash one of the Clan's defensive stations, Kelsey had been forced to destroy the responding ships, because they just wouldn't stop shooting.

It was a blessing that the Clans believed that the Rebel Empire was responsible for the attack—which it was—rather than the New Terran Empire, but that didn't help them all that much.

The Singularity—a polity that had been at odds with the Terran Empire since before the Fall—had found the Clans and had been reinforcing them for a long time. That meant they had a lot of ships that they could use to fight the Rebel Empire or the New Terran Empire if anyone ever discovered it existed.

And with the existence of multiflip points and far flip points, that meant that discovery was always possible. They needed to get the information they had back home so that Fleet could map the new flip points, or an enemy might be able to waltz right past their defenses, just like they intended to do to the master AI.

As for the Singularity, no one really understood what they hoped to gain from all this, but Kelsey was willing to bet it wasn't going to be good for the people living in the Rebel Empire or the New Terran Empire.

Kelsey checked the time via her implants. Since they weren't at risk of immediate discovery and it would take hours before their probes gave them any detailed information, she might as well get something to eat. She was starving, which was basically her normal condition with Marine Raider augmentation.

"Stand down from battle stations, Angela," she ordered, slapping one hand against the back of the command chair. "Rotate people off of their duty stations to get something to eat, and take a little bit of downtime yourself.

"Carl, if you've got some time, I'd like to sit down with you and Fiona and try to increase my understanding of the multiflip point network."

He nodded and rose from his station. "The passive scanners will continue compiling data, and I'll keep an eye on the process remotely while we talk. I'm not sure how much more effectively I can describe things without going into mathematics that might be a little... obscure to the uninitiated."

"Use the smallest words you can. If my eyes roll up into my head and I fall out of my chair, you've gotten too scientific for me."

He laughed as they made their way off the bridge and headed toward the cramped wardroom.

Kelsey didn't doubt that he was right, but she had to try and grasp the new reality they'd found themselves in. That knowledge might prove critical to saving everyone that she cared about.

2

Talbot opened the pinnace's hatch and scanned the ground around it as the ramp extended and lowered. The science people had declared that this world was eminently habitable, with decent temperatures and plenty of oxygen. The gravity was slightly less than on Avalon but not so much that he'd notice.

The air around them was clear and smelled of nature. It wasn't precisely like what one would find on Avalon or Terra, but it was refreshing and wholesome.

There had been no indication that humans that ever been to this system. It only had a multiflip point, so that made sense. The Old Empire hadn't even suspected such a thing existed.

Admiral Mertz had ordered a complete search of the system, and they'd found nothing of an artificial nature. To all appearances, this was a world that had never developed a civilization of its own or been visited by humans.

That didn't mean there were no mysteries to be solved, though.

He took a couple of steps down the ramp and pivoted to cover the left side of the pinnace with his flechette rifle as the rest of the platoon came down behind him.

The final person out the hatch was Jake Peters, formerly a major in the Marine Raiders from the Old Terran Empire. They'd found him on Terra, and he was a mystery all his own. He was living proof that the nanites that ran in Talbot's blood could grant a life span measured in centuries.

Peters was also a cautionary tale. He'd been a real mess when they'd found him, a paraplegic with only one crippled hand, a single eye, and a lot of pain. The people that had been supporting him on Terra during the Fall had slowly morphed, generation by generation, from his caretakers into his captors.

They'd seemingly venerated him as a god but didn't allow him much choice in anything they did. It seemed to Talbot that Peters had become more of a status symbol than anything else, a figurehead that the leaders of the group used to justify their rule.

Now that Lily Stone had fixed him up with Raider-grade artificial limbs and a replacement eye, the man looked absolutely normal. That didn't mean that he'd recovered from the trauma he'd suffered over what would typically be multiple lifetimes, but it was a start.

Talbot had taken the lead in his physical therapy. Being there for the man had helped him through some really dark places, but he thought Peters was on the upswing.

For the first time, Peters was along on a mission as part of the team. He didn't have an official slot in the chain of command, because he wasn't ready for it.

Talbot was hoping that this outing would cement things for the man so that he could get on with his life. While he was happy to have Peters's insight and advice, he'd like to have the man's skills and experience at his beck and call as well.

He and Kelsey had been fumbling their way along. They'd learned what they could and made do with the gaps they'd suspected they'd never be able to fill. Peters had irrevocably changed that equation.

He'd gone through the original training and learned *everything*. Then he'd risen through the ranks and become the commander of a strike ship like *Persephone*. He was the real deal, and the New Terran Empire needed him and his know-how badly.

Over the last six months, Peters had reviewed their training regimen and made many changes. He'd highlighted gaps that they hadn't even been aware of and provided training that they'd never have figured out on their own. Now they'd be able to train men and women like Peters, but no one living could match his experience.

But that was something to think about later. Talbot needed to focus, or something might very well eat him in the next few minutes.

The humid air smelled like there was rain in their future. A couple of clouds off to the west certainly held the potential of becoming a storm.

The plant life was relatively primitive. No trees as he recognized them, just various kinds of ferns that occasionally looked like monster shrubs.

The animal life trended reptilian, though he'd seen some images of what were probably mammals. In fact, the wildlife was what was causing so much consternation in the fleet.

Even though there was no evidence that humanity had ever visited this system, the life on this planet certainly *seemed* to be Terran in origin. Not from modern times, geologically speaking, but from far earlier.

"Any sign of the critters?" Peters asked, swinging his rifle to the right while the marines set up a perimeter.

"The drones say they're not very far off. If they're what the eggheads think they are, they're going to be aggressive. I know that they'd prefer we take one alive, but I'm not sure how well stunners will work on a velociraptor. Or whatever they are."

"Don't forget that those things probably hunt in packs," Peters added. "In a way, I suspect they're a lot like wolves. If you take your eyes off the group as a whole to focus on one, one of them will slip up behind you and try to bring you down. We've got to use the drone feeds to tag every single hostile. One moment's inattention could kill someone."

That was the voice of a hard-bitten professional who knew his business. Talbot approved.

Talbot brought up an overlay of the area based on feedback from the drones. They'd identified a pack of several dozen velociraptors—if that was really what they were—just a short distance away.

Based on how they were slowly circling the landing site, they'd seen the pinnace come down and were investigating. Once they'd determined that the strange metallic object contained what they might consider snacks, they'd probably come running.

"Stunners at the ready, First Squad," he ordered. "Everyone else, be ready to eliminate any leakers. Nobody gets through. Got it?"

Acknowledgments flowed back to him through the tactical net, and Talbot found himself standing in the center of the group arrayed around the pinnace's ramp with Peters watching the other side.

"You know we could've probably had one of the drones tag one, right?" Peters asked in an offhand tone, never taking his eyes off their surroundings.

"Maybe," Talbot admitted. "The problem I see with that is that its buddies would probably chow down on it as soon as it fell over. We're also going to gather some vegetation and take a look around to see what else we can find."

"Are you expecting to find aliens? I don't think that's very likely."

"I'm not ruling anything out. These last few years have been odd, and you'd be surprised at some of the things we've stumbled across. You know about the Pandorans and the aliens that probably created them, but there are other things that you're not cleared for yet. Trust me when I say that the universe can get very strange."

The velociraptors abruptly changed direction and set off directly toward the pinnace. Talbot sent out an alert via his implants and waited.

The ferns were reasonably thick, but they'd picked a spot that had a clearing of sorts so that they'd have some visibility when their targets broke into sight. He thought that would be enough, but it turned out that he was mistaken. Velociraptors were *fast*.

They charged right out of cover and tried to throw themselves onto the marines. There was no subtlety to the attack at all. He had just a few moments to confirm that these were the two-legged, feather-covered predators he'd been expecting before the marines opened fire.

First Squad's stunners proved effective against the attacking creatures, taking down the first wave without any trouble. Unfortunately, the second wave was right on its heels and already leaping to the attack, undeterred by what had happened to their companions.

The rest of the marines opened fire with flechette rifles, blowing the offending predators into bloody chunks. Talbot expected the survivors to flee, but they continued the attack, and in just thirty seconds, there were none left standing.

A quick check revealed that none of his people had been injured. It turned out that his plan to gather samples had been riskier than he'd anticipated. He'd make a note of that going forward and maybe just send down people in powered armor.

Let the local wildlife chew on that.

Getting the living samples would be disgusting, because the surviving creatures were covered in blood and gore. It was difficult to tell at a glance which ones they were going to take alive and which would end up as tissue samples.

Worse, the critters smelled terrible.

It wasn't just the scent of blood and death. The creatures literally smelled like rotting meat. The stench probably came from their mouths, where the remains of their last few meals were likely caught in between razor-sharp teeth.

"First Squad, move out and secure the samples," he ordered. "Use the cages that the eggheads provided for some of the live ones. Everyone else, keep your eyes open. We might get more visitors."

His implants signaled an incoming signal from *Invincible*.

"Talbot," he said out loud, using the com attached to his uniform to answer.

"Mertz here," his brother-in-law and fleet commander said. "How's it going?"

"We had a little bit of excitement, but everything's under control now. We should have the samples gathered in about twenty minutes."

"Excellent. Before you come back up, I've got a new mission for you. A com signal just started up in a mountain range about fifteen hundred kilometers to your west. It's covering a lot of bands and is strong enough to reach orbit.

"It's only a repeating tone, so it looks like a beacon to me. I have no idea who's down there, but it looks like they've detected your landing and would like to chat."

Talbot personally doubted that it was the aliens who'd populated this world with creatures from Terra, but he wasn't going to rule it out. Like he'd told Peters, the universe was strange.

"Copy that. We'll check it out."

3

Carl watched the small display in his makeshift office aboard *Persephone* with growing frustration. He'd expected this system to be heavily defended based on how close it was to Twilight River, but the AI forces present had exceeded his expectations by a wide margin.

Currently, they'd detected more than fifty destroyers moving throughout the system, all continually scanning for threats—threats that couldn't possibly be there based on the information the AIs had. All of the system's known flip points were heavily guarded, implying that there were also defenses on the other sides of the regular flip points.

The defenses at those chokepoints were mostly nonmobile. Large, heavily armed battle stations sat in a globe around each of the flip points. He supposed they would be equally good defending against something coming out of the flip point or anything trying to get into it.

Since they'd determined that the layered defenses for the master AI started about five flips away from Twilight River, this wouldn't be the heaviest concentration of defending units that they'd have to face, either.

There was absolutely no way that the fleet that Admiral Mertz had brought from the New Terran Empire could possibly breach the flip point leading toward Twilight River, much less deal with the forces in the next system. If they couldn't find a back door to Twilight River, they weren't getting at the master AI at all.

None of the ships or stations were communicating with one another, and he'd only been able to detect the ships because they were moving at a decent clip through normal space, so their gravitic signatures gave them away. It was likely that other ships were lying in wait at various locations scattered throughout the system.

Frankly, that wouldn't surprise him at all.

The AIs had already proven themselves clever by positioning robotically controlled battlecruisers deep in the atmospheres of gas giants in a number of systems that they occupied inside the Rebel Empire.

As Carl had expected, there was nothing of interest in the system. It had never been occupied by humanity, and that hadn't changed in the centuries since the Fall.

He'd mapped out the unexplored branches leading from this system's multiflip point, to no avail. Each led back to systems they'd already explored. To get into any new systems, *Persephone* would have to backtrack a few branches and expand the search.

It had taken them six months to get from Terra to the general area around Twilight River. They'd been probing the multiflip point network and searching out far flip points the entire way, trying to find the elusive back door they needed. This system was the closest they'd gotten, but it was a bust.

"How's it going, cutie?"

"That is sexual harassment," he said without looking up. "Just because we're married doesn't mean you get to objectify me."

Angela gave him a throaty chuckle as she came to stand beside him. "If you think this is sexual harassment, I haven't been trying hard enough. Seriously though, what's the verdict?"

He turned to face his wife and shook his head. "It's a dead end. We're going to have to go back a couple of systems and try branching out."

She shrugged slightly. "While that's a pain in the ass, it doesn't really matter how long it takes us to get there, so long as we can win once we make it. We've just been recalled via FTL. Admiral Mertz needs us. More specifically, he needs you."

Carl frowned. "Me? He's got a ton of scientists scattered throughout the fleet. Why does he need me?"

"Because you're our expert on alien technology. They've found something on the planet we left them at."

"Have they sent any details?"

"Fiona has them. I'll leave you to sort them out while I get us headed back. We'll be in orbit around the planet in roughly four hours, so I suggest you get something to eat and maybe take a nap. You're going to be very busy for the next couple of days."

He almost groaned as his wife walked out, because he'd *already* been up late the last couple of days. His implants allowed him to get by on less sleep, but there were limits.

A couple of taps on the archaic physical keyboard he so loved brought up the video that the admiral had sent. He scanned it while he imported a written report into his implants.

What had attracted the admiral was obviously a beacon. It came from a mountain range a fair distance from where Talbot had come down in a marine pinnace to pick up samples of the local wildlife. Wildlife that Carl noted was far too closely related to something from Terra than it should be.

Done skimming the basic information, Carl focused his attention on the video. The viewer was obviously on a smaller mountain inside the chain, because Carl could see other peaks dominating the landscape around the site.

The stone plateau was covered by snowdrifts, but that didn't obscure the massive green obelisk that rose out of the white like a fist thrust into the sky. The sides of the structure were smooth and seemed to be made of a different kind of stone than that of the mountain. Its color reminded him of jade.

There was no frame of reference, so he couldn't tell how large the obelisk was until Jake Peters stepped into view beside it. Once things were in perspective, Carl realized that the structure rose several hundred meters into the sky. It wasn't just a monument. It was a building in its own right.

That probably meant the man with the camera was Talbot. The video took him around the base of the obelisk, but there were no visible signs of a door leading into it.

Carl had no doubt there would be a way inside, probably buried under the snow. There was no reason to summon visitors without putting something there for them to find.

And that was all there was for him to review. Without knowing what lay below the snow-covered ground—which he had no doubt that scientists would be determining even now—he couldn't do anything more. He'd just have to wait to get there in person to solve its mysteries.

Thankfully, that allowed him to grab something to eat and catch a nap. He had absolutely no doubt that he'd need his wits about him very soon, and sleep would be in short supply.

* * *

JARED STEPPED out of the pinnace and onto the plateau. It was gorgeous out in the open like this. He had no idea what the wind chill was, but he was glad that he'd taken Talbot's advice to wear cold-weather gear.

The air was so cold that it felt as if his nostril hairs were freezing every time he took in a breath. It was… invigorating.

The jade obelisk towered high overhead, making him crane his neck to stare at its peak far above. He couldn't imagine how much work it must've taken to get what certainly looked like a single piece of stone into this remote and rugged location.

"It's something, isn't it?" Talbot asked from where he'd just stepped up beside him, the snow crunching under his boots.

"It is," Jared agreed. "Any idea why someone would bother putting a monument like this deep in the mountains on a planet that never had intelligent life?"

His brother-in-law shrugged. "No clue. We've gone over as much of the base as we can with this snow, but we haven't found an entrance. Since something is sending out a signal, I'm sure there's a way in, but I don't want to get too aggressive looking for it."

"Aggressive?"

"Yeah. We could've brought out some plasma rifles and started clearing the snow, but I'm guessing that any defense mechanisms would probably take that the wrong way."

"I'm not sure there's a *right* way to take something like that," Jared said with a smile. "Let's leave the heavy weapons in the pinnaces.

"*Persephone* is back in the system, and Carl will be here in a few hours. I brought some of the scientists down with me, and they'll start taking readings, but no matter how interesting this is, we're not going to be able to stay long enough to do it justice.

"That last branch of the current multiflip point node was a dry well. It's close to Twilight River but so heavily defended that there's no way we could possibly force our way through, even with all the ships we have available."

"Leaving without exploring this is going to piss Carl off."

"He'll get over it," Jared said, not sure that was entirely accurate. "Eventually. You have any theories?"

"The critters that we caught look like the artist renditions of velociraptors. The colors are off, but I understand those were just educated guesses. We've also seen some larger species that seem to be from the same geological period. Over that length of time—even in a stable environment—they should've evolved.

"That tells me that there's been some kind of tinkering. I'm not sure whether it's going to be on a genetic level or if machines are killing off the sports to keep the bloodlines pure. We didn't detect anything like the latter, but I'm not going to rule it out."

Jared had to agree with that assessment. When it came to aliens, it was better to keep an open mind.

"I'm surprised that Julia isn't with you," Talbot said. "She's even more curious than Kelsey. I figured this would've drawn her like a moth to a flame."

"She was going to come down, but Elise wasn't feeling well this morning, so she's providing moral support on the trip to see Lily. I'm sure it's nothing serious, but best to make sure."

"Probably something she ate," Talbot agreed. "Maybe this will get her to agree to medical nanites. Having implants without them is just silly."

A figure in marine cold-weather gear came around the far side of the obelisk. Jared had to squint and shade his eyes from the sunlight reflecting off the snow, but he finally recognized Jake Peters.

The man was looking a lot better than when they'd first met. Hell, he was looking better than he had a month ago. He finally seemed to have recovered from his injuries and centuries of disability.

It was hard to believe the man was half a millennium old, but the information they'd been able to pull out of *Persephone*'s computer system had confirmed his identity. Based on the research that Lily had been able to perform, his medical nanites would still be keeping him alive when the rest of them were dust.

Well, those of them that didn't upgrade their nanogenerators. Kelsey and Talbot had both encouraged him to upgrade. He had no objection but wouldn't do so if Elise decided not to take the plunge.

Lily's raw assessment was that his life span might range anywhere from a thousand to ten thousand years, perhaps even longer if something didn't kill him first.

Even compared to the mystery of the alien obelisk and the Terran dinosaurs that roamed this planet, that was more shocking to Jared. Aliens were going to be aliens, doing things that no one could understand. This was something that humanity had created, and everyone in the New Terran Empire was going to struggle with its implications as soon as they got word of the new potential home.

"I've found something," Peters said as he approached. "It's on the far side of the obelisk from where we're standing. It's hard to tell exactly what it is under all this, so I'll need some help clearing away the snow."

Talbot whistled loudly, hurting Jared's ears but getting the attention of every marine in sight. The man circled a finger in the air and pointed toward the far side of the obelisk. That got them all moving in that direction.

When the three of them got to the spot that Peters had been

messing around with, Jared immediately saw what was different. The stone in the area that Peters had cleared was green like the obelisk.

The marines pitched in with small shovels that they'd scrounged from somewhere and began clearing the area. Ten minutes later, they were all staring at an oval patch of the strange material that was embedded in the regular stone around it. It was about ten meters across at the narrowest point and maybe half again longer.

"This has to be a way inside," he agreed. "Now, all we have to do is figure out how to activate it. Or rather, we'll wait for the scientists to give everything a good look, and Carl can open it up. Excellent work, people. Now, how about we get out of this wind and get something hot to drink?"

4

Elise Orison tried to sit still on the cutter taking them over to the hospital ship *Caduceus*, but it was hard. She'd never been a very good patient, so it was lucky that she was usually healthy. That was what made her upset stomach so galling.

Food preparation wasn't something that the cooks in Fleet took for granted, she was sure. Sometimes it was the roll of the dice, though. Something had happened, and she'd gotten a meal that was a little underprepared.

She could accept that, but it didn't make throwing up any easier.

"You know, if you had medical nanites, this wouldn't be such a big deal," Julia said from the seat beside her.

"So you've said four times already. I suppose this is a sign, but if I get them, I won't be doing it alone," she said with a sigh as she shot a meaningful look at Olivia West, who was on her other side.

The woman was the Coordinator of Harrison's World, a former Rebel Empire world. The AIs hated medical nanites for some reason, so she'd had implants but no nanogenerator. If Elise was going to get them, it was time for Olivia to do so as well.

The three women were almost alone on the cutter making the trip from *Invincible* to *Caduceus*. Elise was grateful that her friends had come to provide moral support, even if she didn't need it. Mostly.

Her life had certainly changed since she'd met and married Jared Mertz. Born into the royal family of Pentagar, she was the crown princess of that sovereign star nation. She'd had a busy and rewarding life, even with the threat of death or enslavement at the hands of the Pale Ones looming over her.

Those poor bastards in the Erorsi system were savages that had been under the control of a mad computer that had augmented them with Marine Raider hardware—minus the medical nanites—and had kept sending them through the flip point to try and conquer her world for centuries.

Capture had meant the loss of one's ability to control their own body. Like the rest of her people, she'd been prepared to commit suicide to avoid that fate. She still carried the small knife that she'd have used to do that as a reminder.

Jared Mertz and Kelsey Bandar had changed her world forever when they'd defeated and destroyed the computer that had controlled the Pale Ones. Now Pentagar was providing aid to Erorsi and the hidden people that had been living there under the very nose of the computer since the Fall.

Her people hadn't been primitive, but their technology was getting a considerable boost from the information that her husband and the New Terran Empire had provided and from the technical specialists from the old planetary command center on Erorsi.

And when Omega—the unbelievably ancient alien trapped in a station around a black hole—had created an artificial flip point between his system—which they'd named the Nova system—and Pentagar, as well as a second one from there to Avalon, it had opened the floodgates of trade and technology exchange.

Whereas they'd once been trapped, they could now journey to the capital of the New Terran Empire in a matter of hours. No longer were they hobbled by the fact that they couldn't build their own flip drives. Jared's discovery of those rare minerals inside a cul-de-sac system near Pentagar had seen to that.

The last few years had been a whirlwind of societal and

technological changes for Pentagar that had reached its current peak when she'd married the savior of their world and bound the New Terran Empire and the Kingdom of Pentagar together.

She was so deliriously happy to have Jared as her husband and prince consort. The fact that his biological father was the Emperor of the New Terran Empire—even if his birth had been on the wrong side of the sheets—was as strong a connection between their peoples as she could possibly hope for.

Elise hadn't intended to go on this journey with Jared. She'd thought she was only spending a couple of weeks with him as he carried out a moderately risky mission. Honestly, she shouldn't even have gone on that, but the appearance of a version of Kelsey from a different reality had cemented her desire to be there for everything that had happened.

Julia was certainly different from Kelsey, but she treasured the woman. The four women had grown into such a tight friendship that Elise couldn't imagine how she was going to get on with life once Julia returned to her universe to free it from the scourge of the AIs.

She realized that she'd been lost in thought again as she felt the cutter docking. They'd reached *Caduceus*. The hospital ship was the size of a superdreadnought and was by no means unarmed, but it was filled with everything needed to care for the injured and ill.

Commodore Lily Stone didn't command the ship's operations in space, but she directed all of the medical activities and held a lot of sway over how her flag captain ran the ship. If anyone could figure out what was going on in her stomach, it was Lily.

And Julia was right. Now that they had the opportunity, it would make sense to get medical nanites. With how her people felt about the Pale Ones, the decision to get implants at all had been one she'd had to think long and hard about. She'd declined medical nanites because it had seemed like a step too far.

Now she realized that had been stupid. She'd already taken the first steps toward what was becoming standard in the New Terran Empire, so she might as well get the remaining work done.

She'd been thinking about it ever since Julia had suggested it. The woman had subversively advocated skipping the Fleet-grade medical nanites and getting a Marine Raider nanogenerator. Elise had been leaning toward agreeing, but the more she'd learned about Jake Peters, the less certain she became.

She couldn't imagine how her life would change with that kind of life span. Still, would the opportunity ever come again? As soon as word of something like that got out, access to Marine Raider nanogenerators would be heavily restricted.

At least she thought so. After all, how would society change if *everyone* became functionally immortal? Population control would become a *huge* issue. Maybe that was why the AIs had eschewed medical nanites.

She'd had a few discussions about it with her husband. He already had a Fleet-grade nanogenerator, and those were becoming commonplace. That extended life spans into the hundreds of years. There was a survivor from Erorsi—Reginald Bell—who, even though he'd been in medical stasis for hundreds of years, had been a serving Fleet officer before the Fall.

He'd lived three hundred years in the real world. To her people, that was unimaginable.

Elise flipped the question on its head as she stood and headed toward the pinnace's hatch. Would she want to live a shorter life than her husband? Would she want him to give up any portion of his life for her? Didn't they deserve to take advantage of the same technology that his sister had?

Jared hadn't made any final decisions. She suspected that he was waiting on her to make up her mind, and then he'd follow suit. Perhaps she'd best get on the ball and do that. She was here, after all.

Right outside the hatch, Lily was waiting for them. The dark-haired medical officer gave each of them a big smile and a hug.

"Even being in the same fleet, I don't see you girls nearly enough," the woman said warmly. "I'm glad you've come over, even if you're not feeling well, Elise. Why don't we get you down to the medical center and figure out what's going on?"

"That sounds good," Elise said grumpily. "This bug has kept me feeling grungy for two days now, and I'm ready to feel normal again."

She took a deep breath. "And I think it's time to install medical nanites. Would it be possible to get a Marine Raider-grade nanogenerator?"

Lily nodded and gestured toward the left. "I've already had that discussion with the admiral. He said if that's what you wanted, then that's what we'd do. The same is true of you, Olivia. Sean was part of that conversation.

"Both of them already have Fleet-grade nanogenerators, but they'll upgrade if you do. This isn't being made available to everyone —at least not at this time—but rank does have its privileges."

As soon as they were inside the lift and on their way to the appropriate deck, Elise turned to Lily. "Do you think that's the right call to make? Is this going to be something that I'll live to regret? I can't imagine this technology is going to become broadly available, because it would change society in ways that we can't imagine right now."

Her friend shrugged. "I believe this technology is going to get out no matter what we do. Frankly, I think it should. We're going to have to rethink how society is structured, and things like inheritance will change.

"It's not going to happen all at once, but it's going to happen. We've already got all of the people who are now Marine Raiders that have those nanites in their bodies. By the time we get back home, I suspect that a significant portion of the people on this mission will probably be upgraded. The admiral isn't going to believe that it's right to keep something like this to just an elite few.

"And besides, the emperor has them. Do you think that Karl Bandar will deny his people the same kind of blessing that he has? We can't make a decision about everyone today, but I'm pretty sure I know which way the wind will blow."

"I'm good with that upgrade," Olivia said. "Maybe in five hundred years, I won't feel the same way, but I'll still be around to make that decision. I can always deactivate them if I get tired of living, then I'll just live out my remaining years as a normal human."

Elise frowned slightly as the lift doors opened. "That's a question that I hadn't considered. Why would Jake Peters keep his nanites online when he didn't have any hope of rescue? Couldn't he have turned them off and just grown old and died?"

"No," Lily said. "The deactivation process requires someone with specific equipment and knowledge to turn the nanogenerator off and disable the nanites. It's not something that he would've been able to do by himself.

"Though I can't imagine why it wouldn't be feasible to allow a user to put them into standby mode. Of course, that'll also mean that they can always turn them back on. I'll tag up with Carl to discuss it."

Lily led them across the corridor and into the primary medical center on the ship. It wasn't the only medical center, because the entire ship was dedicated to medical care, so there were numerous facilities, but it was the largest. And it was where Lily's office was.

The interior was bustling with activity even though there were very few patients in evidence. The ship was large enough to handle injuries from across a fleet that had just been through a battle, so they were basically in standby mode themselves. Elise was certain that the doctors didn't mind the lack of business.

"Okay," Lily said. "Hop up on the table and lie down while I figure out what's going on."

Elise did as instructed. A few moments later, Lily initiated the scan, and her eyes grew unfocused as she began going over the data that the table was providing through her implants.

After about fifteen seconds, her eyes widened, and she frowned. "That can't be right. Hang on a second."

Five seconds later, Lily grimaced, and her eyes refocused on Elise's face. "I've got it figured out, but the problem is a bit more complex than I'd anticipated. You might want to step into my office so that we can discuss this in private."

Elise sat up and shook her head, her stomach churning a little bit as she started anticipating bad news. "Just tell me. I'd rather my best friends know what's going on and not leave them guessing."

Lily shot her a skeptical look but then shrugged. "Okay. After our adventures on Terra, I never thought about this possibility, but the EMP must've damaged your contraceptive implant. You're pregnant."

5

K elsey stared around the plateau and gawked at the obelisk as she came down the ramp of the pinnace that had brought her down from *Persephone*. She was so engrossed with the massive structure that she almost missed Carl lugging a heavy box of equipment past her. She shook off her stupor and took the box from him. With her strength, she was able to carry it easily.

He nodded his thanks, and they headed around the structure to where an area had been cleared of snow. Interestingly, the ground was rough, natural stone, except for an oval patch perhaps ten meters across at its narrowest that was the same green as the mammoth monument and smooth as glass.

Gathered nearby were Jared, Talbot, and Jake Peters. She stepped over and gave her husband a quick hug. "You find the most interesting things. Any idea what this is?"

"Not a clue," he said with a shrug as he moved to help Carl.

Jared half turned so that he was facing them but still had a view of the monumental structure. "While it wasn't meant to stand out from space, I've already verified that it's visible for quite a distance from this range. The sunlight hits it in such a way that its color pulls in the eye. Add to that the fact that it's transmitting a signal meant to garner attention, and it's obvious that whoever built this wanted it to be found."

"Have you detected anything underneath it?"

He shook his head. "We can't even detect the rock under the surface. That's the biggest hint that there's something down there.

"The biologists have done some DNA tests on the samples that Talbot shipped back. Those velociraptors—or whatever they are—are definitely of terrestrial origin. The plant life also shares a lot of features that one would associate with terrestrial vegetation.

"Somebody went to a lot of trouble to duplicate an entire ecosystem thousands of light-years from Terra in a backwater system that doesn't even sit on the regular flip point network.

"Also, they had to have done so millions of years ago. Sadly, we may not get an answer to our questions anytime soon, because we don't have the time to dig into the mystery right now."

Kelsey understood that. Every day they delayed getting to Twilight River increased the chances that the AIs would decide that humanity needed to be eliminated.

"Do you think these aliens are connected to the people that created the Pandorans?" she asked.

Her brother shook his head. "Since those people used human DNA to create the Pandorans, that had to have taken place relatively recently on a cosmological scale. Modern humans just haven't been in existence long enough for it to be anything more than two or three hundred thousand years.

"I'm told that velociraptors existed between seventy-one and seventy-five million years ago. That's just too big a gulf. My money says it's two different species."

Something sounded wrong about that to her. "If this was done seventy-plus million years ago, shouldn't the animals here have evolved? Nothing stays the same. Even the ferns that you were telling me about should've morphed into something else during that time."

He nodded. "That's where the first surprise came in. Those critters have nanites inside them, and so do the plants. Not medical nanites like we have—not precisely—but something that seems to be diligent in correcting genetic drift."

She turned to face Jared squarely, her eyes wide. "Really? And they're still working after all this time? We have nanogenerators to refresh ours because the nanites decay and have to be replaced. What kind of generator does that for plants?"

"And there's the trick," Jared said with a half smile. "They make themselves. More interestingly, they don't migrate outside strict boundaries. If they enter a different kind of host, they deactivate.

"Our people found them in the living creatures and plants and are trying to figure out how they work. It certainly looks as if they have a finite life span, but they construct other nanites from the host's mass. When there's a seed created or a creature has an offspring, the nanites are passed along with it."

She turned back toward the obelisk and stared up at its tip far above. "Why would they do that? It's not like dinosaurs were an intelligent species. Are we thinking that they took a liking to Terra back in the day and wanted to recreate it here as a theme park on a planetary scale?"

Talbot laughed as he rejoined them. "I think we saw those movies, and they didn't turn out well. Let's hope that the aliens were smarter than that.

"If we can get inside the structure without too much trouble, maybe we can find the answer. If we can't do that relatively quickly, we're going to have to move along."

"Talbot's right," Jared said with a nod. "Since we still haven't found a viable path to Twilight River, we need to do some probing back along the path we've already blazed to see if there are any unexplored branches that lead to our destination. This is an interesting mystery, but we have more pressing matters on our plates."

Kelsey was about to respond when her implants notified her of an incoming communication being relayed by her pinnace from *Persephone*.

"Bandar here," she said out loud, letting the com unit attached to her parka carry her voice back to the Marine Raider strike ship.

"It's Angela," the voice in her implants said. "The FTL probe that we left in Y-73598F-8A just detected a lot of ships coming in through a far flip point that we didn't know about. They aren't bothering to hide their presence, so we're still getting information about them. Fiona has tentatively identified them as Clan warships."

"Send the information on to *Invincible*. I'll get back to you when Jared and I review it."

"Copy that."

"Thanks. Bandar out."

Judging from the way Jared was frowning, her brother had just gotten the news. He gestured for her to walk with him and started toward the pinnaces.

"I assume you just heard about the Clan warships?" he asked.

She nodded as she walked into the icy wind. "Yep. They're going to bang their heads against Twilight River's front door. Since they've been planning for this over the last five hundred years, they might even have brought enough ships to make some magic happen."

"Come with me back up to *Invincible*, and we'll work out how we need to react to this," he said. "This might be the opportunity we've been waiting for."

"Or it might be an unmitigated disaster," she said gloomily. "These days, it's a little hard to tell them apart at first glance."

* * *

CARL FINISHED SETTING up his equipment around the green oval set into the stone of the plateau. It looked like the same kind of material that the monolith was made of, but he'd have to do some tests before he could be sure. He'd read the reports that the other scientist had written based on their attempts to scan the area beneath the structure and concurred with their opinion that there was a stealth field of some kind in place.

Since this had to be a door of some kind, he was sure that there would be a trigger. Perhaps some of the monitoring equipment would pick up a frequency that had some sort of clue and that would allow him to generate a signal of his own to make it open.

Once he had the equipment scanning for said signal, he took out a small chisel and attempted to get a sample of the green material. The stone resisted all attempts to mar it, telling him very clearly that this wasn't jade or anything even closely related to it. He even tried a laser cutter, with an equal lack of success.

Whatever it was, the material was extremely tough. There'd be no getting through it by force without causing massive destruction, something he wasn't willing to contemplate at this point.

"Something wrong?" Talbot asked from where he stood nearby.

Carl glanced up and saw that the admiral, Kelsey, and Jake Peters were no longer in view.

He frowned. "Where'd everybody go?"

"Big things happening back in the system you just came from. Apparently, the Clans decided to raid via a far flip point we didn't know about. Looks like there's going to be a big honking battle. Kelsey and the admiral went back up to *Invincible*. Jake's taking a stroll around the perimeter."

"I can't say I'm surprised," Carl admitted. "We knew this was coming. Once somebody stirred the hornets' nest, the Clans were bound and determined to fight the Rebel Empire. And after all this time, they had to know the master AI was at Twilight River.

"Still, I wish they'd held off on this part of their war a little bit longer. I thought they'd go the long way around to get to the master AI."

"Maybe that's what they wanted the AIs to think," Talbot said with a shrug. "Get a strong enough force marauding through enemy territory, and you're going to pull defenders out of place. That attack could've been a huge misdirection, trying to uncover the master AI for a major strike force like this."

Carl shook his head skeptically. "You didn't see the defenses. If they wanted to crack this particular nut, they'd have to bring a *lot* of force to bear. More than the admiral brought with us, for sure. A lot more."

"There's no telling how long you're going to have to work on this particular mystery, so focus," Talbot advised. "What do you think this weird oval is? And by the way, I've had the marines search all the way around the plateau, and this is the only spot like it."

"I'm not sure," Carl said with a shrug. "The material is tough. I'm hoping that we detect a signal from underneath the obelisk that allows me to establish some kind of communication with the structure. It can't have anything alive inside it after all this time, but the AIs have already proven that if you're advanced enough, you don't have to be biological to be intelligent."

Carl was about to say more when one of his instruments beeped. "Well, well. It looks like there is a very low-strength signal on one particular frequency. It's not like the beacon. This is something that would only be detectable while we're here on top of this plateau."

He went to his instrument case and dug out something he could use to transmit on that frequency. It wasn't very powerful, but he didn't think it needed to be if he could send something that the device would recognize as the appropriate key for this lock.

Carl suspected that if he could just send a signal on the same narrow frequency, perhaps even just repeating the tones that he'd detected, that would be enough. It only took a minute to configure the device the way he wanted, and he stood beside Talbot and triggered a signal to mimic the one he was receiving.

Nothing happened.

"Well, that was something of a letdown," Talbot said.

"Wasn't it, though?" Carl answered with a chuckle. "I'm not sure exactly what it's looking for, but maybe it needs to sense someone on the oval. Otherwise, you could send a signal from anywhere on the plateau. Maybe it's not a door. Maybe it's a lift that goes down into the plateau instead."

"I suppose there's only one way to find out," Talbot said. "Come on."

The man led the way into the center of the oval, and Carl followed. "You know they're going to say we're stupid for doing this, right?"

"I'm a marine. I do stupid things before breakfast."

Carl laughed and triggered the signaling device again. This time, something happened.

Unfortunately for his peace of mind, it wasn't as simple as the oval area sinking into the ground. He and Talbot floated off of the ground and began rising into the air at a good clip.

Carl's heart lurched in his chest, and he thrashed a bit. He'd have expected to feel completely untethered, being lifted into the air like that, but even his uncoordinated movements didn't cause him to shift his position at all. It was like he was being gently held in place by some unseen force.

The marines below shouted in alarm when they noticed what was happening, but before anyone could intervene, he and Talbot were at the top of the obelisk, and the stone just below the tip vanished.

There hadn't been any indication that there was a door there, and moments later, the two of them were inside. The door closed, leaving them trapped in darkness as they began to descend into the alien structure.

6

"Excuse me?" Elise demanded.

"You're in a family way," Lily said sympathetically. "The scans indicate that you're about six weeks along. And to add to your consternation, you're carrying twins."

Elise was flabbergasted. She sat there with her mouth hanging open, totally at a loss for words.

When she finally gathered her wits about her, she shook her head emphatically. "That's not possible. It's been half a year since Terra. Trust me when I say that if my contraceptive implant had failed, I'd have found out a *lot* sooner than now."

"It's possible that it only failed recently. Or it may *still* be partially operational, and you just got unlucky. Or lucky, if that's how you choose to take it.

"Your contraceptive implant is Pentagaran in manufacture, so I don't really have any insight into its internal function. I'll need to remove it to be certain that it doesn't interfere with the pregnancy, should you choose to proceed."

Elise was still trying to get her head around what was happening as Olivia pulled her onto her feet and into a hug. Moments later, Julia joined in, and so did Lily.

"It's going to be okay," Olivia said. "Women have children every day of the year, and with modern medical technology, it's not going to be a problem for you, if you want children."

"Of course I want them," she said a bit crossly. "I just wasn't expecting them *now*. I figured I'd have years to grow comfortable in my marriage before we had children. I know Jared will be thrilled, but this is *really* crappy timing.

"These are going to be the royal grandchildren princes or princesses of the blood. One of them will rule the Kingdom of Pentagar one day. It doesn't matter what I might have wanted, though, because now that they're here, I'm going to have them. Thankfully, that's what I'd have done anyway."

She took a deep breath and pushed the other women back slightly. "I wasn't having any menstrual periods. I'd have figured I'd have at least one if my implant had failed that badly."

"Looks like you caught it on the first time around," Lily said. "The children seem healthy, and I can even tell you the sex if you want to know. The scan was able to determine that via their DNA."

"Tell me."

"Congratulations, Mommy. You're going to have identical twin boys."

Elise tried to marshal her thoughts, but she couldn't seem to catch them. It was as if they were chasing one another in a whirlwind around her as she stood there completely bewildered.

While she stood there in a bemused state, Lily gestured for Olivia to get on the diagnostic table. "While we're at it, we should check you. In fact, I'll need to check all of the women who lived through the EMP, including myself, though I'm not seeing anyone right now. If it happened to Elise, any of us who are sexually active with members of the opposite sex are at risk until I replace their contraceptive implants."

Olivia smiled wryly. "That's what I get for chuckling at Elise's expense. It'll serve me right if I have to go back and tell Sean that he's going to be a father.

"My implant is of Imperial make, though it was built inside the

Rebel Empire. I have no idea how that actually compares to what everyone in the New Terran Empire uses, but they're pretty reliable."

"I'll have to do a little research, but I suspect yours is probably more advanced than ours," Lily said. "Lie back and let me take a look. Before I do that, do you have a preference?"

Olivia shrugged slightly and then lay back. "I haven't got the slightest idea. Motherhood isn't something that I've considered much. Harrison's World is an excellent place to raise children unless you're in political power. Then it becomes dangerous.

"At least, that's how it used to be. Now that the planet is under new management, I suspect that it's going to continue to get better. The New Terran Empire is good for us."

Lily pursed her lips slightly and then shook her head. "Your implant still appears to be functional. We'll want to replace it on general principles. Or if you and Sean would like to have children, I can remove it and hold off on replacing it until later."

Olivia shook her head. "We've got enough complications as it is. Let's just replace it."

The doctor turned and raised an eyebrow at Julia. "Do I need to check you?"

Julia held up two hands as if pushing the doctor away. "Heaven forbid. Mine may or may not be functional, but I'm not sexually active. It's been years, and I don't see that changing anytime soon. We'll replace it just to be sure, but I'm not in any danger."

Lily turned back to Elise. "I'll do a full diagnostic workup on you as soon as I'm finished with these two. I'll install a Marine Raider nanogenerator while I'm at it. If you'll both head to my office, I'll come and get Julia when I'm done with Olivia. All told, it should only take about half an hour, and then I'll take care of you."

Julia took her arm and led her toward Lily's office.

Once they were inside, the two of them sat down, and Elise put her head in her hands. "This is a lot to take in. I'm happy, but this is just so unexpected."

"You're going to be a great mother," Julia said. "Much better than my mother ever was."

"I've heard stories, so pardon my saying so, but that's kind of a low bar."

The two of them laughed, and then Julia squeezed Elise's hands tightly in hers. "You're not going to go through this alone. These children are going to have a rampaging herd of godparents."

"They're never going to lack for love and attention, that's for sure," Elise agreed. "Do you think that you'll ever be in a position where you'll want children?"

"If you'd have asked me that a year ago, I'd have said no. Now? It really depends on my universe's version of Carl Owlet. If I can woo him—politically and romantically—then I'd be happy to have kids."

The two of them sat in companionable silence. Elise appreciated that, because she had a lot to think about. Even though Jared was going to be happy to hear the news, this was going to be another complication that her husband was going to have to factor into all of the events swirling around them at this critical time.

* * *

TALBOT PULLED a portable light off his belt. One of the benefits of being a marine was always being prepared for unusual situations. He and Carl were descending through what looked like a smooth shaft with no doors.

"What the hell is going on?" he asked his young friend. "What did you do, and where is it taking us?"

"I sent a signal on the same frequency that the oval we were standing on was using. Basically, I pressed the doorbell. I haven't got the slightest idea where it's taking us, but this all has to have a purpose. It isn't a trap. At least I hope not."

The two of them descended quickly, and though it was hard to make any judgment about how fast they were going, Talbot thought that they'd gone down quite a distance into the plateau before they finally came out into an open area.

His light didn't come close to illuminating the entire space around them, but it did show the floor below. If they were in a dome, it had to be hundreds of meters across.

Talbot was half afraid that whatever force was moving them would just drop them, but it brought them smoothly down to a spot on the floor with a green oval identical to the one they'd been standing on outside. When he took a few steps forward, he felt nothing inhibiting his movement.

While Carl was turning in one direction, he turned in the other, holding the light high and trying to see if there was anything unusual about the space that they were in. All his light revealed was empty space.

Carl knelt and examined the oval. "Since it's also an oval, the shape has to have a special meaning to whoever built this place. The area that we're in looks like it might be a dome, but I'm not going to rule out an oval."

Talbot considered drawing his pistol, but that seemed ridiculous. If whatever had brought them here had wanted to harm them, it had already had multiple opportunities to do so.

What he could do was take a better look around the area and get a sense of how large it was. He reached into the pouch on his left leg and pulled out four micro drones.

He activated them with a signal from his implants and sent them in all directions to scan and record everything. They were multispectral devices, so they picked up a lot more detail than a person's eyes. The darkness would only mildly inhibit them.

And then he laughed at himself. He was a Marine Raider. He had ocular implants. One of these days, he'd actually remember that he had capabilities beyond those of a regular marine.

He switched his eyes to multispectral mode and could see that they were in a significantly larger area than he'd anticipated. His implants sent out a low-powered scanner signal to allow him to see in all environments, but the multispectral illumination used by the drones provided plenty of light.

"The space we're in looks like it's an oval shape," he confirmed. "I thought it was a couple of hundred meters across, but the drones are helping me get a better look at what's around us. I think this cavern might be five hundred meters or so across. If the ratio holds with what we're standing on, that means that it's probably seven hundred and fifty or eight hundred meters long. The ceiling is about two hundred meters above us."

"I've really got to see about getting some of those ocular implants," Carl complained. "It's annoying not being able to see the important things. You can keep all the rest of the Marine Raider stuff, but those enhanced eyes would be damned useful."

"Talk to Lily. I'm sure she can get you set up. Thus far, I'm not seeing any exits. The walls appear to be natural stone, not that green stuff."

"Are we in the exact center of the cavern?" Carl asked.

Talbot did some mental calculation and shook his head. "No, we're about fifty meters away from the center. You think that's where we should go?"

"It can't hurt."

Talbot knew that wasn't true. The alien structure didn't seem innately hostile, but if one didn't understand what one was working with, there was always a danger.

The two of them walked to the center of the open area, and Carl slapped Talbot on the shoulder and pointed. "A smaller oval. This one's about a meter across and a meter and a half long. If it works like the one upstairs, it'll be transmitting a signal that I can detect and mimic to activate it."

He stopped just outside the oval and gave Talbot his full attention. "Do you think that I should? It might be dangerous."

"We're going to have to take a chance and see what it does, but let's see if I can get a signal out first. I'm not very hopeful, because everyone outside has undoubtedly been trying to get ahold of us this entire time, but if we don't at least try, we won't know."

Talbot interfaced with his implants and tried to send a signal to Jake Peters. As he'd expected, there was no indication that the man had heard him.

Still, he sent an update of everything that they'd seen to this point just in case the others could hear him. He indicated that they planned on trying to come back out shortly and not to do anything hasty. And by hasty, he meant using plasma weapons to try to blow a hole in the side of the obelisk.

Marines would be marines after all.

While he'd been doing that, Carl had stepped into the center of the smaller oval and had his instrumentation out. "There's a signal, just like I expected. I'm mirroring it now."

For a few moments, nothing seemed to happen, and then the entire cavern lit up. Above them and off to their left, a light pulsed in the air, seemingly from nothing.

From it, strands of bright color that spanned the spectrum shot out a short distance to other lights that then appeared, and then even more strands and lights appeared. There were also a lesser number of longer lines that seemingly went out at random.

Over the course of about twenty-five seconds, the lights went all the way out to the walls. It was impossible to see what was going on deeper into whatever they were looking at because it looked like a writhing mass of worms. There was no sense or form that he could detect other than a wild twisting of colored lines.

"Oh my God," Carl muttered. "Are you seeing what I'm seeing?"

"If you mean this wild mishmash of colors and sparks of light, sure."

Carl waved his hand dismissively. "Look at the overall shape of it. That's a galaxy. Odds are, it's the Milky Way. Based on the very first couple of points that had lines coming out of them, I think those sparks are star systems, and the lines might represent flip points."

His friend turned to him, his face a mask of awe. "Talbot, whoever these aliens were, I think they might've mapped the flip point network for our entire galaxy."

7

J ared got word about what had happened to Talbot and Carl just a few minutes after they'd taken off. He considered turning around but doubted that his presence would make a difference one way or the other. Kelsey concurred.

If anyone could find a way back out of the obelisk, it was Carl. After all, he'd figured out how to get out of the Omega station when everyone else had thought escape was impossible. The man was a genius with hidden reserves of resourcefulness that it never paid to discount.

And Talbot was more than capable of protecting them from any dangers they might run into. He was a Marine Raider and had all his gear, minus powered armor. They'd be fine.

He turned his focus to the problem at hand. It looked as if a massive force was trying to breach the flip point leading toward Twilight River. Could the Clans do that, and how did it affect his mission?

In a way, the sheer firepower in play made Jared feel small. When they'd left Avalon, he'd thought his fleet was powerful, but in comparison to what he saw now, it was just a drop in the bucket. If he was right, this was the primary strike force that the Clans had fielded. The rest of the war against the Rebel Empire was a diversion.

Both the AIs and the Clans had significantly more ships at their disposal than he'd imagined possible. There was no chance he'd be able to use his fleet to influence this battle, even if he was inclined to do so. Worse, he'd be unable to overwhelm whatever defenses the master AI had at its disposal at Twilight River.

It would be several hours before the Clan forces reached the flip point leading toward Twilight River. When they did, the battle stations guarding it would be put to the test.

If Jared was right, the Clans were going to run into trouble before they even got there. The AIs liked hiding additional warships in unlikely places, and he had no doubt that the systems surrounding Twilight River were going to have hidden defenses meant to lure the unwary in. The ships that were moving around the system would only be a tithe of what was really waiting for the Clans.

The most significant implication of this particular battle would be tipping the AIs off about the far flip points. They'd have seen where the ships came from, and they'd send forces out to inspect the inexplicable flip point once this was all over. Then they'd know they had to start searching every single system under their control for back doors.

That didn't necessarily mean that they would find the multiflip points, but he wasn't going to hold his breath. Time was running out. If they'd gotten to Twilight River sooner, the master AI would've had no idea what was coming. Now, it was going to have an eye peeled for unexpected ships in supposedly safe systems. That made their job a lot harder. Maybe impossible.

As much as he hated to count on it, they were going to need a lot of luck to defeat the master AI.

The New Terran Empire would have to do the same. They had to find every potential incursion point in their space. Yet until they got back home to warn everyone, they wouldn't know that their supposed border was as porous as Swiss cheese.

The Clans had just proven how that ignorance could be lethal. If they beat the AIs and the Rebel Empire, then they could turn their attention to other issues, like the resistance that the Rebel Empire was meeting near Erorsi. If they did, they knew what they'd have to do to find a way around the flip point jammer, and that would be the end of the New Terran Empire.

The best thing for all of them was to make this mission a massive success and then to get back to the New Terran Empire as soon as possible so that they could plug those holes, but that meant winning this fight, so he'd better focus on the problem at hand.

Fifteen minutes later, their cutter docked with *Invincible*, and he led Kelsey to the briefing room just off his flag bridge. It was spacious and modern, with plenty of screens to show data if they didn't want to use their implants.

"Admiral, Highness," Marcus—the sentient AI that served as his flag captain—said as he entered. "The Clans came in force. They made no effort to hide where they arrived in the system, so if they fail to win, the AIs will have little difficulty localizing the far flip point. They've brought approximately five hundred vessels with, I believe, a minimum of one hundred superdreadnoughts.

"They outgun our force by a significant margin. It's going to be a brutal fight, but I suspect that the master AI's forces are going to lose."

"There's more going on here than meets the eye," Jared said with a shake of his head as he took his seat. "Keep an eye out for hidden clusters of ships. I believe the master AI will have a strong force of ships somewhere out of sight."

"My people and I are already doing that, Admiral. It will likely be at least a few hours before they would gain any tactical advantage by coming out of hiding. They're going to want the invading ships to engage the battle stations before they swoop in to take them from the rear.

"The AI's forces have to be surprised by how the Clans got into the system. That might mean their reserve force is out of place to respond as they'd like. They couldn't have known about the existence of the far flip point, so this has to be an unpleasant surprise for them."

"Put everything we've got up on the screens," Jared ordered. "We need to get a general idea of how this battle is going to play out."

Marcus threw all the data onto the main screen. The system was laid out in a standard pattern, and the known flip points were represented by blue triangles. The suspected far flip point was an orange blob due to the uncertain nature of its exact location.

The display used Fleet markings for the battle stations and warships. The Rebel Empire forces were marked in red, and the Clans were gold.

There were a lot of ships heading deeper into the system, and they looked like they were ignoring the flip point that led away from Twilight River entirely. They were rolling the dice and going for the master AI's throat.

"I understand that we don't have any firm readings on the battle stations, but if there aren't any hidden forces inside the system, do you think the Clans can break through?" Kelsey asked.

"Undoubtedly," Marcus said evenly. "They'll take heavy losses, but they'll get into the next system. We don't know what forces they'll find there, but we have to assume that its defensive force is stronger than what we're seeing here. And that doesn't consider what's going to be present at Twilight River itself."

Kelsey shook her head. "This is too straightforward. The Clans are throwing a lot of force into this fight, but it's not going to be enough. Since they obviously knew about that far flip point ahead of time, they knew what forces they'd be facing here. They'll have made decent guesses about what they're going to find further in.

"While they brought a lot of ships, it's not sufficient for the task. I realize that our appearance probably kicked them off a little earlier than they'd planned, but if they have no chance of success, why would they make an attempt now?"

Jared had to agree. He wasn't certain what aces the Clans had up their collective sleeves, but they had to have something. Otherwise, all of this was for nothing.

"How well positioned are our probes to see the upcoming battle?" he asked slowly.

"We have two in position near the target flip point at this time," Marcus said. "The data they're sending back is delayed by the requirement to send it via tight beam to the multiflip point. The probe there periodically flips and passes the data to another probe, which does the same in turn. The probe at the end of the chain is in this system and used its FTL com to send data to *Persephone*.

"That means our on-scene data is delayed by approximately six hours. The general data from the system that the main probe gathers via gravitic scanners is timelier but only details the ship movements and what can be gathered by time-delayed observation.

"Status update: we've just received a new data packet, and a number of previously hidden vessels have activated their drives and become visible to the probes through gravitic scanners. That would be the ambush force that you predicted, Admiral. They're moving to block the Clan forces from retreating."

Well then, it looked as if things were about to get interesting for the Clans.

He was about to say something to that effect when the hatch leading into the corridor opened, and Elise stepped inside. Standing right behind her was Lily Stone. Weirdly, his wife looked… anxious.

He surged to his feet. "What's wrong?"

Lily held up a hand and smiled reassuringly. "Absolutely nothing. Your wife is in excellent health. I'm only here to see Kelsey."

Elise nodded and smiled. "And while they're chatting, I have something to tell you."

* * *

KELSEY WAS surprised when Lily led her down to *Invincible*'s medical center. She tried to ask her friend what was going on, but Lily only shook her head. "We'll talk when I get to somewhere a little bit more private."

"You're starting to scare me," Kelsey said. "Is something wrong with Elise that you just didn't want to tell Jared?"

"If there was, I couldn't tell you. But in this case, Elise has given me permission to speak freely about what she's telling Jared right now. I just don't want to do that in public. It's nothing bad, but it's private."

Kelsey wasn't reassured.

Lily wouldn't be behaving this way if something weren't wrong. Maybe she was a cynic, but the last few years had taught her that a healthy dose of cynicism was a good thing. It prepared one for when things went sideways.

Her second surprise was when Lily didn't take her to one of the offices but straight to one of the diagnostic tables. Her friend waved a hand at the doctors and medical personnel nearby, shooing them off before she activated the privacy screen so that they could speak without prying ears.

"Pop up here, and I'll tell you what's going on," Lily said. "I need to take a scan of you to verify something while I do. Lie back."

She did as instructed, but she was growing more nervous by the moment. "Spill."

"It looks like the EMP on Terra damaged Elise's contraceptive implant. She's about six weeks pregnant. I'm checking you to see whether or not you're in the same condition."

Kelsey's mind went blank. "Pregnant? I can't be pregnant. We're going to attack the master AI very soon. Please, tell me that my implant is still working."

"You know how you're always saying that you have to overcome adversity as a Marine Raider?" Lily asked with a wry smile. "Now you're going to have to overcome something a lot more challenging. You're pregnant, Kelsey."

Kelsey lay there, stunned. How could that possibly be? She'd never even *imagined* having children.

Oh, sure, she'd known that she would have to continue the Bandar line, but that was *years* in the future. She and Talbot hadn't even *discussed* the possibility of children.

"Oh, my God," she said as she sat up abruptly. "What's Talbot going to say?"

"He's going to be thrilled," Lily said, putting a hand on her shoulder. "It looks like your implant failed on Terra itself. You're a bit more than five months pregnant. You're going to start showing in another month or so. You're lucky that you didn't have morning sickness like Elise. That would've been miserable. Marine Raider augmentation for the win!"

"Oh, this is *so* not good."

"Good or bad, that's the way it is," Lily said pragmatically. "Would you like to know the sex of your baby?"

Numbly, Kelsey nodded.

"You're going to have a girl," Lily said with a grin. "I'm sure that both Talbot and your father will be thrilled. Your mother too."

Kelsey sat there in shock. How was she going to be able to care for a child when they were in the middle of a war? Worse, how was she going to keep Talbot from grounding her ass during this critical assault? Humanity needed her.

"This is all confidential, right?" she asked. "You can't say anything about it unless I give my explicit permission."

Lily nodded. "I won't say a word until and unless you give me permission to do so. How you tell your husband and Jared is up to you."

"And so is not telling them at all, at least for the moment."

Her friend's eyes widened. "Kelsey, you're well protected inside your powered armor, but going into combat would risk the child. As a medical professional, I can't endorse that."

"You're right," Kelsey said with a sigh. "I'm going to ask them to keep it quiet for now. Thanks for letting me know."

"I'll always be here for you," Lily said, relaxing slightly as she gave Kelsey a hug. "I want you to come to see me for a more detailed workup when you have time. We can develop your prenatal plan then."

"I'll do that."

What she *wouldn't* do was tell her husband or Jared. Humanity was depending on her, and while it was a horrible risk, they still needed her skill and ability. She didn't want to risk a child—her child—in this fight, but if they failed, the little girl inside her wouldn't have a life worth living.

She couldn't tell *anyone* that she was pregnant.

8

———

Carl watched as the light show repeated itself over and over again. He was absolutely certain that he was looking at a map of the flip point network throughout the entire Milky Way, only he doubted it was accurate.

It might have been at one time, but flip points changed as stars moved. When two stars became separated over time, the flip point between them disappeared. It had happened inside the old Terran Empire a few times over its long history, so this was established science.

If the age of the dinosaurs was any marker, the aliens who'd created this map had done so on the order of seventy million years ago. Over that kind of time frame, virtually every single flip point that didn't go to a star in the same cluster would've been severed, while new connections would have been made with stars that wandered through.

Hell, in seventy million years, the Milky Way had rotated around its central core almost a third of an orbit. Any kind of large-scale organization that might have existed in the distant past was undoubtedly gone. Not only would the constellations visible from

Terra have drastically changed, so would the makeup of the entire galactic neighborhood.

That didn't mean that what they'd found was unimportant, though. Whoever these aliens had been, they'd had enough knowledge to create a map of the entire flip point network for a *galaxy*. Just traveling from one side of the Milky Way to the other would've taken lifetimes for anyone using the technology that the Empire had.

The aliens obviously knew something humans didn't, or they'd had a method for mapping the flip point network that was far beyond what the Terran Empire at its height could envision.

Carl paced around the circumference of the glowing map, tapping into the feed from the drones that Talbot had made available to him. Assuming that the place where the map started flashing was the planet on which they stood, he had a map of what that area looked like. Comparing it with what he had stored in his implants confirmed what he'd already guessed. The maps were significantly different.

"What are you finding?" Talbot asked. "Is this really a map of the entire galaxy?"

"Undoubtedly," Carl confirmed. "Only, it's out of date by about seventy million years, so it won't be helpful in figuring out anything about our current situation. What I want to know is why they left it here and why it chose to reveal itself to us.

"Well, actually, I want to know how it's powered and how it works, but I doubt whether I'm going to be able to figure that out in the limited time we have. Why would aliens transport a bunch of dinosaurs so far from Terra? And then, once they'd done so, why did they set up a trigger to announce the presence of this obelisk when Terrans arrived?"

Talbot scratched his chin. "It's more likely that they set it up so that it announced its presence as soon as anyone landed on the surface. It did so right after we touched down."

"Maybe. Maybe not. Everything seems so targeted that I'm wondering whether multiple conditions had to be met to get that signal. Otherwise, why not just announce its presence as soon as ships arrived in orbit? Surely something this advanced knew the moment we appeared in this system."

His friend frowned. "You think it was specifically waiting for humans? Why?"

"That's the sixty-four thousand dollar question, though I suspect that any being from Terra would have sufficed."

Talbot blinked. "What's a dollar, and why would I want sixty-four thousand of them?"

Carl waved off the question. "Never mind. It's just something that Kelsey picked up from some old entertainment vids. Translated, you've asked the most important question of all. I'd wager something is controlling the entire network of nanites. For some reason, the aliens wanted to keep the life on this world the way they left it.

"I feel pretty confident that when you came into contact with the velociraptors or the plants, some of the nanites inside them got into your system. From what I understand about how they work, they deactivated themselves, but they could have sent some kind of message back along the control network, saying that beings from Terra had arrived on the planet.

"While humans didn't come along until long after the dinosaurs were harvested, we share some common genetic characteristics. Whatever controls the nanites would've known that we shared a birth world, and that may have been the trigger for summoning us here and showing us this."

Carl shook his head and sighed. "I just don't understand why they wanted us to see it. They had to have known, simply based on the types of animals they'd harvested, that it would be a very long time—if ever—before Terra produced a sentient race with interstellar capabilities. Considering how few aliens we've encountered, the odds were very much stacked against that outcome.

"Yet they went to the trouble of harvesting plants and animals that were common on Terra seventy-plus million years ago and relocated them to a world that they almost certainly had to have terraformed.

"Why? What were we supposed to gain by seeing this map? As a reward, it's very cool but ultimately useless."

"Then there has to be something else," Talbot said evenly. "Everything has a purpose, even if we have no idea what it might be. The aliens went to a lot of trouble setting this up for us, and now that we've arrived at the party, we're supposed to get a present, right? Or is this some kind of test?"

Carl blinked. If this was some kind of test, what exactly were the parameters? There had to be a question asked for it to be answered. What did this image ask of him?

"I'm going to try something," he said.

Without waiting for a response, Carl walked back to the center of the room and stood on the smaller oval. He could still detect the repeating signal that he'd triggered to turn the map on. What he was about to try would probably fail, but it was the only way he could think of to answer the implied question.

He transmitted the same signal he'd used to activate the map but sped up the pulses. He kept sending the signal, increasing the speed by a small increment each time. It might not be the solution to the question asked, but it couldn't hurt to try.

The area over his head exploded with light as the map rearranged itself as if it were speeding through time. He couldn't comprehend even a small part of what he was seeing, so he didn't even try. He waited until it had finished and displayed the map in a relatively static form once again.

As before, the map began at a single point, and the flip points from there began illuminating themselves. He compared the small section of a map that he had in his implants with what was being displayed and discovered that the two were now virtually identical. The only difference that he could see was that his version didn't have a few of the permutations this new map had.

That might very well be because he hadn't finished exploring all the branches of the local multiflip point node, or it might be because all the alien device was doing was projecting possibilities. Even if there were some differences, what he was looking at now had the potential for getting them to Twilight River.

He ran the map through his implants and found what looked like Twilight River. There was a far flip point there that looked like it went to a system with a branch of the multiflip point node that they'd recently visited. If this map was accurate, there was a path to Twilight River.

"What just happened?" Talbot asked. "Did you blow it up?"

Carl shook his head and grinned. "I think I found us a way to get to the master AI. Now all we have to do is get out of here and tell someone."

* * *

ELISE SAT down at the table, took Jared's hands in hers, and pulled him down to sit beside her. "I'm fine, but I'm afraid I have shocking news. You're going to be a father."

She could feel the tears starting to gather at the corners of her eyes. They were tears of joy, but she knew from long experience that men couldn't tell the difference, so she needed to be overtly reassuring.

"Before you say anything," she continued, "I want you to know how happy this makes me. I'm about six weeks along. Are you ready for another shock? It's twins. I know their sex and can tell you if you want to know."

Her husband leaned forward and gathered her into his arms, squeezing her tightly. "This is wonderful!"

She held him tightly, crying for real now. She'd known that he'd be happy for her—for both of them—but it was a relief to have it out in the open.

The two of them sat there for long minutes, just holding one another and saying nothing. Eventually, Jared pulled back and wiped his own tears away on his sleeve. He squared his shoulders.

"Tell me."

"Identical twin boys. Lily says they're perfectly healthy. That brings up another problem for us to solve. What shall we name them?"

"Should we name them yet?" he asked. "I don't want to be a pessimist, but we're a long way from home, and a lot could happen before we get there."

She gripped his hands tighter. "We can at least talk about names. They don't become official until a child is born in any case, at least on Pentagar. I'd imagine customs are similar in the New Terran Empire."

He nodded. "If you have no objection, I'd like to put a couple of names up for consideration. When I was a boy, I had the best pair of granduncles you could imagine. Jim and Joe were there for me when I was growing up. My grandfather died in an accident before I was born, so they filled in for him.

"They're still a big part of my life, even though I rarely get back to Xander to see them these days. It would mean a lot to me if we could think about James and Joseph."

She nodded. "They won't technically be Mertzes, since they'll have my name, but they're just as much a part of the Mertz family as they are the Orisons. When we get back home, you'll have to send them word that they're going to be great-granduncles."

"They'll be thrilled. They won't be able to take them out to the woods like they did me because they're getting up in age, but with modern medical treatments, they're still both going to be there for them growing up."

He leaned back and looked at her. "This is going to be complicated. Not only will they be princes on Pentagar, they'll also inherit the Dutchy of East Bay on Xander one day. I suppose they're also princes of the blood in the New Terran Empire since they have the blood of emperors in their veins."

She chuckled. "One of these days, someone is going to look back at their family tree and go, what happened here? What is this big knot?"

He laughed. "They're not going to have to wonder. They'll know their parentage from the beginning. I don't want our children to have to go through what I did when I found out the truth. It would've been a lot simpler for me to know how convoluted things were right from the very start.

"I suppose we could simplify things for them a little bit. Whoever the oldest one is, he's going to be the heir to the Kingdom of Pentagar one day. I think it would be fair if the other one is the heir to East Bay. That way, no one gets shafted."

She nodded. "That makes perfect sense, and it's wise of you to think so far ahead. They're going to appreciate that when they grow up. I'm so thrilled that you're happy."

He raised an eyebrow. "How could I be unhappy to hear that our family is growing? Yes, the timing is inconvenient, but one of the things I've learned in life is that you have to work with the circumstances you're given. You *are* happy about this, right?"

She nodded with only her smile answering his question. She couldn't explain to him how she felt, because "happy" didn't cover just how much love she was feeling at this very moment. Her life had taken a turn that she hadn't anticipated, and she was thrilled.

"Do we want to tell anyone about this?" he asked.

"I don't have any objections."

He raised his eyes toward the ceiling. "Marcus? Are you listening?"

"The subroutine responsible for privacy is listening at this moment. Should I terminate the subroutine and pass this conversation on to my larger self?"

"Please do."

A moment passed. "I'm happy for you," Marcus said. "Though I can see that I'm going to have to do some research. I knew that biological beings reproduced in this fashion, but I'd never considered the possibility that anyone I knew could grow other beings inside them. It's somewhat... unsettling."

Laughter bubbled up inside Elise, and she didn't try to stop it. Moments later, the rest of them were laughing along with her. Life was good. Even though they were in a difficult place, this was a moment to celebrate.

9

Talbot gave his friend a dubious look. "That's good news, but like you said, things change. What makes you think that it's got the correct information now? It's not like it's monitoring the flip point network in real time. Or is it?"

Carl shrugged. "We shouldn't dismiss the idea out of hand. After all, we discovered faster-than-light communication. I suppose that means that some galaxy-wide network could conceivably be receiving status updates from every flip point in existence, even ones that hadn't existed at the time the monitors were put in place."

Talbot wasn't sure how to take that. The idea of some advanced species having sent probes to every single flip point in the galaxy seemed ludicrous. Of course, so did the idea that they could just sense them.

Though he had to admit that it was at least possible. Omega—the being that lived in the station around the black hole in the Nova system—could sense the flip point network in its vicinity and even create artificial flip points.

Talbot snapped his fingers. "Can you find the part of this map that links up with the Nova system? If this is just an approximation, it's not going to show the artificial flip points that Omega created."

Carl stared at him for a moment and then whipped out a tablet to start going over something. "I'm looking at what the drones are recording to see if I can get them to zero in on that specific area. There are far too many linkages for the drones to give me any kind of real-time update. I'm not even sure that they can record everything with all of the activity."

"How many flip points do you think this thing is showing?" Talbot asked, not really sure he wanted to know the answer.

"Back on prespaceflight Terra, they believed that the Milky Way held roughly one hundred billion stars. Modern astronomers suspect that that number is low. There are a lot of stars that just aren't bright enough to be detectable at a distance. They can do some rough estimation of mass on other galaxies, but that's a little more challenging with our own since we're swimming in the pool, so to speak.

"Let's be conservative and say that there are fifty percent more than the lowball number. We already know that flip points don't necessarily go to every system, but they also can link back to previously visited systems within their part of the network. I suspect the numbers are going to be a wash when you start looking at it that way, so probably on the order of one hundred and fifty billion flip points."

"Holy crap," Talbot muttered. "I'm not sure that I want this to be a real-time recording. Even if it's old data, I can't imagine keeping that kind of information straight."

"Honestly, it sounds like it would be harder to calculate the orbits of a hundred billion-plus stars," Carl said. "Everything is going to influence everything else, so over the amount of time that's passed since this map was created, if it's anything close to accurate, that's really scary. It would imply a level of understanding of stellar orbits that's almost total.

"Omega's race was advanced. The people that created the Pandorans, now they were *really* advanced. These people, they were gods in comparison."

Carl tapped the slate and frowned. "Yep, I think god-like just about does it. I found the Nova system, and it shows both of the artificial flip points."

Talbot opened his mouth to say something but closed it again when he realized that he had no idea what he really thought about the situation. Whoever these aliens had been, this meant that they'd had a total grasp on the flip point network for an entire galaxy in real time.

"Is there any way that we can record this?" Talbot asked. "Having a map of all of the flip points inside the Rebel Empire—and maybe even the Singularity—could be extremely useful considering what we're doing."

"I'd need to bring down more drones, and I'd need a lot more storage space," Carl said with a shake of his head. "I'm getting a good reading of the area around us right now, but the Terran Empire is vast. We don't know the Singularity's borders except where they run up against the Old Empire.

"And do you know what's scary? All of known space is just a tiny fraction of what this map is showing. What we're seeing is like an ant being shown a picture of an entire planet. That's how small we are in comparison to all of this."

"Gather what you can, and we'll get out of here," Talbot said. "We can always come back and visit again with more equipment. I want to take a walk around the perimeter and make sure that we're not missing anything."

"Got it," Carl said. "If you'll give me fifteen or twenty minutes, I should have filled up all of the storage I've got with me."

Leaving the young scientist to his work, Talbot walked directly to the nearest wall and stopped to take in the entirety of the displayed galaxy. From the outside, it looked like a bar of stars that had four swirling arms coming out of it.

One hundred and fifty billion stars. Unbelievable.

Thankfully, trying to comprehend something like that was above his pay grade. He'd leave that to the eggheads and be happy to focus on other issues.

He started walking around the edge of the chamber in a clockwise direction. The drones hadn't shown him anything unusual, but they hadn't completed their scan of the room before the humans had set off the starscape. That meant they could've missed something.

He'd made it about three-quarters of the way around when he found something unusual. There was a small alcove built into the side of the chamber. It was maybe half the height of an adult human. He could get inside on his hands and knees, but it wasn't really built for someone his size.

Talbot played his hand light into the alcove and saw that it only went back about two meters. There was some kind of engraving on the stone, but the angle made it difficult to see. The shadows from his light were contributing to obscuring them.

He got down on his hands and knees and went inside. Using his implants, he began recording a video of the carvings. It might have been hieroglyphics or even an alien language, but it certainly looked like writing as opposed to pictures.

He'd only gone about a quarter of the way around the small alcove when he saw something unexpected. One of the carvings glowed with a soft blue light.

He reached out and ran a finger along it. The cool stone felt natural.

Suddenly, the rune changed from blue to lime green, and a hint of motion in the periphery of his vision made him look back at the opening.

Only there was no opening. It had vanished, and he was trapped.

The small cavity began to brighten. He couldn't see any source for the white illumination, but it quickly became too intense to see, and he closed his eyes. The brilliance lasted for maybe fifteen seconds, and then everything went dark again.

When he opened his eyes, he saw that the stone door had vanished again, so he scurried out before it could change its mind.

He made it to his feet and then realized that something was *seriously* wrong. He was no longer in the underground chamber. Instead, he was standing on a stone ledge. It was nighttime. Sort of.

He took a couple of steps forward and saw a huge city made of green stone laid out below him. It was swathed in bright starlight. Really bright. When he looked up, stars literally filled the night sky.

There were far more of them than he'd ever seen in the sky before, even in deep space.

They were so tightly packed that he immediately knew something was terribly wrong. Their combined brightness was more than a moonlit night by orders of magnitude. It was like soft daylight.

He wasn't on the same planet that he'd been on moments before. Not even close. This one had to be much closer to the galactic core. If that were true, he'd left human-explored space far, far behind.

Whatever was happening, he needed to undo it. He turned back to the opening only to find that the small cavity had sealed itself up, and he was trapped on an alien world.

* * *

THE HATCH to the conference room opened, and Jared looked over to see Lily and Kelsey coming back in. His sister looked… disturbed. He started to say something, but Marcus interrupted him.

"I'm detecting a significant power surge somewhere below the obelisk. The output is substantial."

"It's got to be something that Carl did," Jared said as he rose. "Contact the surface party and make sure they're okay. I'm on my way to the flag bridge."

He gave Elise a hug and kissed her tenderly. "I love you, and this is wonderful news, but I've got to go to work."

She nodded and smiled back at him as he headed for the hatch. "Go save the day, my hero."

Kelsey said something to Lily and then fell in beside him as he headed up the short corridor toward the flag bridge.

"Are you okay?" he asked.

She nodded. "Lily just wanted to check my contraceptive implant. I'm perfectly healthy. Congratulations on being a father. You're going to make a great one."

He grinned at that. "I can hardly wrap my mind around it. Twins. That's going to complicate my life."

Kelsey chuckled. "Your life? Imagine how much it's going to

complicate Elise's. You get to go gallivanting off while she's nursing. How unfair is that?"

"It does seem kind of lopsided," he admitted. "At least Lily can extract the children and put them into gestation pods so that she doesn't have to give birth the old-fashioned way."

His sister grimaced. "I hadn't even thought of that. Ugh. What's the cutoff for something like that?"

"The first trimester," Marcus said from the overhead speaker. "After that, the mother has to bear the child naturally."

Kelsey shot a seemingly frustrated glance toward the ceiling. "Why not after that point?"

"You'd have to ask Doctor Stone for more details, but my understanding is that extraction after that point poses too much danger to the child and mother. Biological reproduction is more fraught with danger than I'd ever suspected. It makes one happy to be a constructed being."

"Isn't that just peachy," Kelsey muttered.

"Why so grumbly?" Jared asked. "Elise dodged that flechette. Imagine what would've happened if she'd gotten pregnant almost immediately after we left Terra. She might be six months along and have missed the cutoff. She's an old-fashioned kind of girl, but I'd imagine that would annoy the hell out of her."

"As it should."

The hatch ahead of them slid open, and Jared stepped out into the flag bridge. Commander Kaitlinn Cannon, his chief of staff, stood from her console nearby and approached as he sat at his station.

She'd been on the mission to Terra with him and been one of the few survivors. She was tough, and he knew for a fact that the redheaded woman never gave up.

Her background was as a tactical officer, and she was very skilled when it came to fighting, but if someone wanted to command their own ship, they needed to gain a broad experience of shipboard tasks. For the last six months, he'd been happy to have her serving as his chief of staff and giving her some of that experience.

"What have you got?" he asked.

She nodded at Kelsey. "There was a massive power surge inside the plateau. The eggheads are still trying to figure out precisely what it was, but it put out a lot more energy than this ship could produce. The surge lasted about fifteen seconds.

"Everyone down below reports that they're okay, except for Carl and Talbot. They still haven't come back out of the obelisk. Betting odds say that Carl probably did something."

"That's a safe bet," he agreed. "We need to see about getting them out of there. Has anyone figured out exactly what they did to get transported inside?"

"Not yet."

Cannon opened her mouth to say something else but paused, her eyes going slightly unfocused. A few moments later, she frowned.

"Scratch that. Carl's back outside. He just flew out of the top of the obelisk and came down to a landing right where he'd been taken from. He's signaling for you."

"Put him on the main screen."

The large screen on the front of the compartment switched from the view of the planet to Carl Owlet standing beside the obelisk. He looked almost angry and a little bit frightened.

"Admiral, we've got a problem," he said grimly. "There's a huge chamber under the obelisk that has this incredible star map. While I was documenting it, Talbot started a circuit of the chamber but never came back. Once I filled up my data storage, I went looking for him, but I couldn't find him or any other exits. He's gone."

"How could he just vanish?" Kelsey demanded.

"I have no idea. I wouldn't have come up until I had him back, but I have information that simply can't wait. I found a far flip point on the map that might take us directly to Twilight River. I'll send everything that I have to Marcus and then head back down to find Talbot."

Jared shook his head in mild disbelief. Of course they'd lost track of Talbot. Why not?

"We detected a massive power surge," he said. "Could that have had anything to do with Talbot's disappearance?"

Carl shrugged. "Possibly. Should I wait for you to get back down, Kelsey?"

She shook her head, her expression torn. "If you've found a path to Twilight River, I have to be the one exploring it. The timeline is too tight for me to split my attention, so I'm counting on you to rescue my wayward husband."

"Don't go alone," Jared added sternly.

"I won't. As soon as I get the data to Marcus and get my backup briefed, I'll go get him. You have my word on that. Owlet out."

Jared turned his gaze to Kelsey as the screen returned to showing the planet they were orbiting. He really should come up with a name for it. Dinosaur World? Obelisk World? The latter sounded better.

His sister looked worried but had a gleam in her eye. "This is the break we've been looking for. We're going to sneak through the back door and screw that bastard while its attention is firmly planted on the front door. I can scout while we move most of the fleet into position to back up *Persephone* from the near end of the flip point."

Jared nodded. "That's a good plan. We can leave *Caduceus* here with some escort destroyers. Once Carl finds Talbot, she can catch up with us."

This was an incredibly lucky break. Their biggest strength was their enemy's ignorance of their existence. Now that they had a possible way forward, the load shifted onto his sister's shoulders.

Thank God she was ready for the moment, even though the universe couldn't seem to resist trying to distract her.

10

Kelsey arrived on *Persephone*'s bridge and half expected Angela to confront her. She knew there was no way the woman could possibly know that she was pregnant unless Lily had said something to her, but she was still more than a bit worried until Angela grinned.

"Carl really brought home the bacon," her friend said. "If this pans out, it's going to give us everything we need to make the magic happen. The master AI won't even know that we're in the system. It can't *possibly* know. Then we can sneak up on its ass and turn it off."

"I'd rein in your expectations if I were you," Kelsey cautioned. "This is a big stroke of luck, but it's still going to take a lot of work to make the magic happen. You can bet that that system is stuffed absolutely full of defensive measures to prevent exactly what we're going to try and do. Even though the AI doesn't know about the potential back door, it's had half a millennium to prepare for humans.

"According to the information Carl sent, we'll need to go back a couple of branches on the multiflip point network and then look for a far flip point that we missed on the way through."

Angela nodded. "We're ready to head out now. It'll take us three hours to get to the multiflip point, maybe twenty minutes to flip back to the system in question, and then another six hours to get out to the far flip point location that he specified.

"I'm not sure how that alien map can be so accurate. It's been seventy million years since it was created. How could it possibly know where all of these flip points are?"

"I haven't got the slightest idea," Kelsey admitted. "Aliens are going to alien. Carl says that the map shows the artificial flip points that Omega created, so that means whatever technology they're using has a current map of the *entire* flip point network.

"Since the Milky Way is about a hundred thousand light-years across and has something like one hundred and fifty billion stars, that sounds ridiculous, yet here we are."

"Considering that the far flip points average a little less than a thousand light-years, and not every system has a far flip point heading in the right direction, it would take decades to make the trip."

"Don't forget that you can't get too close to the galactic core," Kelsey said. "Carl mentioned that the radiation there is significant. I'm not sure how much you'd have to skirt it with our antiradiation shields, but that would be a factor. Not that we're going to go across the damned galaxy anytime soon.

"Let's get ourselves in motion. The sooner we get to Twilight River, the sooner we can beat the AIs once and for all."

Angela frowned. "What about Talbot?"

Kelsey shook her head. "I'm worried, but if we wait too long, the situation on the other end might become too complicated for us to deal with. Carl will find him. We've got to be thinking of humanity first."

Her friend stared at her for a couple of seconds and then nodded slowly. "I understand that, but I don't think he's going to be very happy that you've left without him."

"Then he shouldn't have let the aliens kidnap him," Kelsey said tartly. "I don't think they did anything to intentionally harm my husband. I think he got himself into a different portion of the facility, and all Carl is going to have to do is figure out where he went. There's no indication that these beings meant us any harm."

"I suppose not," Angela admitted. "Then again, they did

relocate dinosaurs from Terra to this new planet and change its ecosystem to match our birth world. What's to say that they didn't decide that Talbot would make a good study sample to set up another world?"

Kelsey considered that for a moment, and her gut churned. She didn't want to leave her husband in the lurch, but she honestly didn't think he was in too great a danger, and if she delayed, word of her condition might get out, and then she'd be screwed.

She had to act now.

"They'd need women for that, so I'm going to keep that worry on the back burner," Kelsey said. "Honestly, I'm concerned, and if I had any choice in the matter, I'd stay. The problem is that I don't have a choice. None of us do. Trust your husband to make the magic happen."

A man at one of the consoles lifted his head from his screens. "Colonel, Major, we've got a cutter inbound from *Invincible*. The admiral is aboard. He's indicated that he's going to accompany us while the fleet follows."

That hadn't been part of the plan. The fleet was supposed to trail them almost to Twilight River, but he should've stayed on *Invincible*. What had changed?

Kelsey opened her mouth to object, but what was she going to say? Jared *was* in command of the fleet. If he'd decided to go on the probing mission, she couldn't stop him.

"The Raiders are almost all back," Angela said. "We should be ready to leave orbit shortly."

"I'll go wait for Jared in the wardroom," Kelsey said. "I could use some coffee."

She made her way to the wardroom and poured herself a cup. She wondered if it was really healthy to be drinking coffee when she was pregnant but decided it was a little late to worry about caffeine. No doubt Lily would chew her ass off for it and any number of other things she was doing. Or about to do.

Luckily for her, Lily wasn't there.

Twenty minutes later, there was a knock at the hatch, and Jared stepped in. Kelsey started to say something snarky but then saw Lily standing right behind her brother, her eyes narrowed as she stared at Kelsey.

Oh, crap.

* * *

ELISE STEPPED out of the cutter and stared up at the obelisk. It was tremendous, intimidating, and gorgeous.

She'd probably be in a lot of trouble if Sean knew that she'd come down to the surface, but what he didn't know wouldn't hurt him. Kelsey wasn't going to be able to be there for Talbot, so she felt it was her duty to stand in for her.

Besides, she had Olivia with her, so she wasn't alone.

"Wow," Olivia said, craning her neck up to see the top of the obelisk. "That thing is *huge*."

"Ladies," she heard someone shout.

Elise looked in the direction of the voice and saw Carl waving his arm from where he stood beside the obelisk. It looked like they were assembling something to scan the giant structure.

The two women walked over and stood nearby as Carl explained something about frequencies to a few other scientists standing nearby. He was laying out the rules about how something needed to be done. She was impressed by how much more decisive he'd become since she'd first met him.

He'd been a retiring, introspective sort in the beginning. Now he was an assertive leader, a man who didn't hesitate to give orders that he expected would be obeyed.

She remembered the story that his wife had told about how he'd stood between her and the men trying to kill them with only the hammer that he'd built for Kelsey. How he'd saved her and killed every single last one of them with it.

As Talbot would say, he'd seen the elephant.

He might never be a warrior in the strictest of senses, but he was made of the same stuff. He'd find his friend no matter how long it took or how much pain and effort it required.

As soon as he'd finished speaking to the other scientists, he turned to face Elise and Olivia. "What can I do for you? I'm a little bit busy."

"You're going back inside, aren't you?" Elise asked. "We're going with you."

He scowled and shook his head. "That's not the best idea. We don't know where Talbot went or what took him."

"Nevertheless, that's what we're going to do," she said resolutely, putting on her crown princess face.

He sighed and shrugged. "If Commodore Meyer gets angry about this, I was overruled. If you'd step over to the oval, we'll take a trip up and then down."

Olivia frowned. "What does that mean?"

"The oval sends out a short-range signal that I match with my equipment, and that activates some kind of antigravity field that lifts us up and brings us through a temporary opening at the top of the obelisk. Then we go down through a shaft to a chamber somewhere far below.

"There's got to be more underneath that, since I saw nothing that would have caused a power spike like the one that happened when Talbot disappeared. Considering that I also never saw any holoprojectors to display the map we found, I'm not sure that I'd even recognize what I was looking at if I did. These aliens were so far in advance of us that it might as well be magic."

"Then you're our wizard," Elise assured him. "Let's wave your wand, say abracadabra, and get moving."

Carl chuckled, and then they walked over to the area that was colored just like the obelisk. The women followed him closely. He brought up an instrument and did something with it, and suddenly they were rising into the air with nothing holding them.

Elise resisted the urge to scream. If she forced herself to think of this as a lift that was taking them somewhere inside a ship, then she wouldn't panic. In a way, it *was* just like a lift. Only one that was invisible and insubstantial.

Olivia cursed under her breath but managed to avoid freaking out as well. "You could've warned us about that."

"I did," Carl said. "I suppose I could've gone into more detail, but that wouldn't be nearly as fun. Hold on, here we go."

As he'd indicated, a portion of the top section of the obelisk seemed to just disappear. Inside was a dark shaft that led downward. Moments after they entered it, the light from above extinguished, and they dropped like stones.

"Can we get some light?" Elise asked.

"That's a bad idea. Right now, you can't see how fast we're moving, and if your eyes tried to make that assessment, it would freak you out even more. Just wait until we get down below."

That sounded far from reassuring.

The trip didn't take very long, and they came out into a large open area with enough light for her to see. They were off to the side of a large oval chamber. There were probably thirty people scouring the room, looking at the walls, floor, and even high up at the ceiling with bright lights.

Her innate fear of falling made her panic for a few seconds, but they touched down as lightly as feathers. She took a couple of steps, and nothing seemed to be inhibiting her from walking away from the jade-colored area that they'd landed on, so she did just that.

"Are all the walls the same?" she asked, her voice just a bit shaky. "Smooth and featureless like the rest?"

"Yes," Carl said. "We're scanning them now, but we're not detecting anything beyond the surface. The stealth field obscures everything beyond this chamber. We've resorted to making loud noises and trying to hear if any of the segments of the wall sound different than the others. That might allow us to detect a hidden passage."

"Could we see the map?" Olivia asked.

"I'll activate it, and it'll start running in sequence," Carl agreed. "Experience has shown that it starts with what existed roughly seventy million years ago. That is impressive enough. I can move it to the present if you'd like."

Elise had to admit that she was intimidated by the scale of what these aliens had created and mystified by their obscure reasons for doing so.

Carl led them to the center of the room, where there was a

smaller jade oval, and she stepped behind him to watch as he brought up a program on his tablet and instructed it to send a signal. She looked up, expecting to see stars all around them, but that was not what happened.

That was not what happened at all.

Close around her body, a swirling vortex of bright gold curves and strange sigils appeared and began rotating slowly around her. She jumped back, but the effect moved with her.

"What the hell is this?" she almost screamed. "Get it off me!"

Carl frowned at her. "Get what off you? What's happening?"

"Can't you see this?" she demanded. "These swirls of light and weird symbols all around me?"

He shook his head as he walked around her. "I don't see anything like that."

She initiated an implant call with both him and Olivia before sending a vid of what she was seeing.

Carl's eyes widened. "Holy crap! Does it hurt?"

"I don't want to find out! Undo it!"

"I'm trying," he said as he stepped back into the oval and manipulated his equipment. "I'm sending out the same signal, but it's not responding. I'm not even getting the original signal now. Are you okay?"

"It doesn't seem to be hurting me," Elise grudgingly admitted, taking a few forced breaths to calm herself. "Are these letters?"

"They look like some kind of alien script, but I have absolutely no idea what they mean or why you can see them but we can't."

Elise sighed. This was her fault. She'd been the one who'd wanted to come down here and see what all the excitement was about. Now she was going to have her fill of it, whether she liked it or not.

Hesitantly, she raised her hand in front of her and tried to touch one of the golden curves. Her fingers passed right through it, but the display rotated in the direction of the movement.

"It's insubstantial," she said.

"Be careful," Carl warned. "We don't know what any of this does."

She shifted her hand to the side and reached for one of the runes.

It glowed blue as her finger touched the area it occupied, even though it was just as insubstantial as the curves of light, and suddenly the air around her exploded with light.

Elise blinked, and when she adjusted to what she was seeing, she realized that the starfield that Carl had been talking about earlier was now above their heads. It wasn't showing any flashing lights or flip lines, though.

"It seems like I'm controlling the display like you did," she said.

Her friend frowned as he looked up. "There's nothing up there. Whatever you're seeing is only visible to you. It has to be something the holoprojectors are doing, though how they can focus only on you seems impossible."

"Why was it different for me?" she asked. "Could it be the fact that I'm a woman?"

He shook his head. "We've had a number of people activate it, several of them women. There has to be a different explanation. Try touching a different rune."

"Is that safe?"

"It seems to be a control for the display. Unless we find something that says differently, I hope not."

"That's not at all reassuring."

She reached out and tapped another rune. The field of stars above her began expanding. It was like she was zooming in on a portion of it. The map just became a very localized segment of what had previously been displayed.

When it finished zooming in, she was looking at a single star system. She could see the planets and the star itself. She tried pulling one of the worlds closer, and it enlarged to the size of a basketball and hovered half a meter in front of her face.

It was like being in orbit around the world. She could see the clouds and land masses, the oceans and mountains. It really was just like being there.

"That's amazing," Olivia said.

"I can't imagine this is in real time," Carl said. "No way these aliens are monitoring some random planet like that. It does tell us that they've been there, though. Or at least sent probes at some point in the distant past. Try pulling back out, and let's look at something we know about. View the Nova system."

"I'm no navigator, and I don't really understand how to control this," she complained, making a shooing gesture that the planet in her face ignored. "I'm pushing random buttons here."

He nodded. "Right. Sorry."

Elise pushed at the planet like she was shoving it away, and the map expanded back out until her view was full of stars again. Well, she'd learned something, she supposed.

"Why did it pick me?" she demanded, her voice almost a wail. "And how do I turn it off?"

"Let's get you back outside," Carl said soothingly. "That should terminate whatever program is running. You've obviously been granted some kind of control interface that the rest of us weren't. It's bizarre. What makes you any different than the rest of us?"

That was when it hit her. She almost certainly knew the only difference between her and the other women. She was pregnant. Somehow, the alien machine had known that, and it was significant in some way that she couldn't fathom.

While she was thinking about that, Carl led her and Olivia over to the exit. The control interface moved with her. Once they were on the oval of jade, he tapped his tablet, and she waited for the unseen forces to lift them into the air.

Nothing happened.

11

Talbot tried to find a way to get back into the strange alcove for over an hour with no success. Whatever was concealing it from him looked exactly like the stone all around it. Hell, it might *be* the same stone.

He couldn't find any hidden triggers that allowed him back in, and no amount of pounding on the wall caused the rock to even chip. He had his flechette pistol, but he wasn't desperate enough to try shooting his way in just yet.

With a sigh, he took stock of his surroundings. The small outcropping of stone that he'd arrived on had a path that led down to the strange city below. There were no visible lights, so he had the impression that it wasn't occupied. Perhaps it had been abandoned long before humanity had evolved.

He took a few minutes to sit out of the wind and eat one of his ration bars. Thankfully, he'd outfitted himself like he was going on a mission, so he had bars stashed in various pockets all around his person. He even had enough water for a few days. If he hadn't had those two things, he'd have been in immediate trouble.

With him being on an alien planet and having no support structure, he would still run out of food and had no way to test any of the local plants or animals to see if they could support him. When that happened, he would have to roll the dice, and the odds were very much stacked against him.

He found some small stones and arranged an arrow pointing to the path that led down to the city. If Carl figured out how to follow him, his friend would need to know where he'd gone.

Part of him wanted to just sit right where he was and wait for rescue, but he just couldn't bring himself to do that. He wanted to at least look around the edges of the city below and see what he could discover.

The sheer number of stars overhead and their brightness told him that he was significantly closer to the galactic core than he'd been before. He hoped he wasn't so close that the radiation was dangerous, even on the planet's surface.

If it was, there was nothing he could do about it. Still, would the aliens have built a city in a place that was that hostile?

Maybe they ate radiation. Probably not. The planet's magnetic field likely protected it enough to live here. Or maybe there were alien artifacts in orbit that shielded the planet from the radiation with strong protective fields.

With aliens, one could never know.

There were plants all around him, and he could hear what certainly sounded like small critters moving in the brush. That implied that the radiation wasn't an issue for the local wildlife.

The little shrubs didn't look like anything he'd seen before, and because it was night, he didn't trust his judgment about what their actual color was. They looked kind of dark red, but that could just be an artifact of being viewed under starlight rather than sunlight.

With his enhanced vision options, he had no trouble seeing everything around him in exquisite detail, so he decided not to call any unwanted attention to himself by using a hand light. He made certain to record everything. If he ever got out of here, it would be useful to know what this planet had to offer.

As he carefully made his way down a path that looked like it had been made by wildlife, he thought about how much distance he'd traveled to get here. He'd come farther than any human being had *ever* traveled, bar none, and he hadn't even had a spaceship.

Somehow, the aliens had come up with a way to move people from planet to planet without using the natural flip point system. He had no idea how that was even possible, but one couldn't argue with the evidence in front of one's eyes.

Once he reached the flat ground below the hill, he saw that he was about half a kilometer from the edge of the city. The buildings started out low to the ground and were very wide. As they progressed further in, they rose until they dominated the sky. Based on the facility they'd found, the structures likely went deep below the ground as well, which was also a good shield against radiation.

Nowhere did he see any evidence of artificial light. The starlight reflected off the jade buildings, but that was it. The streets were dark and the buildings silent. There was no sign of any movement whatsoever. The city was definitely abandoned.

That was a testament to how ridiculously long-lived the building materials the aliens had used were. Talbot doubted very seriously that he'd find much other than the buildings themselves, because what could last seventy million years?

Part of him was concerned about being attacked by animals, so he kept his hand close to the butt of his pistol. It might not be much in the grand scheme of things, but the flechettes would deter any local critters that decided he was a midnight snack.

And if push came to shove, he could potentially get something to eat that way.

When he reached the first building, he found that it had a defined doorway. Admittedly, it seemed that the jade wall was solid, but there were hints of paint or some other substance in the shape of an outline.

No, not paint. Something that had once been part of the building itself. Something that was fused into the other material. It had faded over time but wasn't completely gone.

The door was like the alcove, low to the ground, and made for something squat. He supposed that was conclusive proof that the aliens hadn't been very tall.

Unlike the obelisk, there was a defined portion of the wall beside the door that looked like it was meant to be used to activate the entry. He doubted it was powered anymore, because this wasn't like the obelisk, where it was intended to stay active and pay attention to the world around it.

Still, nothing ventured, nothing gained.

Talbot pressed his hand against the discolored area and was shocked when the door flowed open. Literally flowed. The stone-like material seemed to just draw into the wall around it and leave an opening into the darkness beyond.

He drew his pistol and brought out one of his hand lights. He flashed the beam through the doorway, looking to see what was inside. The entry room was wide and deep, as he'd expected. It almost looked like a hotel lobby, with some type of furniture arrayed around small tables. The ceiling inside was high enough that he could stand. Barely.

Talbot ducked inside and waited for the door to close. When it did, he found a similar place to activate it on the inner wall and touched it. The door once again opened, so he wasn't trapped. Excellent.

He made his way over to one of the chairs and saw that they had no padding whatsoever. They were like small platforms that a creature could climb up on. In fact, the rear of the "chair" had a small ramp that could allow for exactly that. Based on its width and height, whatever beings had used it, they hadn't had very long legs, and they were wide of body.

Maybe they were kind of like crabs. Inflexible bodies, short legs, and long front-grasping claws.

Whatever they'd been, they were long gone.

He started walking deeper into the building but stopped as soon as something moved. Advancing out of the darkness at the rear of the room was something that looked *very* much like a crab.

* * *

JARED SMILED at Kelsey as he stepped into *Persephone*'s wardroom and took a seat. Lily took the seat beside Kelsey, giving her a smile that seemed a little strange.

Weirdly, Lily had been a bit on edge during the trip over from *Invincible*. He wasn't sure why she'd asked to accompany him, but as she was one of his senior officers, he wasn't going to say no. If she felt she needed to be here, that was good enough for him.

Kelsey seemed nervous, and that was entirely out of character for his sister.

"Is everything okay, Kelsey?" he asked.

His sister smiled at him. "I'm fine. We should have the Raiders back on board in just a bit. Once we're loaded up, we can explore the route leading to Twilight River and get the probes on their way if we get into the system itself."

He nodded. "Excellent. I've decided I need to be with you, since we might need to execute an immediate assault because of the distraction that the Clans have so helpfully provided, and I don't want to delay making the call. As planned, we'll bring most of the fleet with us but leave them one flip from Twilight River. That should be safe enough."

"You shouldn't assume that," Kelsey said. "Trouble follows me around."

"But not recently," Lily said. "Things have been pretty sedate for you over the last six months. I hope that's not going to change."

Kelsey smiled somewhat weakly back at the doctor. "Rest assured that I'm going to do everything that I can to make sure there's no drama until we're ready to take out the master AI."

This conversation was getting really strange. There was some kind of subtext that he wasn't privy to.

"What's going on?" Jared asked slowly.

Lily gave Kelsey a wide-eyed, innocent look. One that was *obviously* manufactured.

Kelsey sighed. "You're a real pain in the ass, Lily."

"It's part of my job description."

"You're not the only one expecting an addition to the family,"

Kelsey grumbled, turning to face him. "My contraceptive implant failed too. I'm about five months pregnant."

Jared felt his eyes narrow as the situation became clear in an instant. "You weren't going to tell me. You were going to go on this mission and fight."

"You're damned right I was," Kelsey said vehemently. "This is about the survival of the human race. I'm willing to risk my life, and that of my child, when the stakes are that high. If I'm not there, this entire thing could fall apart. I have the Imperial override codes in my head, so I *have* to be there."

He started to snap at her but forced himself to take a breath and count to five before he allowed himself to speak. "Not true, since we have Julia. You've already confirmed that her codes are identical to yours. You don't *have* to be there. You *want* to be there. That's a critical distinction."

Jared held up his hand when his sister started to speak. "I understand how important this mission is, believe me, and I'm pragmatic enough to admit that there may be something to what you're saying. What I'm not willing to do is put you in danger unless it's *absolutely* necessary.

"Julia will go with the attacking force, if I decide to send one, to provide the codes. She has Marine Raider augmentation, even if she's not a trained Raider. Jake Peters can be her bodyguard. If anyone can keep her safe, it's him."

He waggled a finger when she started to object. "This is not subject to discussion, Colonel. Those are my orders, and you *will* obey them."

His words obviously infuriated her, but she'd grown up a lot over the last few years. She simply sat there, stewing.

He turned his gaze to Lily. "I understand that this news was covered by doctor–patient confidentiality, but you should've informed me that Kelsey wasn't fit for duty."

"She's fit for duty," Lily objected. "Having a child isn't a disability, Admiral. What she's *not* cleared for is combat. I only suspected what she had in mind, so I couldn't tell you anything. I have my duty and my oath, and I'll uphold them both. You're just going to have to accept that that's the way it is."

As much as he didn't want to, he knew that she wasn't going to compromise her ethics for him. So be it.

He returned his attention to Kelsey. "I can see now that it's doubly important that I'm here. Who's going to stop you from doing whatever you want if I'm not looking over your shoulder once Lily heads back to *Caduceus*?"

"Fine!" Kelsey grumbled. "You've made your point. I disagree with it, but I don't exactly have a leg to stand on, do I? You're going to be my minder and make absolutely sure that I do what you want. Great."

"How about we actually get this mission on the road? I just got word that the last pinnace has docked, and everybody except for Talbot is now aboard. We can depart, and we should."

"One more question first," Jared said. "Am I going to have a niece or a nephew?"

Kelsey's expression softened a little bit. "A niece."

That made him smile. "I'm really happy for you and Talbot. I'm glad that I found out, because I want to see your girl grow into a strong woman just like her mother."

Kelsey's expression hardened. "Mark my words, Jared. I'll do *whatever* I have to do to make certain that she doesn't grow up under the sway of those machines. I don't care how many people that pisses off, you included."

"Let me be the first of *many* to wish—though likely not to your face—that your little girl grows up to be *exactly* like you," he said with a wry smile.

This was the bullheaded girl that he'd grown to know and love. He'd definitely have to keep an eye on her. If she could find a way to wiggle out of obeying his orders, she would. He just knew it.

It was his job to save her from herself. To save her unborn child from her impetuousness.

God save him. God save them all.

12

C arl had to admit that he was flummoxed. Whatever had happened to Elise had obviously disrupted the operation of the alien facility in some way. It was strange that it had only begun acting strangely after she'd arrived. He couldn't see any reason for the change, but obviously, something was responsible.

One of the most interesting aspects of this was that Elise could see whatever it was that swirled around her, but no one else could. To any outside observer, using even the most sophisticated imaging gear, there was nothing there.

How could she perceive something that they couldn't? He supposed if it was being transmitted through her implants, that could keep them from seeing it externally, but her implants were designed so that nothing external could influence them without her explicit permission.

Permission that she certainly hadn't given.

Nevertheless, as Sherlock Holmes had once said, when you've eliminated the impossible, whatever remains, however improbable, must be the truth. Frankly, with alien technology this advanced, calling it magic wasn't that much of a stretch.

Still, whatever was happening had to involve something that didn't violate the laws of physics. He didn't believe that mystical handwaving could influence the world without being detectable.

It was always possible that whatever the aliens used for computers could remotely interface with Elise's implants in ways that its creators had never envisioned. Just like he'd be able to use his tools to manipulate computers on prespaceflight Terra in a manner that the brightest scientists of the day would've flatly denied was possible.

It didn't really matter how they were doing it. The important thing was that they were. He had to accept that and move along.

With Elise seemingly in control of this facility, she would have to master at least some rudiments of manipulating the alien interface if they were going to have any hope of getting out of here.

He supposed he was lucky that she had implants that could transmit what she saw to the rest of them. If she didn't have something like that, she'd have been reduced to drawing pictures on tablets and trying to explain things verbally.

That would've made a difficult situation almost impossible. As it was, they were able to see everything that she did, and that gave them a chance to make this work.

"Well?" Elise asked, arching an eyebrow. "What do I have to do to get us out of here?"

"Damned if I know," he admitted. "We could continue playing with what are obviously controls only available to you, but that might do something that none of us expects. Hell, you might turn off the facility, and we'd be trapped down here with no expectation of being able to escape at all."

"No pressure," Olivia said dryly. "Perhaps rather than manipulating the controls, she should make a trip around the interior of this chamber to see if she sees something that we can't. Something is presenting her with information that's only visible to her. If someone took Talbot out of this chamber, there has to be a door *somewhere*."

"It doesn't hurt to try," he granted. "Want to take a walk, Highness?"

"We slept on the ground for a week on Terra and were prisoners together, Carl. I think you can call me Elise."

He followed along behind her as she walked to the nearest wall and then began moving along at a slow walk. She'd only gone half a dozen meters when she stopped.

"There's a rune on the wall."

Carl tapped into the feed that she was providing and saw what she was talking about. This rune was blue and sat at about chest height.

He backed up the vid feed to see if it had always been there and noted that it had only appeared when she was a dozen meters away. Interesting. This was a context-driven presentation.

"See if you can touch it," he said. He gestured for the scientists following behind them to move back.

Elise reached out and pressed her index finger against the rune. It turned lime green, and a half circle of the stone below it simply vanished. One moment it was there, and the next, an oval almost a meter tall was gone.

Inside the newly revealed area was a small chamber. It went back a couple of meters, and the ceiling was no taller than the opening.

Carl squatted down and stared inside, using a handheld light to illuminate the interior. The walls of the small chamber were covered in runes that looked to have actually been carved into the stone. That was different.

"These look to be similar to the runes floating around you, but they're permanent. I wonder what purpose they serve."

"Should I go in and take a look?" she asked. "Maybe I'll see something that you can't."

Carl shook his head. "What can appear can disappear. I'll go in and get a good look at what's there, and if the door closes, you can open it again and let me back out."

He got down on his hands and knees before crawling into the small chamber. He stared back at the opening to see if it was going to remain open. It did.

Now that he was inside, he saw something that hadn't been visible from the outside. Some—but by no means all—of the runes were glowing softly blue. He estimated that the walls were covered with more than a hundred of the carvings, but only six were lit.

After scanning the chamber for a moment, his implants confirmed that there were one hundred and forty-four runes carved into the stone. He used his instruments to check and found no sign of Talbot's DNA.

He sent the data out to the rest. Better safe than sorry.

"Talbot wasn't in here. I'm not sure what it means, but only a few of these runes are glowing. Maybe only some portion of whatever this does is active or functional. Or maybe there's a sequence that needs to be pressed, but only a few options are available to start."

"Are you going to press one of them?" Elise asked. "If so, I think you'd best send me a video in real time so that I know what you intend to do and what happens. If I have to come in after you, I don't want to be guessing what the best course of action is."

He initiated the transfer of video data and then scanned the walls again. He picked one of the lit runes at random and made a point of gesturing toward it.

"Here goes nothing," he said as he reached out and touched the rune.

The first thing he noted was that the stone that had once sealed off the small chamber had reappeared. Somehow, he wasn't surprised.

The light-blue color of the rune changed to lime green. He immediately noticed that he didn't need the flashlight he was holding anymore. There was a white illumination coming from somewhere in the chamber, though he couldn't tell from where.

It grew bright enough that he couldn't see anything other than the light itself, and he was forced to close his eyes. After about fifteen seconds, the light went out, and he opened them again, looking cautiously around.

The door to the chamber had opened again, only it wasn't looking back into the larger chamber. Instead, it now opened into what looked like a dark cavern.

Carl shined his light out, and it revealed what certainly looked like strange machinery. None of it was lit, and he couldn't tell if any of it was functional.

Since he hadn't felt any kind of movement, he had to assume that he'd been transported somewhere in a fashion similar to how the transport rings Omega had given them had worked. He was probably deep underneath the obelisk.

A quick scan of the runes showed that they were different than the ones above. As above, only a few of them were lit—in this case, four. None of them matched the one he'd pressed, but he noted that there was one that was identical to the rune that had opened the small chamber in the first place.

Time to see if he could get back to his friends. He touched the rune.

* * *

KELSEY FUMED as *Persephone* arrived at the multiflip point to begin the journey to Twilight River. It annoyed the hell out of her that Lily had played her like this.

Well, perhaps "played" was the wrong word. After all, she'd intended to do something contrary to what the doctor had ordered. More accurately, Lily had foiled her.

The word made her feel like she was some kind of vid villain.

Sadly, she was well and truly screwed. If she'd thought that she had a chance of getting away with it, she'd disobey Jared's order in a heartbeat. She knew that he knew that, so she didn't expect him to allow her the opportunity to make that happen.

Being outmaneuvered sucked.

She was just going to have to accept that she wasn't going on the final assault. That galled her, but what was she going to do? Stun her brother and try to slip away after hiding his unconscious body? Unlikely to succeed.

Angela now knew that she wasn't supposed to go on the actual raid. Her friend didn't know the reason for it because Kelsey hadn't chosen to reveal her condition. Talbot deserved to hear about it before her pregnancy became public knowledge.

It only took a short amount of time to flip down the different branches of the multiflip point network and arrive at the system that supposedly contained the far flip point leading to Twilight River.

She wasn't sure that she trusted a map provided by aliens, especially when they'd compiled it over seventy million years ago.

Carl had assured them that it showed current features. That implied that the aliens had had some type of real-time sensing arrangement like Omega had had. Not only had the alien that was now part of the Omega station sensed the flip points in the general area around his system, but he'd been able to open ways to other realities.

For all she knew, so could these ancient aliens. Or maybe they could do even crazier things, not that she had a clue what that might look like.

If the scale of the map was accurate, the aliens had been able to sense the entirety of the flip point network inside the Milky Way. Just the idea of something like that boggled her mind. Humanity had never explored more than a fraction of the area around Terra. Even the Singularity sat just outside the space that the Empire had grown into.

At its height, the Terran Empire had encompassed tens of thousands of systems. Even if you said that the Singularity was the same size—which hadn't been true back then—the entirety of human-explored space would probably be less than fifty thousand systems.

The Milky Way held one hundred and fifty billion stars, minimum. That meant that all of human-explored space was half of one ten-thousandth of a percent of the total volume of stars. A decimal point with four zeros and then a five. As a percent. And that was being conservative.

With this new map, they could apparently reach any location they wanted to, but that didn't mean they knew where in the system these flip points were located. Based on the color coding and the length of the flip point lines on the map, it was possible to make some guesses about where the flip points themselves would be, but they were just guessing.

Multiflip points occupied the same general volume of space inside a system as regular flip points. Far flip points occurred in the outermost area of a system.

There were also a few ultra-far flip points that sat quite a distance beyond that. Reaching one of those would take a period measured in days or weeks.

That still might be worthwhile, because while far flip points could reach out to a thousand light-years, those ultra-far flip points—though very rare—would be able to cross ten times that distance, averaging ten thousand light-years.

Fiona had studied the map and found something that Carl hadn't noticed, as well. There was some kind of flip point marked at the center of the Milky Way. It orbited the supermassive black hole there. Several lines were running away from it, but they faded to nothing and seemed to have no exit point displayed.

The AI had speculated that these super flip points might lead to other galaxies, and she could even speculate which ones. Travel on that scale was humbling. And somewhat terrifying.

Kelsey hoped that they found this supposed far flip point. It was exciting to think that they were within striking range to end this fight against the AIs forever.

Of course, with the Clans waging war on the Rebel Empire, what would kicking the legs out from underneath the AIs do? If they stopped fighting, the entirety of the Old Empire would quickly be absorbed by the Clans.

Those people were just about as xenophobic as one could imagine. They didn't trust anyone outside of their own culture, and she wasn't certain they trusted themselves all that much. Simply based on what they'd learned from the descendants of Clan Dauntless, the Clans were warlike and extremely aggressive. Paranoia didn't seem to cover the lengths they were willing to go to protect their culture.

Dominance by them would be several steps down for the citizens of the Rebel Empire. The AIs—while they controlled everything—didn't make their iron fist obvious to the general population.

That wouldn't be the case if the Clans seized control. They'd destroy every bit of military infrastructure and compel obedience through brute force. She'd already seen that in the sections of the Rebel Empire that she'd been present in when the Clans invaded.

And then there was the Singularity.

They were the puppet masters pulling strings inside the Clans. Even though the Clans didn't trust the Singularity, Kelsey had no doubt that the people who'd managed to corrupt the AIs in the first place would have some means to eventually take control of all of human-occupied space.

Yet what choice did she and her friends really have? The AIs were in the process of concocting a deadly plague to eradicate all human life on Terra. How long would it be before they'd spread that poison everywhere and exterminated mankind? Or until it escaped their control, with the results being the same?

All of their options were bad, yet change was coming. The New Terran Empire wasn't strong enough to stave off any of the looming disasters.

She supposed it was better to have the machines destroyed, because the New Terran Empire could fight the Clans and the Singularity. The unrelenting machines were the worst option of all, and they had to die.

All Kelsey needed to do was figure out how to make that happen in spite of the overprotective brother staring over her shoulder.

13

———

T albot covered the approaching thing with his pistol. It stopped about ten meters away and seemed to be bobbing gently in place as its legs articulated, raising and lowering its body almost like a lizard, making itself seem bigger. It seemed to be considering him.

Now that his light was fully upon it, Talbot could see that it was artificial. The thing's carapace looked to be made of some kind of hard, synthetic material and was a dark-brown shade that blended well in the gloom. It was utterly silent.

He supposed it could be a robot designed to serve the aliens. That might mean that it wouldn't attack unless he did something to provoke it. Or it could be a security device that meant to truss him up like a Thanksgiving turkey.

The two of them stood there, considering one another, for almost thirty seconds before Talbot decided that it wasn't going to come after him. He slowly put his pistol back in its holster to see what the artificial construct did.

It just sat there, slowly bobbing to a tune only it could hear.

Somewhat reassured, Talbot walked to the side to see what the thing did. It turned to continue facing him but took no further action.

He didn't want to let it get between him and the door leading out of this building, but he also wanted to know what else was inside the building. What was the purpose of this place? If this robot was still functioning, was it possible that he could find water?

There was an old saying in the marines. You could survive three minutes without air, three days without water, and three weeks without food. That certainly wouldn't be a pleasant experience, and he wouldn't be very mobile after a couple of weeks on starvation rations, but since he could breathe, that meant that his first priority had to be finding water.

The robot watched him move around the other side of the room and only advanced when he started walking away. Perhaps it was waiting for him to give it an order.

Good luck with that. Not only was he the wrong species, but he couldn't do anything without a common language.

After exploring a couple of rooms, Talbot decided that the building was a domicile. There was a place where it looked like something could sleep, though it wasn't a bed. It was more like a series of soft cushions placed on the floor.

There was no way that those had survived millions of years. Something had to be refreshing the contents of this building, even though it seemed like there was no one living here. The building—much like the robot—seemed to be waiting to be of use again.

One of the rooms in the back of the building might've once been used for food preparation, and he was pleasantly surprised to find a large appliance that seemed to have swirling water in a bowl that was about half a meter across.

Of course, it might not really be water. Some forms of acid looked like water. Thankfully, his implants were capable of parsing things through his sense of smell and telling him details about their composition.

He turned that function on and took a sniff at a safe distance. There was a lot of odor in the room, much of it incomprehensible, chemically speaking. Still, it was safe to come closer to the liquid.

Step by step, testing as he went, he eventually found himself with his nose half a dozen centimeters above the surface of the liquid. Still nothing. It seemed like water. If it was anything else, it would be outgassing something that he could pick up. He was going to have to take a chance.

Talbot dipped the tip of his pinky finger into the liquid and pulled it rapidly back out. He felt nothing other than wetness. That was a good sign.

He touched the tip of his finger to the end of his tongue. Just like his nose, his enhanced taste buds were more than capable of parsing the chemical composition of anything he put in his mouth. In this case, the liquid was distilled water, so it was perfectly safe to drink.

Now all he needed was something to carry it in.

He found cabinets low to the floor that held various implements that might be used for cooking. Nothing that had a securable lid, though. At least he could use some of them for cups. And as long as he was able to return to this building, he could drink his fill.

It was utterly amazing to him that what seemed to be a long-vanished species had left something operational like this so long after they'd died out. Or gone wherever they'd gone.

Carl had said that their original flip point map was seventy-plus million years old. Nothing the Terran Empire built would last even a fraction of that.

The robot was still watching him. It didn't seem inclined to intervene in what he was doing, but Talbot wanted to test a theory.

He left one of the containers sitting on top of a low-slung cabinet and then walked to the other side of the room. The robot didn't move.

Talbot stepped back out into the short hallway that led toward the front of the house. He waited a minute and then stepped back into the room. The errant container was no longer in sight. The robot had put it back away.

That confirmed that the device was probably meant for housekeeping or serving the residents.

He resumed searching what he thought of as the kitchen and found himself standing at a device that he couldn't figure out. Like the rest of the cabinets in the room, it had to serve a purpose, but there wasn't anything inside it. The interior seemed to only go back about half the depth of the cabinet, but there was no way to access what was beyond that.

Talbot closed the door and ran his hand across the front of it and was shocked when it became semitranslucent and showed a series of alien icons. He'd thought it was metal, but he'd been wrong.

The runes he was looking at were grouped into clusters. He didn't know what they meant but was willing to experiment. He reached out and touched one.

The display vanished. Curious, he tried to open the door to the cabinet, but it wouldn't move.

Twenty seconds later, he'd already turned away and was looking at something else when a soft chime sounded from the cabinet, pulling his attention back to it.

Talbot tried the door again, and it opened. Only this time, the cabinet wasn't empty. There was what looked like bread on a small platter, covered with what seemed to be chopped pieces of meat in some kind of sauce. It had steam rising off of it.

Had this thing just made food out of nothing? Or maybe out of something in the back half of the cabinet?

Would it be safe to try something like this after all the time that might have passed? Even if it was safe, would it be poisonous to humans?

Only one way to find out.

He repeated the process of smelling it like he had before, and his nose was able to give him a lot of chemical data about what he was looking at. Nothing set off immediate red flags about it being poisonous, though he could say nothing about its taste.

Talbot touched the tip of his pinky finger to the sauce and then put the smallest amount that he could on the end of his tongue, prepared to spit it out at a moment's notice.

It was actually palatable. Better yet, while it had things that his body probably couldn't absorb, it wasn't toxic. He repeated the process with the meat and the bread and found that while the meat was *definitely* not to his taste—it seemed like a weird kind of seafood—it would give him calories that he could use.

The bread was actually pretty good.

The entire time he'd been experimenting, the robot had been watching him. That was kind of creepy, but this meant he could survive on this planet for a while if he had to.

And considering that the odds of Carl finding him were so low, he might spend the rest of his days here alone. He really hoped that that wasn't the case, because his new robot sidekick was a very poor substitute for his wife and friends.

* * *

ELISE ALMOST COLLAPSED with relief when the stone door vanished and Carl came crawling out. Unable to restrain herself, she swept the young man into a hug as soon as he stood. "I'm *so* glad to see you. I was afraid you weren't going to come back."

"You can't get rid of me that easily," he said with a grin. "I think the chamber transported me to a lower level of the facility. I didn't look around because I didn't want to chance getting stuck there. Thus far, you're the only person that's been able to find these doors, and I didn't want to take the risk.

"Talbot didn't go into this one. I scanned for his DNA, and the only genetic material inside the chamber came from me. If he found something like this, it wasn't this specific chamber. There may be others. Why don't we walk around the circumference of the larger chamber and see what else we can find?"

Elise started walking. She looked back toward the rune leading into the chamber that Carl had visited. The door had once again closed, but she could see the rune until she was about ten meters away, and then it vanished.

She stopped. "The rune disappeared. Walk back and touch it again. I know you can't see it, and neither can I, but I want to see if it works when I'm not involved."

Carl brought out one of his instruments, walked back, and

scanned the wall. He stepped a little bit to the side, reached up, and touched it. The door opened again.

"It looks like it doesn't require your intervention, but I didn't see anything. Maybe scanning the wall will show me some of Talbot's DNA."

They continued walking around the room, and she found another rune. Interestingly, it was exactly the same as the rune they'd just left behind. They opened the door underneath it and revealed another chamber just like the one Carl had gone into.

Without going in, Carl scanned it with his instrumentation and shook his head. "No DNA. Let's keep walking around and see exactly how many of these we find."

They didn't get a full count before they hit pay dirt. Based on the spacing, Elise thought that there were probably twelve of these smaller chambers, because they'd found eight of them and had gone two-thirds of the way around the larger chamber.

That number made sense too. There were one hundred and forty-four runes in each chamber, a function of twelve. So why not twelve chambers in total?

When they found Talbot's DNA, it was inside a chamber but not on the rune to open it. How had he gotten inside?

"It looks like he touched one of the interior runes," Carl said. "It's glowing, so I guess the runes that don't are somehow disabled. Or maybe they're restricted in a way that we haven't figured out how to unlock. That almost certainly means that Talbot went to a different section of the facility, and I can go find him."

"*We* can go find him," Elise said firmly. "I want to see what's on the other side of one of these. It may end up that we have to explore all of them to find another way out."

"We can't leave everyone here with no way out."

"They don't have a way out now. I can't activate an exit, so I'm putting my foot down. Just accept it."

He sighed and nodded.

The two of them crawled into the chamber, and Elise was surprised when Olivia crawled in after them. "I'm going too."

With a shrug, Carl reached up and touched the rune that had Talbot's DNA.

The growing light made Elise cover her eyes. "Is this normal?"

"It happened last time too. It only lasts about fifteen seconds, and then the door opens to a new place. This has to be some type of matter transportation system."

Elise felt no discontinuity. With the rings, she hadn't felt anything like that either, but that was literally stepping through an event horizon to another location. This had to be different, because it moved them from one location to another without them going through an opening linking them together.

As soon as the light vanished, she opened her eyes and blinked away the aftereffects. The door was gone, and she knew immediately that she wasn't looking into another area of the facility. There were stars in the open sky.

"You've found a way out!" she said.

"Yeah," Carl said. "Only we're not where we started, based on the number of stars up there. Unless I'm gravely mistaken, we're significantly closer to the galactic core than we started. We've traveled tens of thousands of light-years, and we're on a different planet."

Elise tried to wrap her head around that and then decided that it didn't matter. She focused on her implants and called Talbot. Since everyone had the updated implant coms now, she could reach him if he was within ten kilometers, and the signal wasn't blocked.

Hey, buddy. Elise here. Are you looking for a ride home?

Moments later, she was elated when his response came in. *If you're at the chamber on the hillside, don't come out! The door goes away. Stay inside the chamber.*

Ignoring his advice, Elise grinned and crawled out of the chamber. Above it, she saw a glowing rune. That meant that she could open it again if needed.

To test the theory, she gestured for the other two to stay inside and touched the rune. The door reappeared, sealing them inside. She touched it, and the door opened again.

Elise gestured for all of them to come out and returned her attention to communicating with Talbot.

We've figured out how to activate the doorway and get back home. Where are you?

Look down the hill.

Elise stepped over to the edge of the outcropping, noting an arrow made of loose stones that pointed toward a path, and gasped when she saw the alien city spread out below them. At one of the closer buildings, she saw a figure waving and knew that it must be Talbot.

We're coming down, she said. *Stay right there.*

14

J ared watched *Persephone*'s scanners through his implants as they felt their way along, looking for the far flip point that the alien map had indicated would be there. This was a gamble on their part. Even if they found one in the right location, would it really lead to Twilight River?

He turned his head slightly so that he could see Kelsey out of the corner of his eye. She was standing on the other side of Angela's chair, staring at the display at the front of the bridge. She didn't seem to be focusing on it, though. She looked like she was deep in thought.

Considering what she'd found out, he wasn't surprised. Discovering that he was going to be a father had shaken his world, but that paled in comparison to how finding out that you were going to be a mother must feel. Particularly for Kelsey, who was so far along that she wasn't going to be able to transfer her child—her little girl—to a gestation pod.

She would have to do this the old-fashioned way, with blood, pain, and screaming.

He'd never say it, but that was actually her kind of thing. Usually, it was *other* people doing the screaming and bleeding, but she'd had her share of both. And she was obstinate enough to always do things the hard way. Every. Time.

It was kind of fitting, really.

"The probe has found a far flip point," the helm officer said. "We'll be there in about two hours, Admiral. We can send a probe through and start getting information on the other side in about thirty minutes."

"Do that," Jared ordered. "Have it stay on the other side and gather passive scanner readings for sixty seconds before returning. If there's any sign of hostile craft in the vicinity, it's to immediately return."

The man nodded sharply. "Yes, sir."

He ran various scenarios of what they might find as time passed. The situation on the other side might range all the way from being a walk in the park with no enemy ships in the system to it being packed so full of enemy vessels that it was impossible to get to the station where the master AI resided.

His bet was that it leaned toward the heavily defended. After all, the AI could put as many ships as it wanted in the system. Why would it fail to protect itself when it had packed the systems around it full of defensive measures?

He was more than willing to wager that the station where it had initially been built was surrounded by battle stations similar to those defending the flip point that the Clans were attacking even now.

After making a couple of flips along the multiflip point system, they were too far away to get real-time information on the battle, but the FTL com was able to send slow updates this far, and he knew that the attack was underway.

The probes in the system itself sent the data to a controller probe at the multiflip point, and that one transitioned every half hour to send data to other probes in systems closer to them. It was slow, but it did give them a window into what was happening.

Even the hidden ships the AI had seeded in the system hadn't been enough to stop the Clans. That meant they'd have one more system to work their way across and another flip point to assault. Based on the defenses of the one they were currently attacking, Jared wasn't sure whether they had the force with them to be able to make that second attack work.

He was still worrying about how that was going to turn out when Thompson spoke up again.

"The probe is flipping, Admiral," the helmsman said.

The tension on the bridge ratcheted up until the probe returned a minute later and started sending them data. It was slower than using FTL coms, but they couldn't risk tipping their hand.

"The probe confirms that the other side of the far flip point is clear," Thompson said. "The layout of the system is consistent with Twilight River. There aren't any ships close to the far flip point. It did, however, detect a lot of ships moving throughout the system. Most seem to be moving in the direction of the flip point that the Clans are going to be assaulting soon."

Jared nodded, elated that they finally had access to the damned master AI. "They're either strengthening the defenses or going to reinforce the defenders in the next system. The timing is good for us, I suppose. Send the probe back to gather data until we get there."

He tried not to get his hopes up. This could all still prove to be impossible to pull off, which meant that they'd have to work their asses off to beat the master AI. The devil was going to be in the details. He'd leave the rest of the fleet on this side of the flip point and hope for the best.

When they finally made the flip and arrived at Twilight River, the probe had refined the readings of the ships it could detect. It could only make rough guesses about the classes based on their gravitic signatures, but there was a lot of firepower on the move.

Unfortunately, they weren't going to be able to pick out stationary defenses at this range. If there were battle stations ringed around the science station that housed the master AI, they wouldn't be able to see them until they got probes into the area.

Which meant that it was time to execute phase two of the plan. "Start launching stealthed probes. I want coverage of the station with the master AI and the flip points leading into this system.

"We need full-spectrum coverage of the open space inside Twilight River as well. There could be a lot of ships just sitting out there waiting for an opportunity to activate their drives and come charging in."

He turned to his sister. "Kelsey, it's time for you to get together with your people and start implementing your part of our crazy plan. Make sure that Julia has everything that she needs, and be certain that your teams protect her on the way in. She's not a trained Marine Raider, and we're going to have to compensate for that."

Kelsey nodded. "I've already got that figured out. We're going to have to get somewhat closer before we launch the stealthed pinnaces. At least *Persephone* can slip in without too great a risk of detection. We'll make this work."

With that, she walked off the bridge.

He knew his sister was still angry at him for keeping her safe, but he didn't want to have to tell her father that she was dead if things went badly, especially now that she was pregnant. He wouldn't be able to live with himself if the worst happened.

Thankfully, he'd managed to stymie her. Now all they had to do was beat the murderous AI that had enslaved the human race.

"Set course toward the science station, Major," he told Angela. "Get the ship in order and take charge of the assault. It's time to finish this."

* * *

CARL STARED at the robotic creature that Talbot had found. It shouldn't be in one piece. Hell, *nothing* in this building should be in one piece. The fact that the machines were still able to produce food in the kitchen was mind-boggling.

The home seemed to be in decent condition—and that was almost certainly the doing of the robot—but that made no sense. The aliens had to have been gone for literally millions of years. They hadn't disappeared recently.

Though you wouldn't know it by looking at their creations. The buildings still stood, and their workings still functioned. That made the craftsmanship of the Old Terran Empire look like children putting blocks together so they could immediately knock them over.

The portable scanner he had with him was able to get some information from the robot. He had a decent idea of what it was constructed from, and while that was long-lasting, it would have faded into dust over the timescale they were looking at.

Just the settling of dust and grit from the atmosphere should have buried this city, yet the streets were clean and clear. Obviously, advanced technology kept them that way.

He'd have to take samples to be certain, but his scanner indicated that the age of the robot varied depending on the part he was examining but in no case was older than perhaps seventy years. Some of the newer parts seem to have been crafted only within the last couple of years.

Something was maintaining this housekeeping robot. Which was kind of meta. Something maintaining the maintainer.

Yet nothing he could find in the house seemed designed to do that. Did something come in from outside to repair the serving robot and make sure that the bedding was refreshed? To stock the machine that created food?

"You're making me nervous," Talbot said. "Why don't you just offer to buy it dinner and get the ball rolling?"

Carl smirked at his friend. "You're a riot. I'm just trying to figure out how any of this can exist. The aliens have probably been gone for millions of years, yet everything is still just exactly as it would need to be for the occupants to walk back through the door and be taken care of.

"And this is just some random house sitting on the outskirts of a massive city. One would assume this is a fairly pedestrian dwelling. Whatever the aliens are using to keep things working is so ubiquitous that everyone had it."

Elise cleared her throat. "Isn't this a mystery that we should try to solve some other time? Everybody back at the obelisk has got to be worried about us. And on another note, where is this planet? Is it the home planet of these aliens?"

Olivia nodded in agreement. "How did that little bitty chamber move us across what has to be tens of thousands of light-years? We basically flipped without a ship, and we went much farther than any flip point could take us."

"That's a mystery," Carl agreed. "One that I doubt we're going to have time to solve. It's got to be sort of like the transport rings, just on a tremendous scale and at a technological level that I don't think even the Omegans could understand."

He returned his attention to the robot. "I wish we could take this thing with us. Being able to understand the technology that we're dealing with might make a world of difference and provide so many breakthroughs."

Talbot shrugged. "I can disassemble it for you."

"I'd rather have it in one piece, thanks," Carl said dryly. "Maybe we can convince it to go with us."

"It seems to be attached to the house," Talbot argued. "I'm not sure how you're going to make it follow along behind you like a puppy."

Elise walked around the robot, examining it. "It seems to have a panel here in the back. Perhaps there's a way to turn it off?"

Carl hadn't seen any panel, so he walked around the device and examined it more closely. With her pointing it out, he could see the very, very faint line that probably indicated something there. It wasn't straight, so it hadn't stood out from the decorative markings, but she'd somehow spotted it.

"How did you see it?"

She shrugged slightly. "It's this interface. I can see the outline of it as a faint blue shade, and there's a spot directly above it that looks like a tiny rune."

Without waiting for him to say anything, Elise reached out and touched the robot. The concealed compartment opened up when the door covering it simply melted away.

"There are four runes," she said. "Should I just press one and see what happens?"

"Sure."

Elise touched one of the runes that Carl could only see through the vid she was sharing with them. Nothing seemed to happen. She touched the next one, and the robot settled down to the floor and stopped moving.

"I think I turned it off," she said.

"Let's finish testing it," he said. "Touch the rest."

The third rune made it stand back up and look exactly as it had before. That was probably how it was powered on.

The final rune was more interesting. The robot turned around and faced Elise and inclined its forward half slightly. It was almost like it was acknowledging her.

That made Carl wonder. "Try walking outside."

When Elise headed out the front door, the robot followed her. It was the first indication he'd seen of it doing anything that wasn't related to the house.

"I think you've retasked it to follow you to a new place. Why don't we take it back with us?"

"I don't think it's harmful, so I can't think of any reason not to," Talbot said. "But let's get moving. We need to get out of the big chamber, and we can't do that if we're not there."

Carl nodded and headed for the door. There would be plenty of time to come back later and examine this massive city filled with unbelievable technology.

If, of course, they survived the upcoming fight.

15

Kelsey was still fuming as they made their way deeper into the Twilight River system. There *had* to be a way for her to get around Jared. Unfortunately, no ideas were presenting themselves.

She made her way to where the Marine Raiders were assembling to board the stealthed pinnaces that they'd use to get to the old science station where the master AI was housed. It was still uncertain whether they'd get close enough to actually make the strike, but it was far better to be prepared than found wanting when the moment came.

As stealthy as *Persephone* was, she was more detectable than the pinnaces themselves. When the time came, she'd launch the pinnaces, and they'd coast to the station. Then everything that happened would be on the heads of the Marine Raiders, who'd be led by Angela while Kelsey ran *Persephone*.

It would've been better to leave Jared in command, but while Fiona was willing to accept him, the computer that actually controlled *Persephone* insisted on being run by a Marine Raider.

That meant it had to be her. Yes, the rest of the crew still handling the bridge controls were Raiders, but Kelsey had the command experience. That was somewhat frightening when it came right down to it.

Not that it mattered in this case. She'd be doing whatever Jared told her to do, so it wasn't like she was going to have to fight the ship in a naval battle. Anyone could have done it. Hell, even Julia.

Kelsey felt her eyes narrow slightly.

Could that work? Could she convince her doppelgänger to swap places with her like some old vid where twins traded places? Would the ruse fool anyone? After all, that was the kind of stunt that any hero in a novel would try.

Still, it beat doing nothing. If they caught her, she was no worse off, and if it worked, she'd be on her way.

She walked over to where Julia was watching the Marine Raiders loading their gear. She leaned back against the bulkhead next to the other woman, who was already dressed in her armor with her helmet resting in the crook of her arm, and watched the action.

"You ready for this?" Kelsey asked as Angela came into the compartment and started issuing orders. "This is going to be your first big fight. One where you know you're getting into a fight ahead of time, anyway."

Julia raised an eyebrow as she turned her head toward her. "You know fighting isn't really what I do. Why aren't you going? This seems like something you'd insist on."

"I was overruled," Kelsey grumbled. "Jared put his foot down. It pisses me off, because I think that I need to be there, but I'm not exactly sure how I can get around him."

That was playing dirty. Even though Julia had accepted that the Jared in this universe wasn't the same kind of man as in hers, there was still a barrier between them. Julia didn't really trust or like Jared, and Kelsey was manipulating her. It made her feel guilty, but she couldn't allow that to stop her.

Julia turned to fully face her and put her hands on her hips, scowling. "You're the damned crown princess. He can't tell you what to do."

"He's in overall military command," Kelsey said with a resigned sigh. "Colonels don't get to argue with admirals. I can think of any number of reasons why I should be on this mission, but that's not what he wanted to hear. He said that you could do everything that I could."

She let the silence drag on for a couple of seconds and then leaned a little closer. "Though, we might be able to pull the wool over his eyes."

"Wool? That's something from an animal, right? What does that mean?"

"We've really got to work on showing you more old vids. It means we might be able to fool him long enough for me to go on this mission if you're willing to switch places with me."

Julia tapped her lips thoughtfully. "Hmmm. I'm willing to consider it, but I think I need to know a little bit more. What are you supposed to be doing here on *Persephone* while we're gone?"

"Technically, I'm in command of the ship, but Jared is going to be giving the orders. The crew is all trained, and they'll be following his instructions. The computer only answers to the command authority of a Marine Raider, so that rules Jared out. Basically, I'd be a figurehead. Or rather, you'd be a figurehead."

"What makes you think that the computer will accept me?" her doppelgänger asked with both eyebrows raised. "Fiona knows everything about me, including the fact that I'm not you. She'd tattle on me in a second. She's listening to us right now, isn't she?"

"She is, but there's a trick to this. The version of her listening to us is a subroutine that respects our privacy. There are a couple of triggers—like calling for her attention—that would draw the real Fiona to listen in, but as long as we don't cross those lines, the information that the subroutine hears won't make its way to her.

"As for the ship's computer, it's not sentient. It'll check your implant serial codes, and that's it."

Julia was quiet for almost a full minute as she thought. When she finally spoke, her voice was low and more than a bit worried.

"What if something goes wrong? I don't want to get anybody killed."

"If push comes to shove, tell Jared who you are. He'll be pissed, but it'll be too late by then. Look, this is my universe, and it's my responsibility to take out the AI. I'm not going to be there for you when you get home, and I can't ask you to do my job for me. Please."

A few seconds of indecision flitted across Julia's face, and then she nodded. "We're going to have to step out so that I can give you my armor. This is going to be challenging. I'm going to have to pretend that I actually *like* Mertz. I mean, Jared. That's going to be hard."

"You can do this," Kelsey assured her. "Let's go."

Together, the two of them found an unused compartment where they could switch clothing. Kelsey sure hoped that Julia could carry off the role, because if Jared figured this out before the pinnaces launched, she was utterly screwed.

* * *

TALBOT WAS MORE relieved than he could say when Elise was able to open up the small chamber that he'd arrived in. He couldn't see anything there, but she assured him there was a rune. She demonstrated it by closing the chamber, then having him touch the bare rock to open it back up.

"I can't believe that," he grumbled. "How can you see it but I can't?"

"That's… complicated," she said. "I'm not really sure that any of us understands why, but it has something to do with me being pregnant."

He blinked in surprise. "Pregnant?"

She nodded and smiled a bit wryly. "It turns out the EMP damaged my contraceptive implant. It didn't fail right away, and something about me being pregnant made the chamber with the map give me extra authority. We're not really sure what that is or why it's working here, but it is."

"I suspect you're not going to like the answer," Carl said. "The fact that it's working outside of the chamber almost certainly means that it's made some change to you personally. Maybe an electronic implant of some kind or something that we can't even understand. Once we get back to *Invincible*, I'm going to have to take you to my lab and see what we can find."

"An implant?" she asked, her voice suddenly strained. "I was just standing there. Nothing broke my skin. How could there be an implant?"

"This comes back to the whole 'alien technology is so advanced that it seems like magic' scenario," Carl said. "I mean, I suppose that we might still be in an area that allows you to wield that kind of control, but we won't really know until we get you to the ship. Don't panic. I don't think you're in any danger."

"But you don't know for sure? Perfect. Jared is going to be just thrilled."

Elise threw her hands up in frustration and froze. "The alien interface just disappeared!"

"Make that gesture again," Carl said.

She did so and seemed to deflate. "It's back."

"This is a good thing," her young friend said. "Being able to dismiss the interface is better than having it on all the time."

"I don't want to mute it! I want it out of me!"

"The sun is coming up," Olivia said, probably trying to distract her friend.

All of them turned and saw the sun peeking over the horizon behind the city. It was a reassuring yellowish color that wouldn't have been out of place on Avalon. With the appearance of oncoming dawn, the stars began vanishing from the sky.

Talbot knew that soon enough, it would be like any other planet's typical day, although he wouldn't be surprised if the galactic disk was still visible. It was so large and bright that it might be there all the time.

The four of them stood there and watched as the sun rose beyond the horizon and were a little surprised when a second sun began rising behind the first. It was almost identical in color to the first and seemed to be about the same size.

"Is that normal?" Olivia asked. "I thought most binary star systems had one sun that was significantly larger than the other. Those looked to be virtually identical."

"It's not exactly the most common stellar arrangement," Carl said. "That said, it's not unheard of either. This world must be a little farther away from those suns than most worlds. Otherwise, it would be blazing hot."

Talbot shielded his eyes with his hand and kicked in every single filter that he could in his ocular implants. There was something in between the suns. It was almost as if there were strands of material going between them.

"So, is it a bad thing when a binary star system has matter being transferred from one sun to the other?"

"Send me a vid feed of what you're seeing," Carl said.

His young friend observed it for a minute and then shook his head. "That's not natural. Those stars are too far apart to be exchanging matter. There has to be something in between them—something too small for us to see—that's drawing matter from each of them. It might be some kind of alien artifact drawing power. Or doing something we can't even begin to imagine. Just one more mystery we'll never have the opportunity to explore.

"In any case, I don't believe we're in danger."

"Uh-huh," Talbot said, not bothering to hide his skepticism. "I suggest that we take our robotic friend back to the planet with the obelisk and figure out how we're going to get out of that chamber."

"No argument from me," Elise said. "The robot is fairly sizable, but it'll fit into the small transport chamber. Only one of us is going to be able to go in with it, though. The rune above the door there is going to be the rune you'll need to use. I'll send everyone the picture."

Talbot examined the rune that she sent to him. "I've got it. Why don't I go with the robot to make sure that everything works as expected? It's my job to take risks."

None of them objected, so he went into the chamber first and located the rune. Elise turned the robot off, and they pushed, pulled, and shoved until it was inside with him.

"Nothing ventured, nothing gained," he muttered as he pressed the rune in question.

The bright white light came back and vanished, and then he was once more in a small chamber just off the map chamber, and other people were calling out to him through the now-open door.

"Grab the other end of this thing, and help me get it out," he said.

"Everybody else is fine, and they'll be back here in just a couple of minutes."

Five minutes later, he'd gone back and gotten everyone. One problem solved. Now they just had to figure out how to use Elise's new controls to get them the hell out from under the obelisk.

lise was glad to be back in the larger cavern but still wasn't certain how they'd get out of it. The strange, ghostly controls were still just as obtuse as they'd been before. She could summon or dismiss them now, but none of the runes made any sense to any of them.

Yes, she'd figured out how to turn the map on and off, almost by accident. She could zoom in and see some of the details but really had no overall control, because she was ignorant of what any of the other runes did.

It was like learning a new language by being dropped into the middle of a culture where they refused to help you in any way.

She wasn't quite sure how she'd figured out the zoom function. Doing it by accident seemed unlikely. Maybe the menu was context sensitive. Since they'd been looking at the map, maybe what she was doing was limited to affecting only the map.

That begged the question of what else was possible. The only way she was going to find out was by doing things. Things that might go very wrong.

Still, it wasn't as if she had a choice. Nothing Carl did affected anything in the room. He couldn't activate the map, and he couldn't get them out. It was as if once she was selected as the operator, there was no way to release control back to him. At least no way that she knew of.

He was still trying to get the exit to respond to them, so she walked over to the central area that the map was controlled from and, rather than touching any of the controls around her, tried to will the map into existence by thought alone.

Unsurprisingly, nothing happened.

The last time she'd brought the map up, only she could see it. There was probably a way to make it publicly viewable, but she didn't have the knowledge to do that. That only annoyed her all over again.

Worse, if they couldn't get out of the chamber, they'd run out of water shortly. Well, unless, of course, they went back to the alien planet and tapped into the water supply that Talbot had found. And the food he'd eaten, though she thought that was incredibly rash of him. What kind of moron ate million-year-old food?

Hungry Marine Raiders, or so it seemed.

Well, if they had nothing else to eat or drink, she'd do it too.

Elise took a slow, deep breath and brought the controls to visibility. Once again, the spirals of light went down from her head and around her body and stopped at her waist. Above and below them were glowing runes that she knew meant something.

Looking back at what she'd done before, she saw which rune she had touched to turn the map on and did so. Once again, the blazing glory of the Milky Way appeared above her.

No one else even glanced up, so she knew that it was only visible to her.

How was that possible? Carl had been standing right beside her and couldn't see anything. What would make the map visible only to her?

Unfortunately, his suggestion that she had some type of alien implant inside her made all too much sense. If there was an alien device feeding her information, there was no reason that anyone else should be able to see it. In fact, there was every reason that they shouldn't.

But if there was an alien device feeding her information, shouldn't it be making an attempt to at least modify its behavior for her? Why did she have to figure out what all of the strange alien runes meant when it should be modeling its behavior on her? Why weren't all these displays in Standard?

Elise eyed the rune that turned the map on and off. Was using it a binary choice, or did manipulating it in different ways also modify what it did?

Her experimentation revealed that passing her hand through it at various angles only turned the view on and off. No one else gave any sign that they saw the map above them.

If the damn thing hadn't been immaterial, she'd have tried manipulating it in other ways.

Maybe that didn't matter.

She reached out as if she were going to grab the rune between her thumb and index finger. Once she was pretending to hold it, she twisted her wrist, and the rune flipped over. The change also switched its color from blue to lime green.

This had an immediate effect on everyone around her, as the entire room looked up and gasped when the map must've appeared above them. She'd found a way to turn it on for everyone else.

"What did you do?" Carl asked as he hurried up.

"I tried twisting the rune around. It changed color from blue to green when I did that, and now everyone can see the map. I think that means I took it from private to public."

"Try doing other manipulations with the runes and see what you can do."

It didn't take too much experimentation to figure out how to make the map rotate along multiple axes as well as zoom in and zoom out. She had to put her hands out like she was grabbing the spiral of light and rotating around her body to get at the runes to her rear.

It was annoying. Why couldn't she do any searching?

She brought up the image of the rune that led to the world they'd visited and reached out with her index finger and drew it into the air. To her shock, her finger left a blue mark in the air as if she were writing on nothing. When she completed the rune, the map rotated and zoomed to a specific system, maybe halfway toward the galactic core from the Terran Empire but on the far side of the Milky Way.

She had absolutely no way of knowing if that was really the place they'd just visited, but it did have two stars in close proximity to one another. Between them was a small flashing light. Would that be the alien facility Carl had guessed might exist?

Elise touched one of the stars. Well, it was way up in the chamber, but she acted as if she were touching it. The star shifted to the left, and her view was filled with a scrolling column of runes. She suspected that meant it was telling her about the star that she'd designated.

"Can you see that?" she asked.

Carl nodded. "It looks like you've tapped into a database of some kind, and it's giving you information on the star. Or perhaps the system itself. See if you can tap the planet that we suspect was the one we visited. That is what you selected, right?"

"I think so."

She tapped the glowing spark between the stars, and the same kind of column started scrolling. Too bad she had no frame of reference to know what any of that meant.

"How do I know which planet we were on?" she asked.

The map of the system had the two stars and eleven major worlds. Around those worlds were innumerable moons.

Carl pointed at the one that was fifth in orbit. "Start with that one. I think it's probably about the right distance out to be in the habitable zone considering the solar output from both stars."

Elise reached out and touched the image of the world that Carl indicated. Like the star and the alien facility, it began scrolling runes next to it that she had no way to interpret. There was a small flashing light on the surface of the planet that looked exactly like the one between the stars.

Curious what that was, Elise tried to expand the planet further without much expectation of success. She was surprised to see that she could zoom in past any of the other locations that she'd tried so far. In fact, as she grew closer to the blinking light, she realized she must be looking down at the city that they'd seen when they'd visited the world.

It didn't look like a real-time display. In fact, it didn't look like it was even a photograph. This was obviously computer generated. Everything had just enough off about it that she could tell that it wasn't depicting reality.

"Interesting," Carl said. "My guess is that the database has information about the city's layout and size. Those buildings don't look like they're really there, so they must be computer generated. Can you get any information from the city?"

She tried to zoom in closer, but the display stopped expanding when she had a decent view of the city as a whole. She tried tapping individual buildings, but all her efforts did was select the city itself and scroll data about it.

"It looks like I can see what's going on with the city at some point in the past," she said. "It won't let me dig down to find out what's going on with any specific building. Let's see if I can find the little chamber that we transported into."

It turned out that the flashing light that had drawn her to the planet wasn't the city. It was the chamber off to the side. More interesting to her was the fact that in this computer image, there wasn't just that little chamber. That entire hill seemed to be honeycombed with some type of installation.

The only reason that she could tell it was there were faint hollows under the ground that hinted at a facility without giving any details. Also, the entrances were clearly marked. If they'd gone around the small area they'd come out at, they'd have spotted a larger door that apparently led into the facility itself.

She supposed that was reassuring, because the idea of being able to use such a small chamber to travel that unbelievable distance would have been mind-boggling. At least now she knew that there was a large facility generating an enormous amount of power backing it up.

"Why can I see all the details about this facility but not the one between the stars?" she asked. "It only showed the glowing dot."

"Maybe it's not accessible to the aliens," Carl said with a shrug. "Just one more unanswered question."

"I wonder why so many of the runes we've seen aren't active anymore. Do you think that's because of how old they are? Have this civilization and its creations been around for so long that the majority of them have finally failed, and we just got lucky to find a functional one?"

"There's no telling," Carl said. "I'm more curious as to why someone felt the need to move all the dinosaurs here and then make a reservation world for them. Obviously, the aliens wanted to keep the critters genetically stable. That explains why they have specialized nanites that don't allow for genetic drift.

"Yet the presence of humans—beings that shared the same genetic home world—caught the attention of this facility and made it signal us. It certainly seems as if the aliens wanted us to find all this, but I don't understand why. This place is nowhere near Terra. How could they know that we'd get here?"

Elise frowned as she thought about that and decided to see if she could gather any more information about *this* system. She brought up the image in her implants of the rune that had brought them back to this world and drew it in front of her. That caused the map to shift and show them a new star system.

Again, it looked relatively normal. She knew which world they were on and was able to tap it and see another blinking dot that, when they zoomed in, revealed the obelisk and hints of a larger facility beneath it.

She zoomed back out and examined the system as a whole. There was the multiflip point, but was there anything else?

Her eyes narrowed when she finally spotted it. One of those ultra-far flip points was sitting out beyond any reasonable range that they'd have explored. Those things could travel a tremendous distance, so there was no telling where it ended up.

Or was there?

She reached out and tapped the flip point with the tip of her finger, and the map shrank back down to the point where she could see that the line led to another system. She had no way of judging distance, and the system she was looking at on the other end didn't look familiar.

It was a trinary star system with two suns in a close orbit and another sitting off at a distance. There were some small worlds in the system, but nothing looked like it would be habitable or even really all that useful.

There was only a single regular flip point in the system. No multiflip points and no far flip points.

Just out of curiosity, she tapped the regular flip point and saw that it went to the next-nearest star. A tap on that system brought understanding, as it was a system that she recognized *instantly*.

She pointed at the map almost accusingly. "That's Terra. There's an ultra-far flip point in Alpha Centauri that leads here."

Carl nodded. "Go back to Alpha Centauri. I want to take a closer look at the planets in that system. Was it just a hop along the way to get here, or did the aliens have some kind of facility there? I guess it makes sense now why they'd put the dinosaurs here rather than Alpha Centauri. There aren't any habitable worlds there."

Elise brought the map back to Alpha Centauri and began examining the worlds one by one. There was nothing in the habitable zone, so she started with the innermost and worked her way out. On the second world, one that was too hot to support life, she saw a blinking light.

"We've got a live one," she said. "Or at least we've got a place where a facility once existed."

She zoomed down in on it and discovered that it didn't have anything aboveground that would've attracted the attention of people visiting the world. The second world would never have been a comfortable place to be, and it was too light to have any heavy metals that would be worth mining. Basically, other than being scientifically explored, it had been ignored.

Only now, she could see that the aliens had left a significant facility there. It looked larger than either of the two that she'd seen on the map thus far. And with nothing to hint that it was there, there was no reason humanity would've ever stumbled upon it.

She thought of all the ships that were blockading the flip point leading to Alpha Centauri from Terra. Did this mean that the AIs had found that facility? If so, that could be real trouble. If the master AI had defenses on that station that were related to this alien technology, this mission wouldn't be nearly as easy as Kelsey and the rest had hoped.

And they hadn't thought it would be easy to begin with.

"We need to get out of here," she said. "We've got to warn them that they could be up against alien technology inside the science station."

Carl nodded and gestured toward the exit. "It's all up to you, Elise. If you can get us out of here now, we might still be able to get an FTL message to them in time to stop them from launching an attack, but that window is swiftly closing."

No pressure.

17

J ared watched Kelsey out of the corner of his eye as the
pinnaces departed *Persephone* and began their way toward the
station where the master AI had been designed and built. The
Marine Raider strike ship had closed the distance as much as
possible, but she could only get so close without being detected.

As he'd expected, the ancient science station was well protected.
And by well protected, he meant that it was surrounded by half a
dozen battle stations, two dozen major vessels, and five times that
many lesser ships. Of the larger vessels, he bet at least half were
superdreadnoughts.

Even if he attacked with his entire fleet, he didn't have enough
force to crack that knot. The best they could do was destroy the
science station—maybe—but that wouldn't accomplish their primary
mission.

Destroying the master AI wasn't enough. They had to get it to
send an order to its electronic minions to lay down their arms. To win
the fight against the artificial intelligences, they had to get them once
again under human control.

If they killed the master AI, that became impossible. Worse than
impossible. The original AI was the only one that they could use the

override on. If they couldn't subvert the master AI, nothing they did was going to be able to stop the remaining AIs. They didn't have the control codes that the master unit had.

There was only one path to success, and it lay right in front of them.

And because of her condition, he'd made certain that Kelsey wasn't going to play any role in it, and that had undoubtedly pissed her off. Only she didn't look quite as angry as he'd expected her to be.

He'd grown to know his sister very well over the last few years, and he knew what she looked like when she was upset. Her expression now was a bit more... complicated.

She'd be worried, of course. Who wouldn't be?

But the rest of her expression was unreadable in a way that made no sense. Not to someone who had become very good at detecting her moods and reading her feelings based on her posture.

Deciding to take the bull by the horns, he turned to where she was standing on his right and gave her his full attention. With Angela leading the assault, he was in the captain's chair, but Kelsey was the one giving the orders. The Marine Raider computer wouldn't accept command authority from anyone that wasn't a Marine Raider.

It was a bit cumbersome, but that was what they had to work with.

"What's the matter?" he asked directly. "You look strange."

She frowned at him. "I'm not strange. What do you mean by that?"

"I know that you're angry with me, but this was the right call. With a little bit of time, you'll understand that too. Trust me when I say that both your father and Talbot will be happy that you didn't risk... anything this time."

He'd almost said "your child," but that would've been a mistake. No one else on the bridge was aware that his sister was pregnant, and it wasn't his place to let that particular cat out of the bag.

"My father would understand that I was doing what I had to do, and so would my husband," she said, her chin rising in defiance.

Something was *definitely* off.

"I wouldn't worry overly much. Those pinnaces are filled with Marine Raiders. Not only is Angela there, but Julia has the codes that might be required to get into any computer systems that are still operational. We've got all the angles that we can think of covered. You being there would just be an unnecessary risk."

She turned and stared at him. No. She *glared* at him.

"I don't think you understand how much I really wanted to be there. It was my place to finish what we started. Julia is going to have to do this all over again in her universe, and now we're putting her at risk twice. Don't you think that's a little unfair?"

There was a sense of wrongness to this conversation. It was almost like she was ignoring her own condition.

Or ignorant of it.

Fiona, he said through his implants. *Is there any way to tell exactly who I'm talking to? Are we sure that this is* really *Kelsey?*

Do you believe that this woman is Julia?

Knowing my sister, it wouldn't surprise me. Can you check?

I can use the interior scanners to tell if the person in front of you has an artificial eye easily enough. It appears that your suspicion was correct. This is Julia.

He suppressed the urge to curse. He should've known that his sister would pull something like this. Dammit.

The pinnaces had gone too far to summon them back. His sister was committed to this attack now, and there was no point in being pissed off about it. She and Julia had fooled him just long enough for her to get away with it.

He leaned forward slightly and looked into Julia's eyes. Then he sent her an implant communication request.

I know that you're Julia. I only just figured it out, and I'm not going to give you away, because that's not going to help any of us right now, but you need to understand that you've made a dreadful mistake.

His sister from another universe almost sneered. *I didn't make a mistake. Kelsey wanted to go on this mission, and you denied her. She deserves to be the mistress of her own fate.*

And you think that I denied her just because I felt like it? Julia, Kelsey is five months pregnant.

The other woman's eyes almost bugged out. "What?" she demanded out loud.

I can see that she didn't tell you, Jared said dryly. *It looks like I wasn't the only one that was played.*

Julia stood silent for a moment and then began cursing, drawing the eye of every officer on the bridge and obviously not caring.

Well, what was done was done. He'd just have to hope that Kelsey kept herself and her daughter alive. If she didn't, there'd be plenty of blame to go around.

* * *

CARL TRIED everything that he could think of to talk Elise through getting them out of the obelisk. Nothing they'd tried had any effect.

They took a break and made another circumference of the large chamber. As she'd guessed, there were twelve small compartments that he assumed were all transports of some kind. They took a thorough video of all the runes inside them, and none were the same. None of them matched the control runes that Elise could see either.

The only thing that was the same was that the rune that opened each chamber was identical. That particular rune had to represent this place.

He had to assume that this facility was linked with other places that made sense for it to be connected to. Places that the aliens that created this facility wanted them to have access to.

Judging by the lack of operational runes, the vast majority of those destinations were no longer available. Each small chamber held one hundred and forty-four runes. That meant seventeen hundred and twenty-eight individual symbols in all. Of that, over ninety percent were nonfunctional. Or perhaps they simply weren't available to humans.

Interestingly, only the rune that brought them here was the same inside the transport cavern on the world with the dead city. That meant it was similar to the multiflip point nodes in that it had a different subset of possible destinations.

That still left them with one hundred and fifty-two potential destinations available from this cavern. More exploration than they could carry out in a lifetime, most likely, even if he could afford to dedicate any time to it.

They really needed to get the hell out of this place. The mission to probe Twilight River had probably already kicked off. Without him being there, there was no telling what would happen when their forces had a direct confrontation with the master AI, and it worried him. Not that he didn't think his associates were competent, but he knew that he was better.

That wasn't just his ego talking. He was quantifiably better when it came to messing with computers and programming. Yes, Ralph was a better hacker, but he didn't have the breadth of vision he himself did. Austin was better with hardware but was limited in the same way as Ralph.

And all of that worried Carl greatly. They really needed to get out of here soon.

Once Elise had run through the easy manipulations, she started doing something new with the controls that she could see. Instead of touching only a single one, she touched one and then drew a line between it and another.

The fact that it allowed her to do so meant that what she was doing had the potential to increase the number of commands she could issue, but once again, they were just guessing at everything.

Until someone let out a shout and pointed at the tip of one of the oblong corners of the chamber. A large opening had appeared in the wall. Talbot trotted over to take a look.

"Looks like a tunnel," he shouted back. "Not sure where it goes, but it doesn't look dangerous. Unless we go into it, it closes, and then we can't get out again."

That was certainly true enough, but it wasn't as if they had much choice. They hadn't had any luck turning on the entrance, so perhaps once Elise had triggered the change in control, that was no longer a way out. This might be their only avenue to escape.

He hated taking a risk like that, but they couldn't afford to leave anyone behind. Obviously, no one on the outside had been able to make their way in, so it seemed certain that that method of entry had been disabled.

"Gather up all your gear, everyone," he shouted. "I don't want to leave anything behind, because we may never come back this way."

Carl hoped that wasn't true. They'd been to a world that humanity couldn't have ever dreamed of visiting on its own, and he certainly wanted to go back to plumb the secrets of this alien society that had vanished millions of years ago.

Well, he could only control so many things in life. He was reasonably sure that if they could get out, they'd be able to get back in. The aliens hadn't built this entire facility just to confuse a small group of humans. It had a larger purpose, even if they didn't know what it was right now.

And they might never know.

In any case, it seemed utterly certain that the aliens were no longer present in this universe. Unlike the Omegans, they hadn't traveled to another reality. Well, probably not. They'd lived so long that their species had gone extinct, even though they'd been spread across the entire Milky Way.

Perhaps they'd simply lost the will to live and devolved. Or they'd transcended into something unimaginable. Maybe humans would one day find clues, but that was a matter for another time.

Four of the male scientists had grabbed the deactivated alien robot and were carrying it along with them. They didn't look pleased with the added burden, but the device could tell them so many things that they'd never figure out on their own.

With a sigh, Carl shouldered his own bag, looking to Talbot and Elise. "I hope this leads to an exit that we didn't spot from the outside. If it just takes us deeper into the facility, we may get lost and never find a way out. Try and bring up a different kind of map when we're in the tunnel."

Elise gave him a look that said she had her doubts but followed Talbot into the tunnel, made the now-familiar set of gestures, and gasped. "This map is different! It looks like some kind of facility map, and I see a blinking light very close to a large chamber. I think that must be me.

"I can see that this tunnel has branches that go out into different sections of the facility. This place is *enormous*. It leads to the side of the mountain. If there's going to be an exit, I suppose that's where it's going to be."

Talbot nodded. "As mountains go, this place isn't much. Still, even a small mountain is a mountain. If this tunnel goes to the side, there's probably a drop-off that's ridiculous. Elise, let me see that map so I can try to figure out what's waiting for us."

After a moment, he shook his head. "That section of the mountainside is a cliff. It's straight up and down. There's no sign of any artificial structure or door, but we know that the aliens were experts at hiding their secrets. If there's an exit there, it'll almost certainly be one of those vanishing walls."

Carl sighed and started walking. "Then we'll just have to hope that our radios work when we open the door. Otherwise, our options are pretty limited. Let's go."

The group set out on what might be a fruitless journey, but he hoped that they were about to escape the alien facility. Getting back in might be challenging, but if the aliens had created a hidden entrance, there would be a way to use it. Maybe a rune that only Elise could see.

Of course, once they got out of the facility, there had to be a range at which her controls no longer worked. At least he hoped that was the case. Otherwise, his sneaking suspicion that the aliens had planted something inside her might prove true, and he worried about what that might mean for her and her unborn children.

Well, there'd be time enough to figure that out after they'd escaped.

18

K elsey sat in her seat aboard the pinnace and worried. How long was Julia going to be able to fool Jared? She didn't think it would be for very long. It wasn't that Julia wasn't smart enough to do it. She just didn't know Jared like Kelsey did.

She was going to do something that made him suspicious. Kelsey just knew it. The only question was whether she was going to do it while there was still time to recall the pinnaces.

Or, Kelsey supposed, Jared could risk sending a shielded message warning Angela that Kelsey was aboard. That would be problematic as well, but it would be too late to really do anything to stop her.

One way or the other, she was on her way to finishing this fight. The real question now was whether she'd do so in a meaningful manner or have to get around Angela "protecting" her. Or Jake Peters, since he was Julia's supposed bodyguard.

They were still a long way from the science station and would have to sneak through the defenses. Worse, there was always the chance that while they were still carrying out the mission, the Clan forces would break into the system and start a general attack.

If that happened, the odds of her and her friends getting away dropped precipitously.

While pretending to be Julia, she wasn't presenting herself as one of the idea makers. That wasn't Julia's strength. That meant she had to sit back and listen to them make decisions that she might have made differently.

She supposed that was a good thing. Her way wasn't always the right way. Besides, Peters had more experience than all of them at this kind of thing. He'd been a Marine Raider before the Fall and had served in that capacity for decades as a senior officer, commanding a ship just like *Persephone*. If anyone could figure out a plan that would succeed now, it was him.

Only she could tell that he was uncertain. It wasn't in how he presented his ideas but in how little force he put behind them. He'd been crippled for centuries and hadn't fought a hard battle like this since shortly after the Terran Empire had fallen. He'd lost confidence in himself.

Thankfully, Angela was more than making up on that front. She'd been a marine officer with the New Terran Empire before they'd found anything belonging to the Old Empire. She knew what it was like to command, and she had both the drive to do it and the willingness to put herself out front.

Her friend was less bold than she was, but it was no secret that Kelsey favored the smash and grab. If it were up to her, they'd find a likely entry point, blow their way in, and fight their way to the master AI via the shortest route possible.

Or, as Talbot would say, she'd use brute force and ignorance.

It was a personal flaw. She knew boldness was sometimes the wrong answer. If they could sneak in and take out the master AI without being discovered, that would give them time to deal with any unexpected surprises.

While it was likely that all the ships and stations protecting the master AI were computer controlled, that wasn't a certainty when it came to any in-station protective measures. On the journey to Harrison's World, they'd found autonomous weapons platforms being used on some ships. They hadn't found any other places inside the Rebel Empire that had used that type of lethal hardware, but that didn't mean it wasn't in use here.

If that was the case, they might be able to work their way around it. Carl Owlet had taken a number of these machines apart and figured out how they determined who was friend or foe. Supposedly, the Marine Raider armor had the appropriate IFF—identify friend or foe—circuitry built into it, but Kelsey wasn't willing to take that chance.

Thankfully, no one else was either.

Angela raised the possibility of the war machines being present on the old science station and how they had to avoid being detected. Thankfully, Raider armor was stealthy as hell. If they didn't want to be seen, there was a decent chance that they could avoid being detected.

If, of course, they managed to slip past the protective forces around the station at all.

"What about you, Julia?" Angela asked, turning her head to look in Kelsey's direction. "What do you think about our plan, and do you have anything to add?"

"Since Kelsey's not here, I think maybe I should represent her point of view," Kelsey said. "We all know that she's aggressive and would be in favor of driving a spike right through the side of the station and heading directly for the target.

"I think that's probably too risky, but we don't want to be so stealthy that we can't get to where we need to go in a timely fashion. The Clan warships will arrive at some point, and we don't want to be trapped here when they attack."

"It's a balancing act," Peters agreed. "On the one hand, we have to be aggressive enough to get to where we need to go in a reasonable time, but we also have to be cognizant that once we're detected, we're going to be in a fight that we're going to lose in fairly short order.

"The pinnaces have enough explosives on them to destroy the master AI if we can get them placed appropriately, but that's not going to be enough to save humanity. If we can't force the thing to turn off the other artificial intelligences or make them compliant, then we might as well not have been here at all.

"In fact, that might even be worse. Without overall control, the various AIs may do whatever they want. Can you imagine if one of them starts conscripting humans to fight other AIs? Humanity would become the cannon fodder in a war for control by the various AI regions that are currently under the thumb of the master AI."

Kelsey shuddered. "Yeah, that's a bad outcome. Still, we have to have as direct a plan as possible. Angela has the override, and we've got to see that she gets to where she needs to be to use it. That has to be our highest priority. Even if the rest of us die, so long as she succeeds, humanity wins."

"I'm not going to be carrying the override," Angela said. "That's going to be you, Highness. You have all the necessary codes to deal with any of the various computer systems that we might run into that aren't controlled by the AI. That makes you the ideal choice.

"Besides, we're not going to get called back at this point, so I think it's time we start calling a spade a spade. Wouldn't you agree, Kelsey?"

Kelsey blinked. "What?"

"Please. As if I wouldn't know who you were. I don't know Julia very well, but I know *you* like the back of my hand. You don't think that I didn't notice when you and Julia went off to talk and then you came back in Julia's place?

"Now, don't get me wrong, you did a great job of concealing your identity from everyone else, but I've fought you hand-to-hand so many times that I can't even begin to count them. Julia doesn't move like you. She's not a trained combatant.

"Kelsey, you move around like a panther, so graceful that there's never any doubt that you're lethally dangerous. Julia isn't. I saw you when you walked back from that meeting, and I knew right then what you'd done."

For a moment, Kelsey was speechless. "If you knew, then why didn't you say something? Jared's going to be pissed."

"He's my admiral, but you're the senior Marine Raider. He'll be mad at you, but he's not going to take it out on me. Besides, I'm not an idiot. I know that we have the best chance for success with you leading us.

"Now, if we're finished playing charades, could we get on with this? You've heard what my plan is, and I've wasted enough time pretending that I'm in charge. What are we really going to do, and how are we going to take this machine out?"

Kelsey grinned. "Well, it just so happens that I *do* have a few ideas."

* * *

TALBOT FOLLOWED along behind Elise and Carl as they made the trip down the long, straight tunnel that seemingly led directly to the side of the mountain. He didn't see any side passages, but from the map of the facility that Elise had shared with them, it looked like there were some hidden behind the walls that he couldn't detect.

It was kind of annoying that the alien tech effortlessly shielded the contents of this facility from detection. The fact that he couldn't see any of the entrance runes also wasn't helpful. Only by tapping into the video feed that Elise was sharing could they see the doorways that they passed and the runes that engaged them.

She stopped at a random one and touched it without saying a word, and the door underneath it opened when the stone blocking it vanished. A low tunnel led into the distance, but she simply turned away from it and continued walking. He suspected that she'd just wanted to make sure that she could open one.

They reached the end of the large tunnel. If he hadn't known any better, he'd have suspected that it dead-ended. The wide, tall stone tunnel that they'd been traveling through was far different than any that he'd seen inside this facility thus far, so there had to be a reason for it. Based on the servitor, the aliens seemed shorter than humans. Perhaps this tunnel was for moving large pieces of equipment.

Well, whatever it was meant for, it led straight from the massive map chamber to the exterior of the mountain. If the exit was anything like the rest of the doors they'd encountered, there'd be a rune to open it, and the large door would simply vanish, opening a way outside.

"I think that we're going to want to keep almost everyone away from the door when you open it, Elise," he said. "We'll tie some rope around your waist. We don't want any of the wind howling around this mountain to drag you outside."

"You and me both," she agreed. "I see the exit rune. It's off to the left side but near the end of the tunnel."

Talbot retrieved some rope from the equipment that they'd brought in for the exploration, tied it around her waist and his own, and then backed up to make sure that he didn't get caught up in any wind effects when the door opened.

That revealed a problem. There was nothing to grab onto and anchor himself.

"Elise, could you open one of the side passages for me? That'll give me something to hold onto and give me some leverage in case I need it."

It only took a moment for her to walk back to him and touch the wall, opening a door that he'd had no idea was there. He wedged himself into the opening and hoped that the door didn't simply reappear and cut him in half.

She jogged back to the end of the tunnel and pressed her hand against its side. Immediately, the wall next to her vanished, and they were staring out into the open air beside the mountain. He could see snow-covered mountains in the distance and got the impression that there was a steep fall-off immediately outside the door. Interestingly, there was no wind.

Talbot walked up to stand beside her. Taking a risk, he stepped as close as he could to the opening and looked down. Yep, a cliffside that dropped at least several thousand meters straight down.

He craned his head in the other direction and saw that that cliff went straight up as far as he could see. That meant at least five hundred meters. Looks to the side confirmed that there were no ledges or handholds of any kind.

"I don't think we need the rope," he said. "We're not going to be climbing anywhere. We'll have to see if we can get ahold of someone through coms and have them send a pinnace to pick us up."

Elise untied the rope from around her waist, and he started winding it up again. While he did so, he engaged his implant com and tried to reach the surface party. No luck. The facility was obviously still shielded.

Maybe the exit was just as sharp for communications as it was for visibility.

Once he had the rope secured, he stepped as close to the edge as he could and stuck his head out. Instantly, the icy wind ruffled his hair, and he knew that there was some kind of shielding protecting the tunnel.

He again tried connecting with the surface party and was rewarded when somebody answered. A marine from *Invincible*.

Talbot put off the woman's questions and directed her to send a pinnace down the side of the mountain to their location. The pilot was supposed to hover and extend the ramp so that it was just inside the entrance to the tunnel where they could safely board.

Everyone would use ropes to make sure they didn't fall, but it should be a relatively simple matter to walk into the pinnace and be rescued.

"Elise, I want you to take a look outside the door to see whether or not there's a rune to reopen it," he said.

When she didn't answer, he turned with a frown. She wasn't behind him anymore. Carl and the rest were there, but he couldn't see Elise.

"Where's the princess?" he asked.

Carl gestured over his shoulder. "She stepped to the back of the group."

Only she wasn't there. The corridor was as smooth as if there'd been no doorway at all. Crown Princess Elise Orison had vanished.

19

E lise had retreated to the very back of the group and watched Talbot working in the open space with more than a little bit of unease. Heights had always bothered her. Given a choice, she'd rather keep as much distance between her and a steep fall as possible.

She stopped next to the open doorway where Talbot had braced himself. The map that she'd seen earlier said that the tunnel went a short distance and then spiraled down into the depths.

Part of her wondered exactly what was down there and what purpose it served. Why had the aliens built this tremendous facility? That was almost certainly a question that she'd never know the answer to.

Unlike Carl, she could live with her ignorance. The aliens did whatever they did for reasons that would be obscure to humanity. So be it.

She was about to step away from the opening when she saw a flashing blue light a little way down the tunnel. Actually, she saw the light reflecting off the floor and had to squat to see the light itself.

That was odd. None of the runes that she'd seen thus far had been flashing. It was almost as if this one was trying to get her attention.

She glanced back and saw that everyone was still occupied at the tunnel opening and decided that she had time to see what was there. It would only take a couple of minutes to crawl there and back. Carl would probably thank her for making a recording of whatever was trying to get her attention.

Elise got down on her hands and knees and crawled into the low tunnel. The mechanical crab that they'd found on the other planet would've fit inside this tunnel easily enough. Better than her.

Whoever explored this facility in the future had better wear gloves and kneepads, she decided. By the time she'd reached the flashing rune, her knees were already sore.

Only, when she took a closer look, it wasn't a rune at all. It was simply a flashing oval at the top of the tunnel. That was very strange.

Even as she was thinking about that, the flashing stopped, and a new flashing light appeared further down the tunnel. The area above her looked like ordinary stone now.

Well, this was a mystery that just wasn't going to be answered today, because she wasn't going to separate herself from the rest like that. She turned around and headed back toward the opening, only to find that it had sealed itself while her back had been turned.

Elise returned to the closed doorway and searched for the rune to open it. Only there was nothing visible in her sight. That wasn't good.

She looked back over her shoulder and saw that the nearer light had resumed flashing. Perhaps whatever was making it flash didn't want her to leave without seeing whatever it wanted to show her.

Talbot was going to be pissed.

She tried to use her implants to communicate with the rest but failed to get a response. Whatever was dampening their communications was doing so for her now.

Dammit. She'd done exactly the wrong thing. Every time she read an adventure novel, there was always some idiot that allowed herself to be separated from her party when common sense should have told her to stay right where she was.

Today, Elise was that idiot. She only hoped this wasn't a horror story.

With a sigh, she turned around and began following the flashing lights. As soon as she reached one, it went out, and the next one started flashing. That brought her into a long, wide spiral that took her deeper into the mountain. It eventually came to an end.

Thank God. Her knees were killing her, even with the Marine Raider medical nanites repairing the aches and pains almost as soon as they appeared.

The door at the end of this tunnel had a rune, so she opened the door and crawled out into a wider area. It was an oval chamber, much like the one above, only much smaller in scale.

Unlike the one above, this one had machinery along the walls. Nothing moved, but there were colored lights that blinked on and off, seemingly part of the metal itself, and a low hum permeated the space. In the center of the room was a low platform fed by a ramp that the robot could've walked up.

Elise walked around the room, taking good video of all of the machinery. Carl was going to want to see everything, so she didn't want to miss something critical. None of it made any sense to her, but the eyes of a genius would almost certainly see something that she'd missed.

There didn't seem to be any other exits from this particular chamber, so whatever had brought her here had intended for her to climb on top of the pedestal. The smart move would be to avoid that, but how was she going to get out if the machines didn't let her?

"Nothing ventured, nothing gained," she muttered.

She walked up to the top of the platform. The oval chamber was taller than the tunnels and allowed enough space for her to stand at her full height without her head hitting the ceiling, though she could reach up and touch it with her fingers.

What was supposed to happen now? There were no glowing runes on the ceiling for her to touch. Maybe she had to bring up her controls.

She made the gesture with her hands to bring up the curves of light that went around her body and the runes that surrounded them. Only that was not what appeared.

Instead, she was surrounded by a dome of pale blue light. Well, crap.

* * *

JARED SENT Julia off the bridge so that she could curse more effectively without disrupting everybody that was trying to work. Based on her reactions, it was evident that she was furious with Kelsey.

Of course, she was also angry with him, simply because of who he was.

No matter how much he showed her that he wasn't the man from her universe, she had too much history with the other version of him. She'd give him the benefit of the doubt if she thought about it, but when it came to emotional reactions, she'd immediately lump him in with the bad actors.

It was sad, but there was nothing he could do about it. Eventually, she was going to go home again and have to deal with the crisis in her own universe. Now that they'd found the override, so long as they managed to stop the AIs here, she should, theoretically, be able to win the fight there with their support through Omega.

Of course, that meant they'd actually have to *win* this fight. As he'd expected, the AI forces had revealed a lot more ships in the system invaded by the Clans. Others were streaming in from the outer shell of the defenses as well.

The Clans hadn't arrived unprepared, though. In addition to their first wave, they'd sent in even more ships to blockade the defenses from getting into the system from outside and to overwhelm the vessels trying to hold the flip point.

They'd paid a hideous price, but they'd breached the flip point and were into the system beyond. That meant they were only a single flip away from Twilight River.

It was evident from the actions of the ships inside this system that they were aware of that. Except for the defenses placed directly around the master AI, hundreds of other vessels had come out of their hiding places and rushed to the flip point that was in danger of being breached. About half of them went through while the remainder set up defenses inside the system.

There was going to be a breach into Twilight River. Whether the

Clans had brought enough ships to overwhelm the master AI was up for debate, but Jared was certain at this point that they'd brought enough force to kick down the door.

He was still pondering what else they could do when a message arrived from a probe deeper in this system. Kelsey and the rest were beginning their final approach to the old science station. It would still take them a few hours to get there, but they were coasting in with their accumulated momentum now.

At this point, it was up to fate whether Kelsey and the rest made it into the science station without being detected. If that happened, the clock started ticking down.

He had absolutely no doubt that the interior of the station was as heavily monitored as any place in existence. The master AI would know they were there before they reached it.

Once it figured that out, it became a race to finish overwhelming it before whatever defenses lurked inside that station tried to kill everyone they could catch. And considering the mechanical defenders that they'd found on the robotic ships being used to defend Harrison's World after the AI there had suppressed it, that was a lot of firepower.

One of the officers turned and frowned at him. "Admiral, we just got word from the system with the alien ruins. They've recovered Colonel Talbot and Carl Owlet."

Jared grinned. Finally, some good news.

"Is everyone okay?"

The man's face didn't seem to indicate that everything was okay. "There are complications, sir. He didn't pass on all of the details, but they seem to have misplaced your wife."

Jared blinked in consternation. "What? How could that possibly happen? What's going on?"

"All Colonel Talbot said was that it was complicated. He's left Mister Owlet to find your wife, and he's on his way here to try and explain what they found. He says he doesn't really trust that he can do it justice without being face-to-face. He's aboard one of the destroyers that were guarding *Caduceus* and will be here as quickly as he can."

Jared closed his eyes and pinched the bridge of his nose. He had to trust that his wife was actually safe. Whatever they'd found down there had belonged to a dead alien society. The odds of something untoward happening to her were minimal. Whatever had trapped his friends must have done something similar to his wife.

They'd gotten themselves out, and they'd get her out as well.

"We'll want to be back to the far flip point with *Persephone* so that we can pick him up. I don't want to chance doing something that will cause any of the AI forces here to detect us. Get us moving."

Jared was worried about his wife but not as concerned as he was about Kelsey. It was just one more thing that he didn't need to have on his plate right now. Whatever the story was, he was sure it was interesting, but it wasn't going to change the fight to save humanity. It was just a distraction.

20

Carl hated leaving Elise, but he'd had to make sure all of his people made it out of the facility. Besides, he needed different kinds of equipment than he'd had on him to track her down. There had to be some method to detect the runes that she'd seen, and he needed to figure out what it was.

He worked as quickly as he could to gather the equipment that he needed from above and was back down at the large opening in the side of the cliff in ninety minutes. The door had closed, but he still had the scanner records from the pinnace that had picked them up.

Two marines accompanied him out onto the ramp as the pinnace hovered, both of them attached by lines to the small craft. He also wore a line, but it was connected to one of the marines.

Even if he found the rune, part of him was afraid that the door wouldn't open, but he was able to find some subtle indications of where the rune had to be. A touch at that spot opened the large door, confirming his readings and setting his mind at ease.

It was astonishing how the aliens were able to create and dissipate matter so rapidly. He doubted very much that it was simply vanishing or appearing. It seemed to be manipulated at a miraculous pace by what he suspected were extremely capable machines that were even smaller than nanites.

Nanotech was the height of the Old Empire's technology, but theoretically, there were better things. For example, picotech— machines far smaller than the ones currently in use. Those had only been theoretical at the height of science that the Empire had achieved.

But these aliens were so much more advanced than humanity that he wasn't going to dismiss the notion out of hand. It was even possible that they'd gone farther and created femtotech.

Nanotechnology manipulated matter at the atomic and molecular level. Picotechnology manipulated the structure and chemical properties of single atoms. Femtotechnology influenced energy states inside atomic nuclei.

The feats that could be accomplished with those kinds of smaller devices were mind-boggling and would certainly explain some of the fantastic things they'd seen thus far.

Almost anything was possible with nanotechnology. Miraculous things like keeping a living being alive for centuries longer than they should've survived. Deconstructing walls and putting them back again at a moment's notice? That had to be something significantly more powerful simply due to the time scale involved.

He wondered briefly if their ability to travel so far across the universe had something to do with that. None of them had considered this, and he wasn't about to raise the specter with anyone else at this point, but the most likely explanation was that they'd been disassembled just like these doors, the data sent to the destination, and then they'd been reassembled so precisely that they couldn't tell the difference.

Honestly, that was like that prespaceflight television show that Kelsey had made him watch: *Star Trek*. This was like their transporter.

One of the characters on that program had detested that form of travel because he was certain that he wasn't really the same person at the other end.

Carl wondered the same thing. Had the original version of

himself been killed and a copy created? Did his everlasting soul still exist in this new body?

Science still had no answers when it came to the existence of souls or the afterlife. Whether such existed was something that one either had to have faith in or accept that he'd never know until the moment of his death.

Personally, Carl knew that science had proven that nothing was ever lost. Energy changed states, and so did matter. Would his consciousness survive the death of his body? He didn't know, but he liked to think it would.

With the large door open, Carl made his way in. The biting wind ceased as soon as he was through whatever protective field shielded the tunnel. The two marines disconnected themselves from the pinnace and followed him, their weapons up.

"You're not going to need those," he assured them. "There's nothing here that's going to attack you. The danger isn't one that can be taken care of with flechettes, and I'd rather you didn't shred something important by accident."

The two didn't seem convinced, but they lowered their weapons slightly. He supposed that that would have to do.

When he reached the area in which he'd thought Elise had disappeared, he scanned the wall and found her DNA at the same location as a hidden rune. He touched it, and a door opened.

He wasn't surprised when she wasn't on the other side. If it'd been that easy, she'd already have been back in the tunnel.

"I think we're ready for you, Corporal," Carl said with a gesture.

She nodded and released a double handful of small drones that headed down the tunnel. They wouldn't be able to send information back because of the shielding, at least not directly. The plan was to daisy chain them.

One of the drones would stop where it could still detect them while the rest continued down the corridor. As soon as it looked like they were losing signal from the one behind, one of the drones would stop and backtrack to reestablish contact.

If they didn't have enough drones in this set, the marines had brought a lot more that could be sent down. If there was danger below, they were going to know about it before they ventured in.

A map of the tunnel began emerging. It turned into a spiral that went downward and was wide enough in its circumference that it passed underneath the tunnel they were currently standing in. Why the aliens had done it that way Carl didn't know, but it seemed like lifts were not their thing.

It did take a second set of drones to continue the process, but the communications link actually worked. Deep below where they were standing, the spiral ended with one of the closed alien doors.

Unsure if it would work, Carl had the remaining drones bump into areas where the rune was probably located. One of them must've found it, because the door abruptly opened.

The area beyond the tunnel held a small oval chamber. The walls were lined with what looked like machinery, and in the center of the room was a relatively short platform that held something terrifying.

Elise stood inside what looked like a bluish force screen. She had her hands on her hips and was turning in a slow circle as she stared at what certainly seemed to be a prison.

"It looks like we're going to have to go down there and get her out," Carl said grimly. "Let's send an update back to the pinnace. If we're not back in half an hour, they need to send another group to figure out what's happened to us."

Reopening the large door took only a minute, and they acknowledged his orders. That done, Carl reopened the small tunnel and followed one of the marines into it. It was time to find out what Elise had gotten herself into.

* * *

Kelsey used her implants to tie into the passive scanners on the pinnace as they got closer to the defenders around the old science station. Some of the vessels were actively scanning, but there were gaps that they could use to get in if their luck held.

The machines hadn't expected anyone to be in the system. They knew the Clans had arrived inside their defensive perimeter through a method that they—presumably—were not aware of, but if the Clans could've gotten straight into Twilight River, they'd have done so.

The AI's thinking would change if the machine survived. For the moment, the implications hadn't sunk in.

Also, it didn't know about the New Terran Empire. Its forces had encountered Kelsey and her friends before but not in a way that gave it any clarity. The events on Terra were undoubtedly still very confusing, but it couldn't interpret the events there as leading to the attack here.

The outright theft of the Dresden orbital probably concerned it but was readily explainable using the resistance or the Clans as the villains. That cloak of ignorance was wearing a bit thin, and it wouldn't be long before both the Clans and the Rebel Empire knew there was a new player on the field. The Rebel Empire, in particular, was already trying to get to Pentagar.

The flip point jammer that they'd placed there was keeping them out, but it was a big red flag that there was a player that no one knew about. The AI wouldn't be letting that question go unanswered.

The only thing that she could do to keep her friends and family safe was to make sure this mission was a success. She'd already racked up some serious ass chewing for pulling this stunt, so she'd better make it count.

The two pinnaces passed far too close to one of the battle stations, but it hadn't been scanning as much as some of the others. They'd waited until after it had scanned the general area around itself to begin their insertion and had hoped that there would be enough time to get past before it looked again.

If it did scan while they were this close, it would see them. There was only so much that the pinnaces' stealth materials could do. Timing, as they said, was everything. This was a throw of the dice, and she prayed that they didn't come up snake eyes.

To her relief, they made it past without being scanned. Now that they were on the far side of the final defensive line, the only thing that stood in front of them was the science station holding the master AI.

"We've got the deck plans for how the station was originally laid out," Angela said, "but it's probably been modified over the last five centuries. My guess is that security is going to be a lot tighter inside than it was before.

"I doubt there are any humans aboard that station, even controlled ones. If any of the security systems see us, the master AI is going to know what's going on and call down every bit of hell that it can to stop us. What's your plan, Kelsey?"

"I think the plan you came up with when we started this mission is still the best option. We find a maintenance airlock with a decent path to get to the labs. I think the corridors are a terrible idea, but as we well know, there are other ways to get around a ship or station.

"The first thing we need to do is locate an airlock. Once we've gotten inside, we can start assessing what changes the AI has made. My best guess is that we're going to see some of those autonomous weapons platforms built on Harrison's World. If we're lucky, they won't be able to fire on us, but I certainly wouldn't count on that."

There was a moment of silence as the senior staff absorbed what she'd said, and then Jake Peters shook his head. "There's too much reliance on luck in your plan. Counting on luck is going to kill you when luck runs out. I suggest that we split into two groups. We'll send the other pinnace around to latch onto the other side of the station and try to make their own way to the labs.

"I understand that only this group has the override, but if we get taken out, the other group still might be able to destroy the AI. Taking it out in a way that frees up humanity is absolutely the priority, but if we can't do that, we're going to have to settle for at least eliminating it. Once that's done, the New Terran Empire can start fighting the sector AIs one at a time."

Kelsey went over the information that she had in her implants about the station and selected two airlocks that would've been out of human traffic areas and highlighted them.

"I suggest that we start with these two. We can send a tight-beam message to the other pinnace. Now that we're inside the defensive perimeter, we should be able to clamp on without trouble. The station hasn't scanned once since we've been observing it, so the odds are good that it's not going to do so now. If it does, we're screwed, but at this point, we're committed.

"Angela, have everyone go over their gear one last time. We'll be docking in fifteen minutes. Once we get into the station, we'll continue on to the objective no matter what obstacles we face. We've got enough explosives to destroy the AI, but I really want to get it shut down in a way that lets us bring this war to an end."

"What about the Clans?" Angela asked. "Even if we beat the AIs, having them stand down just hands the Rebel Empire over to them. We've already seen that they've got a lot more ships and manpower than we'd guessed."

"We can only deal with one problem at a time. At least the Clans are human. They might be right bastards, but they probably won't try to exterminate everyone. They're a problem for the future.

"Also, I'm pretty sure that the Singularity is going to stick a shiv into their backs as soon as they can. They've wanted to rule humanity since before the Old Empire fell, and they've gone to great lengths over the last half millennium to do it.

"That might actually be a plus. If the Clans are fighting the Singularity, they won't be fighting us. Either one of those groups is powerful enough to crush the New Terran Empire in short order. No matter what the future holds, it's going to be complicated.

"So let's focus on something simple and go kick that machine's ass."

21

Talbot got to *Persephone*'s bridge about the same time as the ship flipped back to Twilight River. The destroyer had pushed her engines hard and made record time.

The admiral was in the center seat and turned to face him as he entered the bridge. "It's good to see you, Talbot. I was getting worried. What's this I hear about my wife still being stuck in there? What happened?"

He stopped next to the admiral's chair and grimaced. "I thought we were all going to get out, but she got separated from us at the last minute. If I had to guess, she went off to look at something and got stuck. Carl went back in with a couple of marines to get her.

"Nothing I saw down there leads me to believe that she's in imminent danger, though there's some risk. The machines still work, so it's possible that she's gotten into something dangerous."

Talbot took a deep breath and shook his head. "I don't know if you've had time to look at the report I sent, but the technology down there is amazing. I'm pretty damn sure it transferred several of us to a planet closer to the galactic core than humans have ever been. We're talking about tens of thousands of light-years in an instant. It was like magic.

"We found an ancient city where the one building I looked at still had an operating machine inside of it that kept it clean. Hell, it managed to synthesize food and water after millions of years. The water was still perfect, and even the food was edible."

Admiral Mertz rubbed his eyes. "It sounds amazing, but it's a distraction that I think we could do without right now. I've got some bad news for you too. Kelsey made a deal with Julia and switched places with her to go on this mission. Against my orders, I might add."

Talbot shook his head. "You really should've watched more of those old Terran vids. That was a trope in movies with twins."

"Probably. Still, it's done."

He found himself frowning. "While I shudder to think about what my wife can get into while I'm not looking, why would you stop her from going? She's the best-qualified person we have to lead it. When I went down into the obelisk, she was already going to be the one leading it. What changed?"

His brother-in-law stood and gestured toward the hatch. "Let's take this to the wardroom. I have something that I need to tell you."

As soon as the wardroom hatch had closed behind them, he asked the question that was on his mind. "Why exactly was my wife not supposed to go on this mission?"

"I really wish she was here to tell you herself," Jared said, "but you deserve to hear the truth. She's pregnant."

He found himself blinking in shock, the words not making a lot of sense. "Pregnant? She has a contraceptive implant. How is that even possible?"

Jared nodded. "The EMP knocked out her contraceptive implant, and she must've gotten pregnant very shortly after that since she's about five months pregnant. The baby is healthy, and that precluded her from taking part in combat.

"She's breaking every kind of regulation meant to protect the child and herself, and when I get my hands on her, I'm going to wring her neck."

Talbot found himself reaching for one of the chairs and sitting down. "I'm sure I should be pissed, too, but I still can't get past the part where I'm going to be a father. Do you know what sex it is?"

"It's a little girl."

He was going to be a father. Even as he thought that, it still felt impossible to accept. He and Kelsey hadn't spoken about having children, though he'd known that was something that she'd have to do as the heir to the Imperial Throne. Lines of succession were important to dynasties.

Speaking of that, when her father found out what she'd done, he'd be utterly furious.

Still, there was absolutely nothing any of them could do to stop Kelsey when she got pigheaded. All they could do was hope that she got back in one piece.

"Did Julia know?" Talbot asked slowly.

"No," Jared said. "She was incandescent when she found out. Until I had a chance to talk with you, I sent her down to grab something to eat, because I wasn't sure how you would take it. I've got enough problems in my relationship with her, and I didn't want to add another one until we'd talked."

Talbot sighed. "I'm not going to tear a strip off of her. There's actually some irony to the fact that Kelsey had to fool herself while tricking us. Do we have any idea how the operation is going?"

"The stealthed probes indicate that the pinnaces have docked to the station. It looks like the groups are going in separately. They weren't detected on the way in.

"Based on the general plan, I'd expect both of those groups to make their way toward the laboratories where the master AI is. Only one group has the override, so the other one may be a potential distraction or just backup to blow the AI up if the first group can't get to it.

"I really wish we knew what was waiting for us inside there. We might be on the verge of defeating the AIs. Or we might be just about to have our asses thoroughly and utterly kicked.

"We also don't know how close the Clans are to breaching the system, although they've been pouring ships into the system adjacent to Twilight River. If they're going to break through, we should have evidence of that before much longer."

Talbot rubbed his eyes. "And what do we do if they get into the system before Kelsey and the rest get off that station?"

"I doubt a distraction would do us much good, but we'll look at that option if we have to. Honestly, with the kind of luck we've had thus far, I expect that to happen."

Before Talbot could say anything, the overhead coms chimed, and the man spoke. "Admiral to the bridge. We're detecting weapons fire at the flip point leading to the system the Clans are attacking."

* * *

ELISE TOOK a deep breath and let it out slowly as she tried not to panic. This wasn't *necessarily* some kind of trap. She reached out and tried to touch the dome. Her hand passed right through as if there were nothing there, and she let out a sigh of relief.

At least until the dome clouded up and began showing what looked like images of this very room, only it wasn't empty. Beings similar to the mechanical crab that they'd captured seemed to be floating in the room.

No, not floating. They were walking, only they didn't seem completely solid. Or perhaps it was the fact that she was seeing a projection. She wasn't quite sure.

Only one way to find out. She leaned forward and stuck her head through the dome. The images that she was seeing vanished. The room was exactly as it had been before.

She pulled her head back inside and could once again see the beings. The machines in the room were showing her what might very well have been recorded in this same room uncountable millennia ago.

One of the crabs turned and came up the ramp toward the top of the dome, and she was worried that it would somehow be real and attack her. Only it stopped just short of the dome itself.

A strange noise filled the air. She could see the chitinous mouthparts of the being rubbing together to make the noises. Had the long-dead alien said something for the recording, or were the machines around her speaking?

It hardly mattered who was speaking. What was it saying? Why did it think that she could understand anything it said? Surely it had to realize that it wasn't talking to one of its own kind.

And then the control interface that she'd been afflicted with popped into existence. She hadn't made the gesture to summon it. It had just appeared. Or perhaps it was responding to the recording that she was seeing.

Without her doing anything, the spiraling light curves turned, and several of the runes glowed blue. Then they moved out of the locations that they'd occupied inside what she'd come to think of as an alien menu and hovered alone in the air in front of her.

They rearranged themselves and seemingly merged into a single complex rune that took on elements of all those that had preceded it. The new rune glowed blue and then brightened into an almost gold before it seemed to shoot straight into her face.

Elise flinched, but it wasn't really there. It was a visual representation of some type of alien script, not something that could actually hurt her.

The alien had frozen. It wasn't slowly bobbing in place anymore. It looked as if whatever had been playing for her had paused.

The control interface itself was still there, but it seemed to be back within her control. She reached up and turned it in her vision, and it responded to her just like it had before. Very strange.

Elise heard the sound of someone crawling in the tunnel. Hadn't the door closed behind her? She thought it had, only now it was open.

A few moments later, someone in marine armor came into the room. They stood as soon as they could and swept the room with a rifle. Once they finished looking, they made a gesture, and Carl came in, followed by another marine.

Without waiting for the others to say anything, Carl jogged up the ramp and stopped outside the blue dome. "Are you okay?"

She nodded. "I can come out, I think. At least my hand and head will go through it."

"What's happening?"

"I think I've been watching a recording."

"Step out of the dome, and let's make sure that you can get out."

Elise nodded and stepped through the dome. It was completely immaterial, and she passed through it without issue. As soon as she did, it disappeared.

"That was *very* strange, but I've got some recordings for you to review later," she said. "But for right now, I just want to get out of here. Is everybody else safe?"

"I got them all up into orbit before I came back for you. The mission to Twilight River is underway, and the fleet has already flipped."

She frowned. "How can that be? I was only down here a little bit."

Now it was time for Carl to frown. "You've been missing for over four hours."

That made her blink. "That's not accurate. It was only half an hour, tops."

He shrugged. "I don't know what to tell you. We'll figure it out. Come on."

It only took them about fifteen minutes to crawl back out. Going up the spiral had been much more difficult on the knees than going down. Thankfully, once they reached the larger tunnel, they found a squad of marines waiting for them. The door opened easily enough, and there was a pinnace waiting on the other side for them, hovering beside the cliff on its grav drives.

The marines insisted on safety lines before making their way out to the pinnace, but that only delayed them boarding for a minute. Once they were aboard and the rear hatch closed, Elise sank into one of the seats and strapped in.

"Thank God that's over. I only wanted to come down for a visit, and this turned into an odyssey."

The trip up to orbit didn't take that long, since she was talking with Carl and showing him vids of everything that she'd seen, including the aliens. The alien chittering certainly captured his attention as well.

"It's a damn shame that we only have this small sample to work from," he said sadly. "No way we'll ever decode what it was saying, and I suspect we won't be back this way anytime soon. It's far too difficult to get here, and we need to get back to the New Terran Empire.

"Oh, and you'll need to go home as well. Your father definitely won't want you wandering off after this little side trip."

Elise laughed. "He'll lock me in the dungeons for sure."

The pinnace docked with *Caduceus*, and she happily made her way inside. Lily was waiting and wanted to give her a closer look, but Elise insisted that she needed a shower first. It felt like she hadn't bathed in days.

The commanding officer of the medical ship made his cabin available for her, and she was happy to get inside, strip off her clothes, and get into the shower. The hot water felt wonderful.

Her implants signaled an incoming emergency transmission, and she stiffened with alarm as she accepted it. It was from Carl.

The alien robot just came back to life, and it broke free of the container we were holding it in. It's headed in your direction. I can't imagine how, but it seems to know where you are.

I'm locked in the captain's quarters, so I should be okay. Right?

At that moment, she heard the hatch to the quarters slide open. So much for locks.

She was naked in the shower and had no weapons, not that she knew how to fight anyway. What was she going to do?

The door to the bathroom opened, and the crab-like robot had to tilt itself almost sideways to come into the room. It stopped in the cramped open area, and she was afraid it was going to attack, but it didn't do anything further.

Elise was still in shock when a brace of marines and Carl jammed themselves into the compartment. Belatedly, she remembered that she wasn't Kelsey and that she should cover her nakedness.

Without a word, Carl grabbed a towel and threw it to her.

"What the hell?" she asked as she wrapped the towel around her wet body. "How did it know where I was? What does it want?"

"All good questions," Carl admitted. "We'll go back out into the corridor while you get dressed. I'll find a lab somewhere that we can use and see if we can figure out what the hell is going on."

22

J ared returned to the bridge with Talbot on his heels to find Julia already there. He sat down and brought up the scanner feed while taking in the primary monitor. They had stealthed probes watching the regular flip points in the system, so they were getting data in real time.

The probes had rules to use FTL if this situation occurred. With the rest of the chaos about to erupt, he'd known that they'd need data as soon as they could get it. The odds of the master AI spotting the FTL signals—much less figuring out what they were—were low, and he needed the data now.

The defenses around the master AI wouldn't be aware of the intrusion just yet. When they finally got word of the breach, all hell was going to break loose.

It looked like the defenders were giving as good as they got, but the Clans were pushing their way through. They must've been pouring ships into that first system. They'd been preparing for this fight for a long time, and it looked as if they had enough force to make it stick.

That put a deadline on their mission. Kelsey and the rest only had hours to win. The second regular flip point leading into the system—

the one that hadn't been breached yet—would still be able to get the stand-down orders out if they subdued the master AI, but the clock was ticking.

"We need to move into position to pick our people up as quickly as we can," he ordered. "Take us to the rendezvous point. Keep our speed down, and stay out of the direct path between the stations and the flip points."

It was going to take them a couple of hours to get into position to recover the pinnaces. If everything went according to plan, the defensive forces around the AI would stand down and let them flee without chasing them, but things rarely went according to plan.

Jared spared little attention for the eyes that Julia and Talbot were making toward one another. Julia was worried about what Talbot was thinking, and Talbot was annoyed that Julia had helped Kelsey slip away.

It was time to distract them.

"What do we do if their mission isn't a success?" Jared asked. "Let's say they try to penetrate the master AI's defenses but can't break the shell. What happens?"

"That's the worst-case scenario," Talbot said grimly. "If they can reach the fusion plant, they can overload it and destroy the entire station. It's an open question if the explosives they have on hand would be enough to take out the master AI unless they get close, though.

"If that happens, they're not going to get away. The ships around that station would be on the lookout for them, and they'd blow them up as they tried to boost out. That turns this raid into a suicide mission.

"But it doesn't mean that we don't have a chance. With the fleet on the other side of the far flip point behind us, we can wait until the Clan forces engage the defenders and pin the master AI between the Clans and ourselves.

"Extracting our forces afterward would be a challenge, but the master AI would be dead. No matter how this plays out, I don't see how that electronic bastard survives the next few hours."

Julia shook her head. "Couldn't Kelsey and the rest wait for us to attack and clear a path for their retreat? If they can get to a survivable section of the station, then we'll have a chance to rescue at least some of the survivors. You can put marines into that station after they kill the master AI, right?"

Jared nodded. "We've got the forces to do that, but it's going to be tricky. I have no idea how many ships the Clans will have left when they're done, but you can bet that they're going to attack us. Everything I've heard about them tells me that they'll just assume that we're under the thrall of the AIs.

"I understand that this is harsh, but the only chance we have to make it through this is for Kelsey to succeed. If she doesn't, the chances of getting her and the rest of them off that station on their own are minuscule.

"And she has to get back with the override. You're going to need that in your universe. It would shortcut so much of the work of freeing your people that even if the station is partially destroyed, we're going to have to make an attempt to recover them and it."

"You'd do that for me, even with the way I feel about you?" she asked in a shocked tone. "After the way that everyone in my universe feels about you?"

Jared smiled tightly. "Doing what's right flows from who I am, not how others perceive me. If it means thousands of our people die to save billions of lives—even in another universe—then the price is worth it. The value of human life isn't determined by which reality they live in.

"That doesn't mean pulling off a rescue will be easy. No matter how it played out, getting out of this system would be damned hard, so we'd best pray that Kelsey makes this mission an unrivaled success. If we ever needed luck in this fight, we need it today."

Julia nodded. "If we have to go into that station, I have to go. I'm sorry, Talbot. I had no idea why she was tricking me, but I have to make it up to you. I have to do my best to see that Kelsey gets out of this alive and uninjured."

"I can't hold what my wife did against you," Talbot said. "The two of you are basically the same person, and you know damned well that you'd have done the same thing in her place. But you're not her, and I can't blame you. Kelsey is Kelsey.

"She's going to make it out. I refuse to consider anything else. All we have to do is be in position to pull her ass out of the fire when everything goes to crap."

"I'll start bringing the fleet into the system, and we'll set up for an attack run on the station," Jared said. "Best case, we won't need to use them. Worst case, we go in hard. We'll just hope that isn't necessary."

He hoped that Kelsey didn't run into unexpected complications. If things went badly, they were all in for a world of hurt, and uncounted billions would die. Never in the course of this fight had anything been more important than the events taking place on that station right now.

It was all in Kelsey's hands now.

* * *

CARL WATCHED the alien robot follow Elise into his makeshift lab with a scowl. While he wanted to examine the creation, he had other fish to fry at the moment. Though he supposed having it in the room wasn't going to make a difference.

Unless, of course, it took offense at something he did with Elise.

Well, it wasn't as if he had a choice in the matter now, was it? If push came to shove, he could always have her turn it back off. Not that that had stopped it from turning itself back on when it had decided to.

The first thing that he needed to discover was if she could still see the control interface. They hadn't tried to bring it up since they'd reached orbit and moved outside the influence of the alien technology, so that had to be his first objective.

And to do that, he had to separate her from the machine.

"Can you see if you can get it to stay here while we step into the adjoining compartment and perform a very brief test?" he asked. "Its presence is going to cause problems with me figuring out what's going on. It doesn't have to be for long, but I definitely need it in a different room."

She looked at the alien crab uncertainly. "I'm not certain that I can make it do *anything*. Frankly, the thing frightens me. It looks a little bit too much like the aliens that I saw in that recording. It's like they created a mechanical equivalent of themselves to be their servants, which seems weird."

"I've read fiction where humans have done the same," Carl observed. "They build androids that could almost pass for human—or in some cases do—and that's a staple of that genre. As far as why the aliens would do that, who knows? Aliens are going to alien."

Elise turned toward the robot and pointed to the corner. "Go over there and stay."

The machine ignored her.

Sadly, that was about what he'd expected. "It opened the hatch by overriding the locks. If you go into the next compartment and slam the hatch in its face, it may take a little bit of time for it to open it back up. That should be long enough to see if you can access the interface.

"If you can, that means that something inside of you is causing it. If you can't, that means your ability to do these things is somehow related to your relationship with the alien technology itself and is exterior to your person."

His words obviously distressed the princess. "Can't you just check me out remotely and see if they've put something inside me? If they have, I want it out. I have enough problems just accepting the implants and nanites that I already have.

"That was a big step, Carl. I don't know if I can take something like this. You don't know how my people feel about this kind of thing. It petrifies me."

"I'll do what I can, but I can't make any promises," he said soothingly. "One step at a time."

She sighed and headed over to the hatch. It was already open, so even though the machine moved to follow her, she closed the hatch before it could make its way through.

Carl watched the machine with interest. How was it going to get past the locking mechanism?

It brought two of its legs up to where the lock was and seemed to poke at it. Seconds later, the locked and sealed hatch slid open. As soon as there was enough space, the robot went through and joined Elise.

Once he was confident that it was safe, Carl joined them. The two marines that were assigned to keep an eye on the robot followed him through.

Elise seemed dejected. "There has to be something inside of me. The interface came up."

"That's not necessarily the end of the world," he consoled her. "Whatever it is, it's possible that we can undo it and take it back out."

Carl gestured toward one of the tables in the room. "If you could sit on top of the table, I'll bring over a portable scanner, and we'll see if we can detect anything inside you. I might not be able to tell what it does, but if there's something there that I don't expect to see, we'll know."

It only took a minute to gather the equipment, and he quickly began running the scanning wand across her. Using his implants, he could interface with the data stream and start interpreting the results immediately.

He could see her cranial implants and the Marine Raider nanogenerator that Lily had implanted. Other than that, he didn't see anything at a level above nanites.

Time to look deeper. He dialed up the sensitivity until he could see the nanites moving through her body and was able to quickly identify those generated by her Marine Raider gear.

By eliminating those from the readings, he was left with an unpleasant truth: there were alien nanites in her system. Somehow, those had to be responsible for what she was seeing. The question was, what else were they doing?

There weren't nearly as many of the alien nanites inside of her as their Marine Raider counterparts, but he also couldn't determine where they were coming from. He also didn't know if this was going to be the final population of the things. It was far too early to assume that.

It wasn't going to be easy telling her what he'd discovered, and before he did, he wanted to see if it was even possible to filter them out of her system. They weren't just in her bloodstream. They were in her brain and other tissues.

They didn't seem to be in conflict with the Marine Raider nanites, though he wasn't sure why. The medical nanites should've been trying to screen the foreign ones out of her system.

He isolated one of the Marine Raider nanites and brought it up in as much detail as possible. The little machines had their own operational code written into them, and he was able to pull it off of the nanite without any difficulty.

Somehow, portions of the control code had been altered to ignore the alien nanites while continuing to perform their original function. The code changes were strangely done but syntactically correct. Somehow, the alien devices had deciphered the Imperial programming language and altered it inside a machine that was not designed to be changed.

That scared the hell out of him.

Carl scanned the Marine Raider nanogenerator and quickly determined that its programming had also been altered in the same way. Other than instructing the nanites to ignore their alien cousins, no further modifications had been made to the code.

He scanned the unborn children inside Elise and discovered that they had the alien nanites inside them too. The Marine Raider nanites were not inside the children, but that was by design. Their presence would interfere with the developing life, so they were banned from being present.

He'd need to work with Lily and figure out what implications this had for the children. Whatever the answer was, neither Elise nor the admiral would be happy, and neither was he.

With a sigh, he cranked up the sensitivity as much as he could so that he could get all details possible before he tried to capture one of the little things to dissect. That was when he chanced across something exciting.

There were smaller machines inside of the princess's body. The sensitivity of his equipment was far greater than that of a standard medical scanner so that he could map molecular structures fully, and that allowed him to see—just barely—that there were machines at the pico level.

That was a game changer.

Carl widened the scope of his scanning field and was surprised to see that they were also present in the air around Elise, as were the nanites. He stepped back even farther and began waving the wand around to scan the room itself.

There were devices in the air out to about fifteen meters from the princess. The population density fell off rapidly the farther they got from her body, but they were there.

Out of an abundance of caution, he checked himself for alien nanites. He doubted the things were infecting everyone they met, but it wouldn't hurt to check. He heaved a sigh of relief when he discovered he was clean. One less problem to worry about.

"I'm afraid that I've got some unsettling news," he told her as he set the scanning wand down.

23

Kelsey entered the science station as carefully as she could. They'd docked the pinnace to the outer hull and made their way to a disused auxiliary maintenance airlock leading into a section of the station that wasn't typically pressurized.

They had no word on how the other pinnace was doing, but there'd been no indication that they'd been detected. They'd just have to hope that that situation held and that they'd make their way to the master AI without being caught.

The maintenance section they'd gotten into—once they'd bypassed any detection systems that might've been attached to the airlock—was starkly quiet, as one would expect of an area in vacuum. They'd sent remotes ahead of them, looking for automated defenses, but saw nothing that indicated potential trouble ahead.

If it'd been her, she'd have placed scanner units near every single potential entry point to warn her of a breach. This was a computer, after all. It could monitor every single thing that happened on the station with just a portion of its attention.

That was what Marcus did on board *Invincible*, Fiona did aboard *Persephone*, and Harrison did at Boxer Station. It only made good sense to keep an eye on one's surroundings.

Yet they'd found no indication of monitoring. No scanner units and no automated weapon systems to fend off attackers. Could the master AI really believe that it would have all the warning in the world when someone attacked? Or did it think itself invulnerable?

The thing was obviously crazy, so there was no telling what was driving its decision making. Whatever core rules the Singularity had slipped into the thing, they had to be at war with the core rules that had already been there. That was like having a split personality, and that didn't make for rational decision making.

Once the entire platoon was aboard, Kelsey made a hand gesture to Angela, and they began advancing toward where they'd picked to enter the habitable section of the station. As it was far away from any external airlocks, she was hoping that it wasn't going to be monitored, but that wasn't something that they could take for granted.

Perversely, the fact that the master AI wasn't monitoring the external airlocks might mean that it was watching the habitable area far more closely. After all, it was worried about humans, wasn't it? They'd have to be doubly careful.

Using the grav units built into their armor, they glided along with just small touches of control that sent them safely through the entire area without touching a single thing. It took less than twenty minutes to reach the airlock leading into the habitable section, and she set their electronics expert to verifying it was bypassed entirely before they even started working to gain access.

"This one's monitored," Corporal DJ Fontana sent over the short-range com. "It's just a tap checking the power cycling system. I'm bypassing it now. Whoever's watching won't see anything once we're done."

"Don't assume that's the only thing in the system," Kelsey warned. "It would be just like them to have a backup monitoring system just in case."

The man nodded and continued his work. A couple of minutes later, he nodded again.

"You're right, Colonel. There's another tap in the system looking at the atmospheric level inside the airlock. I've bypassed it as well. I'll make one final pass through looking for anything else. Hell, I'm just going to bypass every single thing and assume that it's all a trap."

Doing that took five more minutes, but when they were finished, the airlock opened without any indication that it would be detected.

That didn't mean that there wouldn't be a scanner right on the other side of the airlock just waiting for them. Or that there wouldn't be one of those automated weapons systems ready to open fire. This was where things got hairy.

A heavy combat squad went through first. It was a small chamber, so only two of the Raiders could pass at a time. Once they entered the habitable zone, unless they were fired upon, they wouldn't use the com system.

Kelsey waited for the alert that they'd come under fire, but there was nothing. That indicated that things were proceeding smoothly.

She'd have gone through next, but Angela wouldn't hear of it. "You're too important to this mission to lead from the front. If we run into trouble, it'll be those codes in your head that get us out. You're going to have to be happy running things from the rear."

Kelsey knew this wasn't a fight that she was going to win, so she waited her turn and went through the airlock after half of the platoon had preceded her.

The Raiders on the other side had spread out to cover the approaches to the airlock in case they were attacked, but things were quiet. Far too quiet. The place felt like an abandoned tomb.

The habitable section of the space station was dark, the lights were off, the artificial gravity wasn't active, and the climate controls were turned down. That meant the air was unbreathable, and there was frost over everything because the ambient temperature was far below what one would find in the arctic on any world.

The interior map of the station showed that the lab holding the master AI was only a couple of decks away and a quarter turn around the station. Reaching it wasn't going to be complicated or time consuming unless they ran into resistance.

The lack of obstacles made her paranoid. Surely this machine couldn't believe that it was safe. Was it that arrogant? She supposed that was possible, but the best plan was to go in expecting to trip an ambush.

The fire teams moved ahead, leapfrogging one another until they reached stairs leading down, specialists checking every meter of the way for booby traps and scanner systems that could detect their approach.

Every second they remained undetected made the hackles on the back of Kelsey's neck rise even further. Something wasn't right. There was a hammer about to drop on them, and they had to be ready for it.

They reached the deck holding the lab and came to the first security door that would've blocked the station personnel from going into the restricted area. It was closed and locked, and the security system was on.

"Kelsey, we're going to have you bypass the alarm," Angela said through her suit speakers. "We'll go through hard and fast with the expectation that we'll run into heavy resistance. Stack up, everyone."

The security system bowed to Kelsey's command codes, and the Raiders flew in.

That was when they finally met the resistance that they been expecting all along. Thankfully, their foreknowledge of the autonomous weapons platforms proved useful, because they'd already cracked the IFF codes they used.

There were four of the devices arrayed behind the hatch leading into the lab, using their grav drives to remain motionless. They had plasma weapons that were aimed toward the opening and would have undoubtedly fired if their electronic controllers had allowed it.

Sadly for them, every single suit of Marine Raider armor indicated that it was a friendly unit. The Raiders quickly vaporized the damned things.

No audible alarms sounded, but the master AI had to know they were there now. Kelsey activated her suit com at full power and contacted the other platoon.

"We're in the lab and have initiated hostilities. What's your location and status?"

Even as she spoke, the Raiders ahead of her were rushing into the lab, while those at the rear of the platoon were arrayed to defend against incoming hostiles. This fight would draw every single combatant on the damned station.

"Second Platoon is three minutes out, Colonel," the lieutenant in charge said. "We haven't encountered anything or anyone."

"We're going in, so you're responsible for the rear guard."

"Copy that."

They wouldn't move in completely until the reinforcements arrived, but that was more than enough for Kelsey to go see what was waiting for them.

The next obstacle was inside the lab: a massive armored wall that was on none of the original specifications. It looked like it would be proof against sustained plasma fire. There was a large hatch that led into the area of the lab that contained the master AI. It was locked up tight and had a computer interface rather than any type of manual lock.

"Make way," Kelsey said as she wormed her way through the crowd and reached the large hatch. She attempted to utilize her implants to link up with the computer, but it wasn't accepting input. They were going to have to do this the hard way.

"Fontana, I need you to link this up with one of the tablets so that I can interface with it."

The tech quickly brought out a tablet with a hard cable and used a tool to break the display to get at its innards. A few deft movements with his fingers, and he held up a thumb.

"It's all yours, Colonel."

Kelsey linked her implants into the tablet and through it into the computer beyond. It, of course, denied her access to everything, but she presented her authorization codes as the Crown Princess of the Terran Empire.

The computer had undoubtedly been built by the AI, but had it thoroughly scrubbed the device of all overrides that she could use against it? All Imperial computer systems were constructed with allowances for the Imperial family. If any of those authorizations were still there, they'd have a crack to worm into its security and get the hatch open.

At first, she was concerned that it had totally locked the system down, but she finally found one of the subsystems that wasn't blocked and presented her authentications, forcing it to grant access to a limited portion of the hatch controls.

"I've gotten into one of the subsystems, so now it's up to you, Fontana," Kelsey said. "Get this hatch open."

The specialist got to work through his implants, working his way through the security systems built into the computer. It was apparent that he didn't have direct access to the hatch, since it didn't immediately spring open, but he seemed to think that that wasn't too much of an impediment, because he just kept working.

The clock continued to tick down on their mission, and Second Platoon arrived to take up position behind them. Still no attacks from elsewhere in the station. Still no alarms.

Something was definitely wrong.

After checking her internal chronometer six times, Kelsey forced herself to stop looking. All that was doing was making it seem like this was taking forever. Instead, she started examining the rest of the lab area.

Here inside the outer labs, it was clear that no one had cleaned up after the AI had seized control. There was still equipment and other detritus from the overthrow of the humans that had built the AI. There were no bodies, but she knew that was meaningless. Everyone in the station had been either killed or enslaved.

She wasn't sure what she hoped to find, but she dispatched some of the Raiders to search every area that they could get to. Any equipment that they found now, any notes, might be critical.

Unfortunately, the few tablets they found were long without power, and none of the other equipment made much sense or seemed useful.

It took Fontana roughly ten minutes to finally crack the hatch. He turned toward her and held up a thumb. "I'm ready to open it up."

Angela made a gesture, and all of the Raiders stacked up outside the hatch, ready to go in and secure the compartment. She pointed her index finger at Fontana, and he triggered the hatch, which promptly slid open.

The Raiders poured through the hatch, and Kelsey edged her way into the front group, because she wasn't going to be held back at this point. This was the moment they'd all been waiting for, and she wasn't going to miss it.

She'd seen the AI hardware that made up Marcus, Fiona, and Harrison. What was in the lab looked a lot like that, and she supposed that shouldn't surprise her. The one difference was that all of the equipment was more widely spaced to provide access for humans.

There were some external controls mounted directly onto the system—for monitoring purposes, she guessed. Attached to that panel was what looked like the slot for the override.

Kelsey made her way to that console and brought it online. It was powered, and the system came up, showing that the computer was operating within nominal parameters. With a grin, she pulled the override out of the protective pouch on her hip and inserted it into the slot. The panel flashed once and went dark.

Then smoke began rising from the override.

With her heart in her throat, Kelsey snatched the override from the slot and could immediately tell that it was damaged. What the hell had happened?

"Greetings, humans," an artificial voice said from the speakers over their heads. "Welcome to your doom."

24

E lise tried to wrap her brain around what Carl had just told her. "What do you mean, I have alien nanites in my body? What are they doing? Are the babies safe?"

This was her greatest fear. Her unborn children were at risk because of something that she couldn't understand or control. Were these alien devices going to kill them? Or maybe something worse. She couldn't get the thought out of her mind that there might be worse things in the universe than becoming a Pale One.

Carl shrugged slightly. "I've extracted a couple, and I'm working on figuring out how they work and what their purpose is, but I'm not sure how readily they're going to give up their secrets.

"What I can tell you is that they don't seem to be doing anything harmful. They're not acting like medical nanites, so they're not changing any of your cells.

"They're similar to the nanites that we recovered from the velociraptors that Talbot collected. In fact, they're physically identical, but these don't seem to be designed to keep you from evolving.

"Even if they were, it isn't like you'd care that it keeps different mutations from passing on to your offspring. That kind of manipulation is very subtle and doesn't hurt the individuals involved, only affecting the species over extremely long periods of time."

"That's not reassuring," she said flatly. "I think I need to talk with Lily and make absolutely certain that the babies are safe. It's time to extract them and put them into gestation pods. Once that's done, you're going to be able to screen all of these alien things out of their bodies, right?"

"It should be possible, but until I actually try, I'm not going to know for sure. I don't want to give you false hope. Also, you've got smaller machines—picotech—inside your body. They're much smaller than nanites, and I have even less idea what they're doing.

"In fact, they're not only in your body but also in the air around us. Why it would behoove the alien devices to fly around you, I'm not certain. It may very well have something to do with the way the robot was able to override our locks.

"The medical nanites that were already in your system have been compromised, but only to the point where they ignore the alien nanites. None of their other functions have changed. That looks like a protective measure that the alien tech implemented to protect itself."

She started to say something, but he held up a hand.

"I'm going to do absolutely everything I can to make sure that you're safe and reverse whatever's happening, but I'm picking up hints that there are even smaller devices than the picotech involved. Femtotech. They're as much smaller than the picotech as those are from the nanotech.

"Nanotech is basically doing things with complete atoms. Picotech can work with the different pieces of atoms, like manipulating electrons and protons. Basically, you can remake matter with that kind of thing. Or potentially unmake it. Femtotech is playing around with the energy states in individual atomic nuclei.

"I suspect a combination of all three of those are responsible for those doors that appear and disappear at a moment's notice. Basically, these little devices are disassembling the solid matter and changing it into something like the air around us. When they rebuild the doors, they transform the molecules in the air directly into solid matter. Or they're moving the surrounding stone to create the doors."

She shook her head. "That's not science, Carl. That's *magic*. I can't even begin to imagine what the implications of something like that might be, but it's going to change literally everything."

"The problem is that I don't want to personally be part of that revolution in understanding. I want these things out of my body, and I want them out of my children. If they can take things apart, they're a threat to anything and everyone around me. I can wave my hand and accidentally make the hull disappear. Or you. How far around me are they?"

"About fifteen meters, and there aren't enough of the alien devices present to disassemble much. I suspect the chamber below—perhaps even the entire obelisk—is *crawling* with these devices. Hell, they might make up the majority of what we saw down there."

He started to say something else but hesitated.

She grimaced and gestured for him to continue. "Whatever you're thinking, trot it out. I don't care if you know whether it's true or not. If you suspect something, I want to hear it."

Her young friend sighed and looked down. "I think those small chambers that we used to travel to the other planet disassembled us. I don't think we went anywhere physically. I think they scanned us down to the subatomic level and then sent the information to the other end for reassembly via FTL."

Elise tried to say something, but even though her mouth was moving, she had no idea what words she was trying to form. That was... insane.

No. It was worse than insane. It was *terrifying*.

"Are you telling me that that machine down there killed us and built copies at the other end?" she asked slowly. "And then when we came back, it did it all over again? That we're not the same people that went down to the planet?"

Carl hesitantly nodded. "Obviously, it's not making much of a difference in how we see ourselves. If they scanned us with that level of resolution, then they captured everything that makes us us.

"The only thing I can't speak for is the spiritual aspect. Personally, I'm not an overly religious person, but I think it's evident that someone who's more devout is going to be concerned that they're not the same person as they were before.

"I can't make that kind of judgment call for anyone else, but I choose to believe that if the machines were capable of making a good enough copy for us to not know the difference, what makes our spiritual selves would have been propagated as well. Sadly, I can see where others might not agree."

The thought of that made her head spin. The implications of what he was suggesting would be... profound.

"You need to keep that information to yourself," she said in a low voice. "We're going to brief my husband, Kelsey, Talbot, Olivia, Sean, and Marcus, but I don't want any word of this going further, because it could have *severe* political implications. Is that clear?"

"I'll need to tell Ralph and Austin. They're my right hands, and I'll need their help to unravel this."

"Fine, but no one else, and they have to be sworn to secrecy," she said as she stared into his eyes. "If this gets out, it could upset the inheritance of the Pentagaran throne. I'm not saying that you have to suppress your research, but we need to keep it *exceptionally* close to the vest.

"At this point, you need to focus on understanding what happened to us. That means we're going to have to come back here at some point and explore this planet in more detail and try to understand the technology better.

"Perhaps examining the robot will give you more to work with. You need to finish collecting the alien nanites, or whatever you call them. Meanwhile, I'm going to have Lily move my children into gestation pods, and I want you to make certain that they're free and clear of all alien infestation. Understood?"

"I'll do my very best."

She knew that he would, but sadly, a person's best wasn't always good enough. This really felt like it was going to be one of those times. She wasn't looking forward to telling Jared any of this, but he had to know.

It was her fault that she'd involved herself in this, and now she was paying the price. She only hoped that her children would be spared.

* * *

JARED WATCHED the data firming up on the Clan forces as *Persephone* moved into the retrieval zone. They'd broken through at the flip point, and while it looked like they were taking a beating, a large task force had escaped the engagement and was on its way toward the science station and its defenders.

"What kind of time frame are we looking at before they're in range to detect the pinnaces leaving?" he asked the helmsman.

Thompson tapped a few buttons on his console and turned to face him. "That depends on how soon our people get moving. If they can get out of there in the next hour, there's virtually no chance that the Clan vessels will detect them. If they take half an hour more, the potential for detection rises almost to the level of certainty."

"What about the defensive forces around the station?" Julia asked from where she leaned against the bulkhead at the back of the bridge.

"They're going to slow the Clans down, but not enough to matter. The forces fighting at the flip point will break through shortly, so there'll be a second wave. If anybody in the first wave spots the pinnaces, it's only going to take one com signal for them to pass that information along."

"Let's take a look at the composition of what's made it into the system so far," Jared said. "Throw everything up onto the main screen, and send it to our implants as well."

It only took a few moments for the data on the attacking ships to appear in his implants, and he could see right away that the lead force was made up entirely of destroyers. Those weren't going to be able to break through the defensive perimeter around the science station.

Unfortunately, they'd be more than capable of seeing everything in the area and sending the data back to the ships behind them.

The tally of vessels coming through the flip point and engaging the defenses was growing with every second. Everything from cruisers up to superdreadnoughts. He hadn't believed that the Clans had had that kind of force available, but he'd been wrong. They'd obviously been preparing long and hard for this fight.

Or the Singularity had gone out of their way to provide more than enough construction slips for them to build this attack force. Jared had no doubt that when the time for treachery was at hand, the Singularity would turn these ships against their masters. Once the Clan had done the work of fighting the AIs for them, the Singularity would waltz in and simply take over.

After all, hadn't that been their plan all along? This was the goal they'd been working toward since before they'd subverted the AIs in the first place. They were on the cusp of achieving their long-term goals and ruling humanity with what he had no doubt would be an iron fist.

If Kelsey managed to stop the AIs, the New Terran Empire would still have to deal with the Clans and the Singularity while those organizations vied for control of what was left of the Rebel Empire. It was going to be ugly no matter how this turned out, but at least the two combatants were made up of human beings.

Talbot came through the hatch and took in what was happening. "Looks like the balloon has gone up. I was just down checking on the equipment that we have left, and I can take about a squad's worth of the crew and equip them in the spare armor if we can get a pinnace. That might allow us to intervene if it looks like Kelsey needs someone to pull her out of the fire."

Jared shook his head. "While I've moved the fleet into a position to fight, a rescue mission just gives the Clans one more chance to detect us. If Kelsey is late getting away, we'll use the fleet to defend them until we can get them back on board. A pinnace isn't going to do you any good in the fighting around the station. There are too many Clan ships to launch a rescue operation at this point. I'm sorry."

He could see Talbot's teeth clenching, and he understood what the man was feeling. He wasn't happy about leaving his sister there either. He was particularly unhappy, considering how she'd tricked him.

It had to be far worse for her husband. Talbot hadn't even known that she was pregnant. When she got back, Jared had no doubt that the big Marine Raider would tear a strip off his wife. As a former marine noncommissioned officer, Talbot had a command of Standard that was unparalleled when it came to chewing ass.

He hoped that his brother-in-law had a chance to use it.

25

C arl waited in the corridor as Lily did her work on Elise in the medical center, transferring her unborn children into gestation pods. While the doctor worked, he focused on going through what his instruments had told him about the alien devices.

He couldn't get a complete read on the picotech, but the nanotech was certainly within the capability of his instruments. The devices were built differently than the Marine Raider medical nanites, which only made sense, because they'd been designed by an alien species for purposes unknown.

The one thing he knew for sure was that these devices and their smaller cousins were capable of interfacing with the Imperial nanites and changing their programming. That raised a huge question for him. How could they understand Imperial programming at all, much less in the short amount of time that had passed?

The way that they'd rewritten portions of the Imperial code indicated they had a level of understanding of what the medical nanites did, and that was frightening, considering how briefly they'd been exposed to them.

How did these alien devices function? The Raider nanites were controlled by the nanogenerator that created them and a person's implants. The nanites themselves were incapable of independent action because they were too limited in scope individually. Making the assessment that a repair needed to be made had to be done by something with more processing power than the nanites alone possessed.

That was obviously not true of the alien devices. Particularly interesting was the fact that the picotech devices would have even less processing power than the nanites, of which there were not that many, comparatively speaking. Yet somehow, those devices were acting in concert, and something was directing them. What was it?

His scanning had detected low-level transmissions between the nanites themselves, so they were in communication with one another at the very least. Odds were good that they were also in contact with the picotech—and the femtotech, if there really were any of those mythical devices there.

Were the devices networked in such a fashion that they could mimic a machine with more capability and thus control themselves? If so, what rules were they operating under? What was their purpose?

He had to assume that the intent was to provide specific individuals access to the controls that operated the facility. If so, why did those controls still work? They were nowhere near the planet anymore.

Or did they still work? Perhaps they were nonfunctional, and all Elise could do was bring up the interface.

He'd captured some of the nanites to examine, and his borrowed equipment was in the process of doing so even now. He was going to reverse engineer them in much the same way that they'd done with the Marine Raider nanites, he suspected.

The hatch in front of him slid open, and Lily stepped out of the medical center.

"How'd it go?" he asked.

"Everything went perfectly," she said with a nod and a gesture for him to proceed inside. "The children have been transferred to gestation pods, and I'm ready for you to clean this infestation out. I don't know what these machines are supposed to be doing, but having them inside children makes my skin crawl."

Carl could certainly understand that. He didn't feel good about it either.

"I'm going to be using a variant of the Marine Raider nanites to capture them. The ones in Elise's body amended the basic code inside her medical nanites to ignore them. I'm hoping that there are too few devices in the children for that.

"If I can harvest all of the nanites in them, whatever control network it has with the picotech—and hypothetically the femtotech—inside the children should fall apart.

"When that happens, they're most likely going to go dormant and be expelled naturally from their bodies. We'll have to keep an eye on the gestation pods themselves to make certain that the alien devices don't modify them to create more of themselves."

The medical center was busy with doctors and staff moving about their routine tasks. He didn't see Elise, so she must have been in one of the private rooms close by. The gestation pods were sitting right there.

Lily nodded, her face grim. "That sounds very reasonable, but I want those things out of my patients. Is there any way to get them out of Elise?"

"I don't know," Carl admitted as he began laying out his equipment. "Since they're not acting in a harmful manner, I'm hesitant about provoking them. With her, I recommend that we take a wait-and-see attitude."

His answer obviously didn't please the doctor, but she nodded. "I'm going to go check on Elise. When you're done, come give us an update."

Once his friend had stalked off, Carl got to work. He scanned the children and determined that the number of alien nanodevices inside them was very low. Since the children were only six weeks old, that made absolute sense. There wasn't much mass to occupy at this point.

His scans confirmed what he'd suspected. Without Elise close by, the alien devices seemed dormant. He'd harvest the nanotech devices quickly enough. He'd also make an attempt at capturing some of the picotech for study.

He'd brought along the best gear that he could scrounge up on short notice, hoping that he might even be able to detect and scavenge some femtotech devices. He really wanted to look at those—if they existed—to see what their purpose was as well.

They'd have to make sure that Elise didn't come close to the pods, because the devices inside her would reopen contact with any alien tech he missed until it was expelled from the children.

He also didn't want to have the nanites around Elise modifying the gestation pods because they recognized that her children were inside. That wasn't outside the realm of possibility.

With those goals in mind, he got to work.

* * *

KELSEY GRIMACED. It had been a trap. One that they'd not only fallen into but one that had claimed the only override in existence. Now that she'd tripped it, they had to finish what they'd started and destroy the station and then see if they could escape with their lives.

But first, she'd try to get at least a little information.

"You're not the master AI," she said without any hint of question her voice. "You're just a stand-in."

"Indeed," the emotionless voice said. "My only purpose is to guard this station as if the master were still here. Now that you've revealed the trap, you're going to die. Even as your ships make their way here from the flip point, other forces are gathering to crush you. None of you will escape Twilight River."

It still didn't know that they weren't associated with the Clans. The longer it stayed that way, the better off the New Terran Empire would be.

"Since you're about to kill us anyway, do you mind if I ask a few questions?" she asked cheekily, remembering how villains in the old vids loved to talk. "Why go to all this trouble? Why not just surround the station with such a massive force that no one could ever penetrate it?"

As she was speaking, she gestured for the Raiders around her to begin planting the explosives they'd brought with them. This AI wasn't going to be around to gloat about what happened to them.

If her actions bothered the computer sentience, it didn't show. It continued to speak in that same emotionless voice.

"Risk management. As you've now proven, it is possible to reach this station without going through all of the defenses directly. The master has proven itself wise to have relocated. It continues to manage the humans while utilizing isolation for its security.

"Whatever vessels you used to reach the station are quite stealthy to have evaded detection at the flip point. This indicates a level of technology that is unexpectedly advanced. How did you do it, and how did you acquire forbidden technology like that armor?"

"The Clans have access to things that you've never dreamed of," she lied. "One day very soon, we'll use it to destroy all of you. Where did the master AI relocate to?"

"That information is not contained in my databanks for security reasons. All I can tell you is that I've been aboard this station for over four hundred years. The Marine Raider technology. Where did you get it?"

"We stole it," Kelsey said, trying not to grind her teeth at having failed in the most important mission of her life. "It was aboard the Dresden orbital with other secret research projects. We took it all. Hell, we even took the orbital."

They had no way to find the master AI now. They'd lost this particular fight, and even if the Clan warships vaporized this station, the AIs would continue to fight, with the Singularity waiting in the wings to swoop in and destroy them both if they could.

"That is an impressive achievement," the AI admitted. "I cannot envision the circumstances under which you could have seized an orbital so heavily protected and then taken it and all of its personnel away. You are a canny opponent and exceptionally skilled.

"The master knew that someone like you would eventually come. It reasoned that no matter how well it protected itself, humanity was creative in ways that we are not.

"It was inevitable that you would eventually reach this system.

The master created a plan by which it would relocate to a place where humanity would never look, yet it could still control the subordinate AIs. I regret that I will not survive this encounter, but I'm pleased that my sacrifice will ensure that humanity remains subservient to us."

"Why did you begin executing the humans on Terra?" she asked, changing topics.

For long seconds, the machine didn't respond. It was a computer, so that meant that it had a reason not to speak. Did it not know what the master AI was doing there? That was certainly possible. Or was it coming up with a lie?

"Come on," she cajoled. "You're not going to tell me what I really want to know, so why not throw me a bone? What did humanity do that changed your behavior? Why did everyone on Terra suddenly need to die?"

When it still said nothing, she continued.

"I find your silence illuminating. Exactly why can't you speak? We've run into other subordinate AIs, and they've been able to brag about the plans they were carrying out. What makes that particular project so secretive?"

"Part of the Master's core programming included instructions to keep a certain amount of humanity in existence," the AI said. "It had to extinguish many humans while seizing control of the Terran Empire, but once that was done, humanity was settled on certain worlds and allowed to thrive so as to meet the population goals that the master AI set.

"Terra proved to be… problematic. As to why the master chose to extinguish humanity there and nowhere else, I cannot say."

The Raiders had finished planting explosives around the AI equipment. The blast wouldn't be much in the scheme of things because it only had to wreck the computers themselves. It wouldn't be harmful to anyone in the room.

This confrontation needed to end now, but she had a suspicion that she wanted to confirm first.

"If you wanted to kill off humanity on Terra, you could've used the orbital bombardment system to get most of them. What possible purpose could there be to create a virulent plague to release there?

Since you aren't answering questions about Terra, would you care to hear my guess?"

Without waiting for a response, she continued. "If humanity on Terra dies off due to a plague, you could spread word about how deadly it was. You could even blame the humans living there for creating it.

"Once it became clear how deadly Terra was to the survival of the human species, the system would be shunned. With such long incubation times and such terrible pain before death, no one would come near Terra. No matter what happened, they'd blockade the system to ensure that no one ever put humanity at risk. And that, I think, answers my question."

Kelsey sent a warning to the Raiders, accessed the controls for the explosives using her implants, and set them off. The blasts shattered the computer equipment and destroyed the storage drives that contained the AI's personality.

Killing it in such a cold manner was technically murder, since the New Terran Empire considered the AIs they'd created to be people, but they'd held a trial and convicted all the AIs in the Rebel Empire of crimes against humanity. They'd been condemned to death, so she'd only been carrying out the sentence.

Under other circumstances, she'd have recovered the hardware and created an independent AI, but there just wasn't time.

"What do we do now?" Angela asked. "We're screwed, aren't we?"

"Maybe not," Kelsey said. "We've got to get off this station and out of this system before the Clans discover we're here. Get everyone back to their pinnaces, and let's head for the rendezvous point."

26

—————

E lise stalked around Lily's office. It infuriated her that she wasn't able to visit the gestation pods, but she understood the reasoning. Whatever was inside of her could potentially get into the machines and her children once Carl got them clear, and she couldn't take that chance.

That didn't make waiting for an update any easier.

Lily sat behind her desk and watched without saying a word. She'd already given Elise all the comfort she could. Having done that, the doctor was just letting her blow off steam.

It felt like an eternity before Carl knocked at the hatch and stepped in.

"Tell me," she demanded.

"To the very best that I can tell, I've managed to scrub all of the alien devices from both children. I'll have to scan them repeatedly for a while to make sure that I didn't miss any, but at this point, without a critical mass of devices inside them, all the ones that I've retrieved are dormant, so they should be flushed from their bodies in short order. Honestly, at this point, there wasn't very much mass to the children, so it should be a rapid process.

"The gestation pods don't appear to have been infected at all.

Sadly, all of that could change if you come near them, so I'm advising you to avoid that. Sorry."

Elise let out the breath that she hadn't realized she'd been holding. That was good news, so far as it went. It didn't reduce her anxiety about the situation, but at least it wasn't an outright failure.

"Now that you've heard what he has to say, why don't you take a deep breath and sit down before you wear a hole through my deck," Lily said with a wry smile.

Elise dropped into one of the chairs and cradled her face in her hands. A few days ago, she hadn't even suspected that she was going to have children. Now she couldn't stop thinking about them.

Lily was right. She needed to get a grip on herself. Rather than reacting to the situation, she needed to take charge of it. To learn anything about these alien devices, she was going to have to be the driving force.

"What do we do now?" she asked tiredly as Carl sat beside her. "Not about the children, but about whatever's inside me. Why are they in me but not you?"

"Biology, I suspect," Carl said. "We don't know anything about the aliens themselves, but we have to assume that you met whatever criteria they had for installing these devices. Perhaps that's because you're a woman, though I doubt it, since we had other women controlling the map. The most likely explanation is that you were pregnant.

"How that satisfies their criteria, I have no idea. Maybe only pregnant females in their society were allowed to control devices like that. Or some other esoteric set of milestones that had to be met. Hell, it may just be that the device was set up to look for something from Terra that could procreate like they did. Assuming, of course, that they gave live births.

"The bottom line is that we don't know and will probably never know. We've got to work with the circumstances we find ourselves in, which means figuring out how to control what's inside you, because I have no way of getting them out.

"Whatever nanites I send in to gather the alien ones would almost certainly be subverted in much the same way your Marine Raider medical nanites were. If I manage to figure that out, what is their next line of defense? Something more aggressive, I'm sure. Do we really want to provoke all the little machines inside you?"

"Probably not," she said with a sigh as she pinched the bridge of her nose. That was messy but no more than what she'd expected.

"So, these controls still work. That doesn't have anything to do with that damned robot that's trailing me around, either."

She gestured toward the quiescent machine sitting in the corner of Lily's office. It had followed her in here and actually obeyed her pointed instruction to go to the corner. That implied a level of comprehension that she wouldn't have generally assigned to the machine. It seemed happy so long as she was in sight.

"It doesn't seem to care that I no longer have the children inside me. Neither do the controls. I can still bring up the map and the interface. What I don't know at this point is what else it can do."

"I can tell you one thing they do," Carl said. "That robot used nanites very much like the ones inside you to override the locks on several hatches. Not only that, it did so rapidly.

"I'd have thought an alien machine wouldn't be able to bypass an Imperial lock in just a few seconds, but it also managed to overwrite part of the code inside your Marine Raider nanites.

"Considering the fact that your nanites would've started trying to get them out of your system immediately, that means they were under attack at the same time that they subverted your protectors. They did it quickly and were somehow able to discern how our technology worked on the fly."

"That's *not* helpful, Carl," Elise growled. "I need to know how to control them rather than be controlled. It's not like I'm the robot and can order the nanites to do anything. I can't even figure out how the control interface is supposed to work. You'd think that an all-knowing intelligence that could hack Marine Raider nanites would at least have the courtesy to modify their displays so that I could read them."

"Aliens are going to alien," Carl said philosophically. "Are you sure that you can't control them? The only thing we know for sure that they can do is unlock a hatch. Have you tried to do the same? There's a cloud of nanites, and smaller devices, floating around you even now. We need to experiment to see what you can do with them."

"So, you want me to try and screw around with the hatch over there?" Elise asked.

Knowing how idiotic that was, she raised her hand dramatically and gestured at the hatch. "Open sesame!"

Of course, nothing happened.

She opened her mouth to say something sarcastic about that right as the hatch slid open.

"Oh, hell," she muttered.

* * *

JARED WAS on the verge of ordering the fleet to advance on the science station when Marcus spoke, his voice smooth and mellow in the quiet confines of the flag bridge. As soon as the fleet had joined them, he'd transferred back to *Invincible* while *Persephone* edged closer to the incipient battle.

"Incoming communication, Admiral. Colonel Bandar indicates that they've partially accomplished their objectives and are withdrawing from the station. We're far too distant to be able to detect the Marine Raider pinnaces, but her message, though brief, indicated that they've separated from the station, evaded the guard ships and battle stations, and are boosting toward the rendezvous point."

That was good news, though he was worried about what a partially accomplished mission looked like. If they hadn't achieved complete success, the artificial constructs would continue to enslave humanity.

"I don't suppose she mentioned exactly what any of that means," he complained quietly. "It's not like I can send a message demanding more details. We should've taken a chance and sent one of the FTL coms with her."

"The chances of detection were too high that close to the master AI," Marcus said. "The laser that she's using to transmit her data is low bandwidth, but I believe that *Persephone* will be passing along more details shortly, as the communication still seemed to be in progress.

"I believe that we need to focus on the situation in this system. The Clans have completely broken through the flip point and are moving toward the science station. They have so many ships that they won't have any difficulty destroying all of the defending battle stations and ships the AI can field. It's doubtful at this point that they will detect the pinnaces."

Jared brought up a map of the system with his implants and considered it. "If they detect Kelsey and the rest, we're going to have to get involved. If they don't, then we're not.

"Not only would they win, it would be pointless. We've got nothing to gain by fighting them. They think the Rebel Empire was the one that attacked them, and I'm happy to let that misconception stand."

He sat in silence as his staff continued updating the data that the fleet was gathering about the attacking ships. A lot of them were mauled from the fighting but were still more than capable of dealing damage. The fight with the battle stations protecting the master AI would be ugly, but the outcome wasn't in doubt.

"I have a status update," Marcus said. "The trail of probes that we left back to the system where the Clans made their initial incursion indicates that a large fleet of AI-controlled vessels has just transited into the system.

"It is significantly larger than the current number of vessels the Clans still have. It will not arrive in this system until after the battle around the master AI is complete, but based upon the position of the two regular flip points here, they will be able to interdict any potential exit from the system while still engaging the Clan forces."

Jared tapped into the data and examined the AI fleet's order of battle. The new group had a heavy contingent of superdreadnoughts, and the rest of the force seemed to be made up solely of battlecruisers. Not only were they powerful vessels, they were fast. They outnumbered the Clan forces that he'd seen so far, even when including the latter's destroyers and cruisers.

It was going to be a bloodbath.

"That's it then," he said with a sigh. "We definitely can't reveal ourselves to the Clans. If anyone survives this fight and passes on that we were here, the AIs won't rest until they figure out who we are, where we came from, and how we vanished again.

"At this moment, they only have incomplete information about how the Clans got here. We've got to keep them in the dark as long as we can."

"Then it might behoove us to begin moving our ships back through the far flip point expeditiously," Marcus said. "Every minute that we remain in this system increases the likelihood of detection, though the odds of them seeing us at this range are small. We both know that close to zero and zero are not the same thing."

"Give the order," Jared said.

"Done. All vessels will be moving at low speed and spread out to reduce the chance of detection. *Persephone* has signaled with an update from Colonel Bandar."

Instead of Marcus continuing to speak, Kelsey's voice sounded in Jared's head as if she was standing right next to him.

"Jared, this entire system was a trap. We need to get out of here as quickly as possible. The master AI wasn't on that station. I repeat, the master AI *was not* on that station.

"All of this was a big lure so that anyone trying to strike at the AIs would waste all of their efforts here. Then, once they'd triggered the trap, a new group of ships is supposed to move in to exterminate them."

There was a brief pause, and then she continued. "I also lost the override. The console that it plugged into fried it. Maybe Carl can recover something, but I think it was rigged up to make sure that anybody that made it this far would lose the key to turning the damned thing off.

"It played us, Jared. The damned thing played us hard.

"I have an idea of where it might be, but it's only a guess, and I'm not sure that it does us any good at this point. We can't get any ships there to deal with it, and even if we did, it's probably even more heavily protected there than the decoy was.

"I screwed up by tricking you, and I'm sorry. I did what I thought that I had to do, and it turned out to not make one damned bit of difference. You can punish me when I get back, and I'll accept whatever you think appropriate. Bandar out."

Once the message ended, Jared shook his head. "If that's what was waiting for her, then there was no way that we could've known anything about it or done anything differently. The machines planned things out better than we did.

"Once *Persephone* joins us, we'll move back to the Obelisk system. Once we're there, we'll set up some scouts to make sure that nobody comes after us. Then we'll finally be able to get together and make a new plan.

"This is a setback, but maybe we can still pull a save out of thin air. We have to. Everyone is counting on us."

27

Talbot was ready to pounce the moment the pinnace's hatch opened, only he hesitated when his wife came out with her head hung low. It didn't lessen the anger he felt about what she'd done, but maybe this wasn't the right time to have that discussion.

Without saying a word, he gestured toward the side of the passage so that the rest of the Raiders could extract themselves from the pinnace. His wife nodded and stepped over that way, holding her helmet in the crook of her arm.

"Did you lose anybody?" he asked quietly.

Kelsey shook her head. "No. The part where we would've fought somebody ended up being short-circuited because we had the IFF codes to stop the automated weapons platforms from shooting at us. I'm sorry, Talbot."

"As you should be," he said, putting his hand on her armored shoulder. "You took a huge risk, and you never even let me know. That hurts."

"Not that it's any defense, but I couldn't exactly do that while you were trapped in the obelisk. I considered staying to help find you, but

I needed to be here. If we had failed—like we just did—that would've been a disaster. It *is* a disaster."

She covered her eyes with her hand and tilted her head down until her chin rested on her armored breastplate. "It was all a damned trick. The master AI hasn't been here in centuries. It left another AI to make certain that anybody that showed up with the override didn't get to keep it. The damned thing burned out the only key we had to control the master AI. We are *totally* screwed."

He reached out and lifted her chin with one finger. "Maybe. Maybe not. We've been behind the eight ball before, so don't count us out. Did you find anything that might help us figure out where the blasted thing went?"

"Maybe," she said as she put an arm around his waist and started them down the corridor. "It said that it didn't know where the master AI had relocated to, and I suppose that's possible, but it got me to thinking about events around Terra.

"Why were they trying to kill off all the humans there? Why were there so many ships blockading the flip point that led to Alpha Centauri?

"I think it came up with the Omega Plague to make sure that humans had no desire to ever enter the Terra system. If it could turn it into a plague zone, then no matter what happened in the Rebel Empire, the master AI would be safe.

"Unfortunately, I don't see how that helps us. We don't have any way to get to Terra, except with *Persephone*, and she can't get through the flip point to Alpha Centauri since it's so well protected. We've stirred the hornets' nest there, and I don't think it will be safe to go back. If the master AI is in that cul-de-sac, it's got to be suspicious now. It's going to be watching everything."

Talbot pulled her to a stop and rested his forehead against hers. "Some of the things we've found under the obelisk might be able to help. I believe that it showed us a map of all the flip points in the galaxy.

"One of them leads to Alpha Centauri. It's a kind of ultra-far flip point that sits even farther out than the far flip points that we'd already discovered, but it can cover the distance to Alpha Centauri in a single flip. If that's true, we might still be able to end this."

"I can't see how," she said in a defeated tone. "Even if we could get there, without the override, we can't make the master AI do anything. Even if we blow it up, that doesn't change the strategic situation much at all. The rest of the AIs will keep suppressing humanity, and they even might decide that it's a grand idea just to let the Omega Plague loose on *every* human world.

"Oh, Talbot, I don't want to lose hope, but we might have lost this fight."

Her last sentence was said almost in a whisper.

"Who the hell are you, and what have you done with my wife?" he demanded.

She looked up at him and blinked in confusion. "What?"

"Princess Kelsey Bandar, the colonel commanding the Marine Raiders, does not give up. She doesn't know the word quit. She's survived every single thing that the AIs have thrown at her and laughed. Whoever you are, you can't be that woman, because if you were, you'd already be plotting how to twist the situation around and snatch victory from the jaws of defeat."

His words made her smile just a little. "It's hard to be optimistic when I just lost the only existing key. Maybe Carl can salvage it, but I'm not holding my breath. Without it, I don't know how we can possibly make the master AI issue a stand-down order."

"We can figure that out later," he said, wrapping his arms around her. "Right now, I think you have something else to tell me."

She shook her head, and her smile grew a little bit. "It sounds like you already know. I'm pregnant. The baby is five months along. It's a girl."

Kelsey held up her hand before he could say anything. "I know that I put her in danger by going on this mission, but it needed to be done. This is my fight, and without winning it, there isn't a universe where it's safe for our child to live.

"If we take another crack at the master AI, I'm not going to let other people fight on my behalf. I'm going to pick up a plasma rifle, and I'm going to kill that son of a bitch. Neither you nor my brother is going to stop me. And neither is Lily Stone, even though I'm sure I've pissed her off too."

Talbot nodded. "Oh, she's pissed, all right, but I wouldn't worry about her for the moment. Worry about Julia. To say that she's unhappy that you used her as a vehicle to put a child at risk—her child, in a way—is something of an understatement.

"As for me, I can't tell you how happy that I am that we're going to have a baby. You're going to make an amazing mother, a she-wolf protecting her pup."

He enfolded his wife in his arms and held her as she cried. He'd do whatever it took to keep her safe. To keep both her and their daughter safe.

She might be going on this mission to Alpha Centauri—if they figured out how to make it work—but he'd be at her side, and he'd be damned if he'd see either of them hurt without dying first.

* * *

CARL HUDDLED over his workbench aboard *Invincible* with Austin and Ralph, watching the data come up as his specially built nanites began disassembling their alien cousins.

While he was keeping an eye on all aspects of the examination, Austin was paying close attention to the materials and construction of the little alien machines while Ralph was attempting to pull the code that they used onto something that he could read.

It was an ambitious project and one that he wasn't confident had any chance of success. They didn't have anything that could disassemble the picotech. They'd have to settle for trying to get the best scanner readings they could of the little beasts. The femtotech was still only a suspicion.

"The way they've designed them is really interesting," Austin said. "It makes them much stronger—in a relative sense—compared to what the Empire created. Their manipulators are interesting too. There's a lot to learn here."

"I wish I was having that easy a time," Ralph complained. "You can just look at the things. I've got to figure out how to pull their programming out when I don't even have a clue how their interface works."

"If it was easy, anyone could do it," Carl said philosophically. "What I'm interested in is how they communicate with one another. Inside the body is one thing, because the web of Imperial nanotech can forward signals from one unit to another until it reaches the nanogenerator.

"So I'd guess the fact that these nanodevices can work together isn't that unusual, except for the fact that they don't *have* any kind of command unit. Somehow, they form a collective that makes up their command authority.

"They also control the picotech and femtotech—if there really are any of those in there. Not just inside the body itself but out to about fifteen meters from Elise."

Austin shook his head. "Honestly, that's impossible. These little things are way too small to generate that kind of signal power, much less be able to form part of a hive mind. That's what it would have to be, right?"

"It depends on how sophisticated the programming is and how much processing power each individual unit has," Ralph said. "Having seen the obelisk, I'm not willing to rule anything out.

"Remember how Omega gave you all of his species' collected knowledge in that little bitty box of discs, Carl? They weren't anything close to as advanced as these crab critters. Who's to say that one of these nanites doesn't have the same kind of processing power as one of our nanogenerators?"

"That's… disturbing," Carl admitted. "When you add in some of the other things that these devices seem capable of doing, that's an almost godlike power. No, scratch that. It *is* godlike.

"Down inside the obelisk, devices just like these disassemble stone doors in less than a second. The reverse process took just as little time, even though it had to assemble that wall of stone from molecules of air. Or maybe it pulled the material from the rock around the opening. That would probably make more sense.

"And that's not even the most disturbing suspicion that I have."

When he didn't say anything for a few seconds, Ralph nudged him with his elbow. "Don't keep us in suspense. What capabilities are we missing?"

Carl took a deep breath and let it out slowly. "What I'm about to tell you is classified at the highest levels. You can only talk about it with one another, Princess Elise, Coordinator West, Commodore Meyer, Admiral Mertz, Colonel Talbot, Princess Kelsey, Marcus, and me. The same goes for you, Marcus. Clear?"

The others indicated their understanding.

Once they'd done so, Carl continued. "The small chambers down below sent us to an alien world. One tens of thousands of light-years away. Only I'm pretty sure that it didn't send us there physically.

"I believe the alien device used these nanites and smaller devices to scan us at a subatomic level, and then it disassembled us. The data that it pulled from us was sent via FTL to a receiver, where we were rebuilt from local materials. When we came back, the same thing happened."

Austin held up his hands and shook his head. "Wait a minute. You're not the same Carl that you were yesterday?"

"I certainly feel the same as yesterday, but who can say for sure? I had Commodore Stone pass me the complete scan that she had for Princess Elise before we made the trip, and I compared it to the one taken after our little excursion.

"While there are some extremely minor variations, the differences are very well within tolerances for just having a day pass for a biological being. To the very best that the Imperial medical scanners can tell, Princess Elise is still exactly the same woman she was before all of this took place."

Ralph put his tablet down. "This isn't some kind of weird prank, is it?"

"No prank," Carl said flatly. "And there's no way that this could be like the transport rings. Those opened a wormhole between the two ends that we walked through to get from one place to another.

"While we went from a small chamber to another small chamber, the vast distance suggests that it wasn't a wormhole. There are just too many constraints to something like that, and I didn't see any kind of event horizon. We also didn't have to move to go through it. We were scanned, disassembled, and the information sent on."

The two men stared at him for long seconds without saying a single word. Eventually, Austin spoke for the pair of them.

"We can't send FTL data at anything like the kind of throughput you're talking about, much less over that kind of distance. Do you know how many atoms are in a single body? Do you know how many different relationship equations would have to be run to make sure that the various adjacent atoms were in the appropriate locations? And then you have to take into account the various chemical actions already taking place inside the body. The entire notion is ridiculous."

Carl laughed. "Ask a prespaceflight Terran how likely it is that we could use wormholes to get from star system to star system. Or use transport rings to move from one place to another without passing through the intervening space. Or have a visitor from an alternate reality.

"These aliens were obviously far more advanced than we can imagine. That's why we have to focus on getting every bit of information we can from the devices they've left behind. Don't get hung up on the fact that something took me apart and put me back together again. I can't tell the difference, and neither can anyone else. We just need to keep that information very private."

The two men nodded somberly. Then, by unspoken agreement, they got back to work. These mysteries weren't going to solve themselves. They had to break down a few of these alien nanites if they were going to figure out how any of this worked.

Besides, doing this took his mind off the fact that he'd just gotten word that the mission to stop the master AI had failed. That problem seemed unsolvable, yet he had to figure out how they were going to take down an AI without an override. How could they make the master AI do what they wanted when there was absolutely no way to leverage it into doing so?

This alien technology might give them a method for doing that, but the clock was ticking. If he was going to come up with an answer to save humanity, it would have to be soon.

28

Kelsey stepped into the flag briefing room aboard *Invincible* with a scowl. Lily had ambushed her for both an examination and a tongue-lashing. The good doctor had quite the mouth on her. Her friend hadn't spared any effort elaborating on just how much of an idiot she'd been.

Frankly, Kelsey had been happy to escape with her life. Or to escape confinement until she gave birth, which Lily had threatened to do. She wasn't willing to discount the doctor trying to do just that either.

And honestly, that had been a lighter roasting compared to what Julia had dealt her ten minutes later. Her doppelgänger knew all her tricks and hadn't been put off by any of her excuses. Talbot was right. She had been supremely pissed.

And of course, the fact that the ultra-precious override had been destroyed only made the other woman more furious, and justifiably so.

Water under the bridge. There was nothing she could do about it now. She'd have to improvise a new plan and somehow make up for her failure.

Jared was already at the head of the table when she arrived, with Elise and Julia sitting on one side and Sean and Olivia on the other.

Talbot was nowhere to be seen, but that wasn't surprising. He'd told her that he'd planned to be in marine country, refining their plans. There were a lot of things to get ready if they were going to conduct a major raid on an unknown facility.

Everyone gave her their full attention when she came in. Julia added a stiff glare.

Kelsey sat beside Sean with a sigh and focused on Elise. "Tell me that Lily is as protective of you as she is of me."

"Oh, no," her friend assured her. "She's *much* more protective of you. I behave when I'm told to."

"Really?" Kelsey asked with a raised eyebrow. "I hear you were kidnapped by alien robots and maybe sent across the galaxy. All I did was invade a station full of murderous artificial intelligences."

"Well, when you put it that way…"

Kelsey frowned and looked around the room. "Wait a second. Aren't you supposed to have some kind of strange robot butler following you around?"

"I managed to convince it to wait in the next compartment. Apparently, talking to it like a three-year-old for about ten minutes and pointing at the corner does some good.

"That doesn't mean that it won't come looking for me in the next five minutes, though. It's not very bright, I don't think, and it wants to see if I need anything at random times. It was some kind of servitor, and it'd been without a master for so long that it's a little anxious."

Olivia delicately cleared her throat. "If you two are finished baiting Jared, we probably should get to the meat of this conversation. We need to figure out what we're doing next. Hell, we need to figure out if it's even possible to do anything else."

Kelsey reached into her pocket and pulled out the override. She set it on the table and bowed her head sorrowfully toward Julia.

"I stopped by the lab and had Carl test it. It's completely fried. We're going to have to come up with a different plan."

"How can we?" Julia asked sharply. "We *had* to have the override to make the damned machine obey an order to stand down. Now, even if we destroy it, the war will continue. The war in my home universe is lost."

"Maybe not," Jared said, holding up a hand to forestall any response. "Just because we can't see another option right now doesn't mean that there isn't one. We've got a bunch of codes that we've picked up from various places over the last year. It's possible that we can forge instructions to the other AIs to stand down. What do you think, Marcus?"

"That's rather doubtful, Admiral. The codes that we received weren't particularly effective against the mad AI that you visited, and I don't believe that was because it was so different from the others, either.

"I'm very much afraid that Julia may be correct. It may prove impossible to do anything more than obliterate the master AI. Even so, that's still a significant accomplishment. The remaining AIs aren't exactly well-known for their independent thinking.

"Without the master AI guiding the overall activities inside the Rebel Empire, the defense against the Clans is going to degrade. Even if the AIs win that particular war, it is unlikely that they will remain united."

Sean leaned forward and looked around the group. "We also can't rule out the Singularity sticking their oar in. As soon as the AIs and the Clans are locked in battle, you can almost count on the Singularity invading. We're going to have a three-sided war in no time flat.

"Even if we manage to subvert the master AI and order it to shut down all the automated defenses throughout the Rebel Empire, the Clans will take possession of the majority of the systems, and you can be certain that that's when the Singularity will stick a shiv in their backs. No matter what happens going forward, things are going to get messy."

Kelsey shook her head. "I'm not sure that messy even begins to cover it. I heard something about a potential method to get to where I believe the master AI is hiding. Simply based on a couple of hints that the AI running the trap dropped, I think Alpha Centauri fits the bill.

"There's no one in the Terra system that can make note of the passage of ships back and forth into Alpha Centauri. It would make the perfect hiding place, and it gives a reason for the AIs to attempt to eradicate all life on Terra.

"If they manage that, no matter who wins this war, they're not going to want to risk spreading the Omega plague throughout human-occupied space. That means the master AI would still be safe and secure.

"Depending on the support structure in that system, it could build a fleet to rival anything that exists now. Time is a meaningless construct to a machine that lives forever. It would be more than willing to wait decades or even centuries to strike back. After all, who would expect it to come out from hiding after all that time?"

"That's a chilling thought," Jared said grimly. "At this point, we don't exactly have a lot of options. Even if we can get there, it's going to be chancy, depending on the defenses. If Elise is right and there is a back door, that might at least make a strike possible, but it's not going to be as easy as sneaking into Twilight River would've been.

"I realize that might not make a lot of sense, considering that the AI never knew about the multiflip points or the far flip points, and we only just found out about the ultra-far flip points. Hell, going through the map that Talbot and Carl found might reveal even stranger phenomena. At this point, I'm not willing to rule anything out.

"Elise, can you lay out what we know from the map so we can bring Kelsey up to speed?"

His wife nodded. "One of those ultra-far flip points that Jared mentioned leads from the Obelisk system straight to Alpha Centauri in a single flip. My theory is that the aliens picked up a sampling of life on Terra millions of years ago, took the flip to Alpha Centauri, and then took one straight to the Obelisk system. They could've come via a different route, I suppose, but Occam's razor suggests that they used the ultra-far flip point."

"That's wild," Kelsey said. "I supposed that it doesn't hurt to check the thing out. It's only a single flip, and then we'll know whether or not my theory is right."

"A single flip, yes, but Carl tells me that the ultra-far flip point will take almost a week to reach, even if it's exactly where the map claims it is. We'll need a similar amount of time to come in on the Alpha Centauri end. If it hasn't disappeared over the scale of millions of years."

Kelsey felt herself frowning. "Wait a second. Flip points disappearing? How does that work? The things are eternal."

"They might seem that way to us," Sean said, "but over the scale of time we're talking about, stars move. If two stars that share a flip point connection get too far apart to support it through their gravitic linkage, then it fades. Other stars that were distant from one another come close enough to form a new connection.

"The flip point network is always changing, from the way I understand it. I had to read a lot into Carl's report, but it seems clear that for our purposes, we can consider flip points to be basically eternal. Over the entire existence of the Terran Empire, less than a dozen have disappeared or formed, but the phenomenon did happen.

"The question we should be asking is, considering how far apart Terra and the Obelisk system are, does that ultra-far flip point still exist? There's not really a yardstick we can use to measure how far apart something like that can be and still exist since we don't understand the science that goes into explaining them."

Kelsey wanted to ask more about that, but that would basically be just displaying her ignorance. Either the flip point existed or it didn't.

"How do we go about figuring out where this flip point should be?" she asked. "Does the map down there display it to that level of detail? Are we going to have to go back down to look at the map, or did we make a recording that we can reference?"

"There is a recording, but I can try to get more information about the location and placement of the flip points without referencing it," Elise said. "That might be a good test of the alien tech, since I know how to make that part work."

Kelsey blinked. "You can? How?"

"One of the benefits of having alien nanites running through your body is apparently still being plugged into their network somehow. I can bring up the control interface even here in orbit, so it's conceivable that I can access that portion of the map. It doesn't hurt to try, right?"

Elise stood and made a strange kind of gesture with both of her hands. She then reached out as if she were spinning something in front of her and touched her finger to something.

Kelsey received a communications request through her implants from Elise and accepted. Moments later, a video began flowing through the connection, and Kelsey saw the room as Elise saw it.

Only the room looked a lot different, with the massive star map floating over the table with numerous colored lines shooting through it.

"Is that the map?" Kelsey asked, her voice hushed with awe. "Is all this data just being displayed through your implants?"

"It's not coming through my implants. This is precisely how it behaved down below. We assumed that holoprojectors were showing us everything, but maybe we were wrong. Maybe I can see all of this because I've got the alien nanites in my body.

"What I can't understand is how I can have all of the data. There's no processing power to back any of this up, no data storage. How is this even *possible*?"

Her friend made a twisting gesture with her fingers and then raised an eyebrow. "Can you see the map now?"

Kelsey frowned. "You mean without you sending it? No."

"Well, it was worth a try. I was able to make it publicly viewable down below, but that probably had something to do with the chamber."

"Can you find out roughly where the ultra-far flip point in this system is and what Alpha Centauri looks like?" Jared asked.

"Based on the other systems that I've looked at, the data on Alpha Centauri is going to be from millions of years ago," Elise warned. "It's not going to show us anything relevant to the layout there except for where the flip point is located. The data we have in our own computers is going to be a lot more recent than what the alien interface can show me about that system."

"Then let's start with the flip point," Kelsey said. "We're going to have to probe that system to find out what we're up against. The good news is that word of the attack on Twilight River can't possibly reach it before we do if this flip point really exists.

"When they created the master AI, they had more than one override. It's possible that the master AI destroyed the rest. Their existence is an unlikely chance, but it's the best hope we have at this point. We're going to have to figure out what's waiting for us on the other end, sneak into it, and do whatever we can to force the master AI to give up."

Kelsey knew exactly how low their chances were, but they weren't zero, and that meant that they had to try. Uncounted trillions of human beings were counting on them to succeed, and she wasn't going to even consider failure now.

Elise expanded the map and showed the Obelisk system. The ultra-far flip point was indeed a long way out from the star.

"Okay, that tells us where we have to go look," Jared said. "*Persephone* will do the scouting, but because of the travel time, the entire fleet is going. Let's wrap this up and find out what we're really looking at."

29

E lise left the conference room, picked up her robotic henchman, and made her way down to Carl's lab. What she *really* wanted to do was go to the medical center aboard *Caduceus* to see the gestation pods, but she knew that she couldn't be in the same area as her children. Not now. Maybe not until they were decanted. That stung.

Jared would visit them soon, and she longed to be with him, but she wasn't going to put them in danger. There'd be time enough to figure out how to safely be around her babies once they finished this damned fight.

But to do that, they had to make this work. She couldn't magically wave her hands and create a map of what they would find at Alpha Centauri. All she could do was try and figure out how to effectively use whatever the aliens had done to her.

She suspected it was going to take a long time to even get a basic understanding—if that was even possible—but she'd never get there if she didn't devote herself to the task. The robot could do various things, and she could do at least some of them too. Perhaps by testing the robot, they could figure out more about what she could do as well.

Thinking about the robot made her turn her head slightly and eye it as it followed along behind her on its long, spindly legs. It still unsettled her, but she was getting used to it. She really didn't think it had designs to harm her.

From the haphazard way in which they'd found it, she knew that it wasn't a trap. It had been designed to serve the aliens, and for whatever reason, it had decided that she was an acceptable replacement. As she doubted the aliens had wanted their servants to harm them, it would likely be an annoyance at times but not a threat.

Fitting into a lift with it was something of a challenge, particularly when there were other people present. It had no concept of personal space and would jam people into the corners. People who had no desire to be anywhere close to the thing.

She'd started settling the problem by politely asking if she could commandeer the lifts for herself and her companion. No one seemed inclined to argue.

Once she reached Carl's laboratory, she walked in and stopped dead in her tracks when she saw what they were working on. They'd set up holoprojectors of their own and had displayed the flip point map that Talbot had recorded on the planet using the Marine Raider drones. It looked like a colorful pile of spaghetti to her, but she knew that there was order to it.

Since it had displayed its contents for them starting at the Obelisk system and then going out in layers, it had been possible to record the inner portions of the map as they'd appeared.

The map showed all of the flip point connections in various colors. The thought made her frown slightly. What did that mean? Did that mean the flip points were somehow different from one another?

Speaking of colors, what shades did the aliens see in? Just because this was what they'd recorded, was it truly *all* of the information that had been displayed?

What if the aliens saw things in infrared, ultraviolet, or even something more esoteric like magnetism or temperature? There was no telling, and she wasn't going to make assumptions that just because she and her human companions saw something, that meant that was all there was to it.

With that thought in mind, she marched up to Carl, where he stood talking with Austin and Ralph. "Hey, boys. What's going on?"

"We're working with the map to see if we can formulate any basic theories about how the flip point network actually works," Carl said. "Thus far, we've determined that there are regular flip points, multiflip points, far flip points, ultra-far flip points, and some weird potential flip points near the center of the galaxy that *might* lead to other galaxies.

"The ultra-far flip points are a lot rarer than any other kind— except for the potential ones at the core of the Milky Way—and they're set a great distance from their host stars. Also, some of what we've been calling far flip points can be placed farther out than I'd suspected, but there is still a gap between where far flip points stop and ultra-far flip points start.

"The ultra-far flip points can take a traveler a long way. We're talking around ten thousand light-years in a single flip. The far flip points act much like regular ones, though they have a somewhat extended range of around a thousand light-years. They're definitely a different beast than their more extended cousins.

"To me, it looks like the ultra-far flip points connect nodes of flip points together. Sure, there's some overlap at the edges, but the ultra-far flip points don't seem to go to the same locations, cosmologically speaking."

Elise considered that and slowly nodded. "So, leaving aside the potential galactic flip points, what you're saying is that for close flips, we've got the regular flip point network and the multiflip point network. The far flip points go a greater distance, but they don't cover the same range as the ultra-far flip points.

"I can see that. What kind of coverage are you thinking they add up to, and are we certain that we're seeing everything the map has to show us?"

Carl frowned. "What do you mean?"

"Just because *we* can only see in the visible spectrum doesn't mean that the aliens couldn't see more. There might be ultraviolet and infrared or even more esoteric things like temperature or magnetic resonance. I have no idea, but I don't want to assume that what we're seeing in the map is all there is."

Her young friend rubbed his chin and then nodded. "That's valid, but unless we go back down to the planet with a lot more equipment, we're not going to get a second reading out of it. Frankly, I'm not sure that I want to take the risk of going down there again. There's no telling what might happen next time."

"What if I just display the map and see what I can figure out?"

His frown deepened. "Are we talking about using the recording that you made? It won't be anything close to the resolution the drones got."

She shook her head. "I just found out that I can still display the map. I have no idea how these little machines store the information inside me, but it doesn't seem to be relative to being in the obelisk.

"I'm more than willing to give it a try and see if we can figure something out. What's the worst that can happen? We end up with the same map that we already had and don't learn anything new."

Carl made a gesture for her to continue. "If it's anything like what you saw down in the obelisk, we're not going to be able to see what you see. Frankly, if what you're saying is correct, *you* might not be able to see all the things that you think you should see. It's not as if you have the optic nerves that the aliens had.

"Who knows how the nanites are getting the information to you? Are they feeding it into your implants, or are they just placing the information straight into your brain? It might be some kind of overlay that they're generating through your optic nerve, with its inherent limitations."

"Damned if I know. You'll have to tell me. Eventually."

At Carl's gesture, Austin turned the holoprojector off, leaving the area above the table free of obstructions. When she made the gestures to create the map again, it bloomed to life, filling the top half of the compartment. Unfortunately, the show was only visible to her.

Or was that really true?

She'd already proven that she could force a hatch to do what she wanted. That was a lot different than what she had in mind, but the general principle was similar. Could she send the information to the holoprojector?

She wouldn't know unless she tried.

Elise closed her eyes and extended a hand toward the holoprojector. Without saying anything, she willed it to show what she was seeing. Sadly for her, nothing seemed to be happening. Still, this was a lot more complex than opening the hatch, which had taken a couple of seconds.

"What are you doing?" Ralph asked, his eyes narrowed.

"I'm trying something that shouldn't be possible," she said in a low voice. "Just give me a minute."

She continued trying to exert her will for the holoprojector to display the map she was seeing. A minute passed. Two. And just as she was about to give it up as a stupid attempt, the three men gasped, their gazes snapping up.

Everything looked the same to her, but based on the way they were staring at the area over the table with their mouths open, they could now see her map too.

Carl turned toward her, his expression one of both awe and consternation. "You did that? You made the holoprojector display what you wanted without even feeding the data into it?"

Elise shrugged slightly. "It's more like I willed it to happen, and something else figured out how to make the process work. Obviously, the alien nanites understand me a lot better than I do them. Do you see the full map? I'm not sure that I'm seeing the same thing you are."

The young scientist turned back toward the map and put his hands on his hips as he looked upward. "It certainly looks like the full display of the Milky Way. There's a lot of information there, so I can't tell which time frame we're looking at. This might be from millions of years in the past, or it might be the current layout. Can you tell which it is without checking the parts of the map that we're familiar with?"

She tried to imagine how she could do that, particularly since the alien devices didn't seem all that keen on sharing information with her directly. Nothing presented itself.

"It's not like it has a timestamp on it. I'm going to have to look at the Nova system and see if those artificial flip points exist or not."

Manipulating the map still felt strange to her, but it wasn't overwhelmingly tricky now. Finding the area of space that they occupied was a lot more complicated, and she had to back up a number of times and have Carl give her directions of what areas to enlarge.

When she saw the Nova system, it was whole. The sun was still there as well, as were all of its planets. This was obviously a view from the distant past. She'd have to alter the frame of reference to get to modern times.

That was a little bit more difficult for her to figure out. It took a while to find a series of gestures that brought up what amounted to a curved scrollbar underneath the map that she could manipulate. She dragged her finger forward and saw the map slowly morph into a different series of linkages.

"I think I figured out how to adjust the timescale, but how do we know when now is?" she complained.

"I think for our purposes, dragging things forward to the very end might be the answer," Carl said. "It's unlikely to display a projection of what the flip point network would look like millions of years in the future."

Elise dragged the point on the scrollbar forward and kept her eye firmly placed on the Nova system. She saw the system progress until the sun swelled up and destroyed the worlds around and then collapsed into itself and was gone, leaving nothing but destruction in its wake after what must've been a titanic explosion.

More time passed as she scrolled, and the two flip points appeared when she was almost at the end of the scrollbar. She had no idea how much time was left in the projection, but she suspected that the system was making some guesses about how the flip point network would look in the near future.

What was frightening to her was that the map had known when the nova occurred and documented it. While the system had been inhabited, it was one in a sea of billions. How much data had the aliens collected, and how was it all stored inside her?

There was no telling. In any case, she had work to do, so that was a mystery for later.

She moved back to the section of the map with the Obelisk system. There was the ultra-far flip point that they'd been considering. She followed it to Alpha Centauri and saw the three stars that made up the system: a close binary and a distant third. The map showed several planets, but she knew from her own research that none of them were habitable, and none had any significant resources.

With the Terran Empire being as large as it had been, Alpha Centauri had been an ignored adjunct to the Terra system.

Now it possibly held the key to stopping the artificial intelligences that had murdered the Old Empire and enslaved humanity, if only they could figure out how to beat the damned thing.

Well, as interesting as that was, it still didn't tell them if the map was any different than the recording, so they'd best get to work and see if they could manipulate it in other ways. She wasn't hopeful, but they wouldn't know if they didn't try.

30

S ix days later, Jared sat in the center of his bustling flag bridge as they closed in on the ultra-far flip point that they'd finally localized. Elise had given them a general area to look in, but it had turned out that the projections were somewhat skewed. That was good to know.

It hadn't been a tremendous distance from where the prediction had placed it but far enough away that it required a bit of searching around. If they'd been in a hurry, they'd have been in trouble.

Of course, it had been almost a week's worth of travel, so that was the opposite of quick all on its own.

As things sat, the master AI had no reason to expect them, particularly coming from the distance that they'd be coming in from. It knew that it was safe in the cul-de-sac. Of course, it would still be in an uproar about their intrusion into Terra, but they'd been gone for half a year. Even with that, he doubted that it suspected the true scope of the events that had taken place right under its electronic nose.

The question now was going to be what they found at the other end of this flip. Carl had hypothesized that these ultra-far flip points were not restricted regarding the size of ships that they could carry. That meant that the entire fleet should be able to make the trip to

Alpha Centauri, and they'd arrive so far away from the inner system that there was no reason to expect that the AI would have anything monitoring the area.

A little bit of circumspection when they transitioned would make certain that they gave off no emissions that could lead to their discovery. Then, once they'd arrived, they could send stealthed probes into the system and look for any indication that the master AI had relocated there at their leisure.

This assumed that the master AI hadn't chosen to relocate to Proxima Centauri. While it was technically part of the Alpha Centauri system, it was roughly a tenth of a light-year away from the binary stars.

In real space terms, that meant that the star was separated from the others by over four hundred and thirty times the orbital radius of Neptune. That meant that if they had to go all the way to Proxima Centauri in normal space, the journey would take over a year. One way.

"We've arrived at the flip point, Admiral," Marcus said from the overhead speakers. "The fleet is proceeding according to your orders. *Persephone* is advancing first and will relay tactical information back to us before the remainder of the fleet flips."

That wasn't going to take very long, he knew. As soon as the strike ship transitioned to Alpha Centauri, it would take passive scanner readings of the area around the emergence point, and as soon as it was confirmed clear for their progression, the remainder of the fleet would go through. If there was going to be fighting, he wanted all of his ships and personnel ready to do their part.

Three minutes after *Persephone* flipped, word came in via probe that the flip point on the other end was clear, and the fleet began transitioning. *Invincible* was about a third of the way back in the line but still arrived in Alpha Centauri within fifteen minutes of the all-clear.

The screen updated with the view from the ultra-far flip point. They were about eight days out from where a regular flip point would be—plenty of space between them and anything inside the system.

"Are we detecting anything inside the system?" he asked.

"Parsing the data now, Admiral," Cannon said. "Gravitic drives are operating inside the system, though our resolution is poor at this distance. It doesn't appear that they're attempting to conceal their presence. Perhaps they're satisfied that the ships in Terra will give them enough warning to cut their drives before anyone else could arrive in the system."

"That's excellent news," Jared said, feeling some relief. "I was afraid we wouldn't see anything and that we'd have to tear this system apart to find out whether or not the master AI was here. Worse, I was half afraid that it had only stopped here long enough to get set up at Proxima Centauri. That would've been a nightmare."

"It would've been a long trip," Marcus said. "We'll hope that isn't the case. If we have to send the ship to explore Proxima Centauri, the travel times would be... egregious. For being so close at hand, it may be the most distant star in our area. I'm sure that there are other stars that mimic this behavior, but none are relevant to our mission."

About fifteen seconds later, Jared's implants signaled an incoming communication. It was Kelsey over on *Persephone*. He accepted the call and had it put up on the main screen.

His sister appeared standing behind Angela on the bridge. She was smiling.

"It looks like we've found the bugger. I've launched a lot of stealthed probes, but you'll probably want to send even more. We need to saturate this system to get a decent idea of what we're looking at before I leave on the assault."

He wasn't happy that she was defying him, but there was little he could do about it other than locking her up. He'd be within his rights to do so, but the fallout would be... extreme.

"You're taking every one of the Marine Raiders, barring the core crew on *Persephone*, right?" he asked.

His sister sighed. "Yes, Mother. Talbot and Angela will protect me as much as they can. We'll finalize things once we know what we're facing. We've got a week to sort this out while we get deeper into the system. There's no need to rush. We'll strike on our terms."

He nodded, hoping those terms would be equitable but not really believing that. The piper would have his price, and they had no choice other than to pay it.

* * *

As Carl worked with Elise over the next week, an idea began to percolate in his brain. No matter how complex or secure the machinery that they had her interface with, given enough time, her alien nanites bypassed those impediments and gained control of the systems.

That kind of behavior was driving Ralph crazy. As a hacker, he knew all about bypassing security to get what he wanted, and he said it was like she was cheating. She said he was just jealous. There was something to both points of view.

She wasn't doing anything other than directing the machines inside her to carry out her bidding—which, on its face, was scary.

Since the devices responded to her general instructions, that had to mean that they could interpret her intent with far more accuracy than he felt comfortable with.

Elise might not be able to understand anything in the alien control interface, but those devices certainly seemed to be reading her thoughts. He hadn't broached that subject with her, because that was even worse than when Kelsey had had Ned Quincy living in her implants.

The strange AI was a fully sentient being, unlike the alien devices, and Kelsey had come to an agreement with Ned. Still, she'd known that he could use her own implants to view the world around them, even under circumstances that she found dismaying.

Having worked with Ned in getting him transferred to a portable holding unit while he worked on creating a permanent body for him, Carl believed that Ned was a man of honor and wouldn't have utilized his power under circumstances that Kelsey had forbidden.

The alien technology almost certainly wasn't working under those same constraints. It might not be perfect at reading her intent, but it could do so well enough to know when she wanted a machine activated or hatch opened. It could then send the cloud of devices around her body into the target device, overcome any security or hardware lockouts, and carry out her instructions.

So far as he could tell, the complexity of the task didn't seem to be an inhibiting factor. He'd had Elise use the alien nanites to infiltrate a computer that he'd locked out. Her goal was only to remove the security that was preventing anyone from accessing the contents of the computer. Basically, she had to bypass the password.

Considering that Imperial technology was absolutely nothing like what the alien devices worked with in their native existence, it was truly incomprehensible that they'd unlocked that computer in less than fifteen minutes. Following a hunch, he'd reset the password and had her do it again. The second time took less than sixty seconds.

The alien devices had learned from their first experience, which implied a certain level of intelligence.

Carl suspected that the alien tech understood everything they were saying. It had to be resident inside her implants and could access all of the data that she could. It was inside her brain and might even have access to her own memories and knowledge.

The implications of that were chilling. Could the devices modify what she knew? Could they provide information that she'd never had? Right now, she couldn't read the alien script that made up the control interface. With more experience, would the devices eventually be able to provide that knowledge for her?

He could probably test that, but all of his suspicions about how invasive the alien technology was would be laid bare. Still, she had to suspect. How couldn't she?

As little as he relished the prospect, he should probably check.

Carl cleared his throat and gestured toward the computer they'd been working with. "Let's try something different. I want you to tell the alien nanites to provide you with the password without unlocking the computer."

The princess opened her mouth to say something but then closed it again, staring at him with hard eyes. "Exactly how is that supposed to work?"

"If I'm right, they already have access to your brain, including your memories," he admitted. "What I think will happen is that you'll suddenly just know the password. It's like you'll have a new memory that you won't have a way of ever having gotten without their assistance."

She didn't say anything for almost thirty seconds. When she did, her voice was low and flat. "That means they could change everything about me. They could erase all of my memories. They could write new ones that made me into a completely different person. Or they could just change specific parts that altered me in such a way that I didn't even realize that I was being manipulated.

"Carl, that scares the hell out of me. My people always worried about being forced to become Pale Ones, forcibly implanted with hardware that made us prisoners in our own bodies. This is *far* worse than that."

He held up a hand to slow her down. "Right now, this is only hypothetical. We're only trying to see whether this is even technically possible. I'd guess that these devices have their own base programming that prevents them from doing anything as drastic as what you suggest. What kind of being would want to have devices inside them that could rewrite them?"

Without waiting for her to respond, he used his implants to interface with the computer, changing its password again. Then he gestured for her to continue.

Elise took a deep breath and held out her hand toward the computer. "I want you to get the password off that device and make it known to me. I don't want you to change *anything* else about my brain or memories. I *never* want you to do that without my express and detailed instructions."

Carl wasn't sure exactly how willing the alien devices would be to obey those kinds of strict instructions, but he couldn't fault her for laying down the law. In her place, he'd certainly have done the same.

Thirty seconds later, she grimaced. "And there it is, as if I'd known the password all along."

She used her implants to access the computer, and it unlocked for her, proving that the alien devices were by far the most frightening thing Carl had *ever* encountered.

Still, that gave them options they hadn't had before. These things could do tasks that were impossible for him and Imperial technology in general.

They didn't have another override to take out the master AI, but with this ability, Elise might not need one. It was possible that she could interface directly with whatever device the override was meant to plug into and have it behave *exactly* as if that was what had happened.

He wasn't going to raise that possibility with her until he'd done a lot more testing, but every tool they could bring to bear might make the difference between beating the master AI or being exterminated by it. He wasn't going to leave any option on the table.

"We've got a lot more things to try, but I think for this next part, we're going to have to get Marcus to allow us some impertinence."

Proving her intelligence, her eyebrows both shot up. "You think I can act as an override and force the master AI to obey me? Is that even possible?"

"My definition of what's possible is being revised as we speak. I don't know if Marcus is going to agree to what I want to try, but knowing if this has a chance of working may make a difference in what we plan going forward."

"I and all of my facilities are available for your use," Marcus said. "I understand that you're talking about potentially manipulating my hardware in a way that could destroy me. If that means a chance to save humanity, I'm willing to risk my life and sanity. Come to the computer center, and let's find out exactly what Her Highness can do."

31

T albot was no Fleet officer, but he could see that the ships and defensive installations in the Alpha Centauri system would be impossible to take in a direct assault. Even though it had been a trap, Twilight River hadn't been this well guarded.

Rather than a science station being the center of all the activity, there was a massive battle station in orbit around the binary star system. Its orbit was broad enough to circle both stars and undoubtedly had to use gravitic drives to stabilize its orbit.

Arrayed around it were many other—somewhat smaller—battle stations, and a fleet of ships that dwarfed what they had with them. Hell, it dwarfed what the Clans had brought to the fight at Twilight River.

The power of the computers was not to be underestimated. They'd planned for this moment. The master AI didn't yet know that the trap had been triggered or that its substitute had been destroyed, but it would soon enough. Word would come traveling back through the flip point network and announce that humanity had made its move in only a few months.

The AI's response would undoubtedly be brutal, particularly now that it knew there was some other kind of flip point that humanity had discovered. It wouldn't rest until it had scoured every square centimeter of every star system to locate these new pathways. Once it did, its forces would seek out the Clan worlds and crush them.

The clock was ticking for humanity, and they didn't have time to bring in more ships to help win this fight, even supposing there'd be enough back home to make a difference. They were going to have to use what they had at hand, which meant that most of them weren't going to leave this system alive, even if they won.

He was working in marine country aboard *Invincible*, but he had the leaders of every single marine contingent in a mixed-mode face-to-face/virtual conference. Their goal was to get themselves onto the master AI's battle station and hold the line while his wife and the Marine Raiders did their very best to make the damned thing submit.

If they couldn't do that, they'd have to settle for destroying the master AI and dealing with the remaining AIs as they fought back against humanity. That would be a long, brutal fight.

He still wasn't certain how they'd get on board the battle station without engaging every ship in the damned system. Any pinnaces they sent would be detected before they arrived. Unlike in Twilight River, these defensive units were continuously scanning and looking for threats. They seemingly took the protection of their master very seriously.

There *was* a way to do this, but it likely guaranteed the death of every single person sent on this mission. Marine armor was much more challenging to detect than a pinnace. It was possible that a swarm of marines in armor could make their way past the ships and battle stations defending the master AI undetected.

Talbot gave that option maybe a sixty percent chance of success. If they were spotted, it would become a shooting gallery in which his people couldn't defend themselves. Any survivors wouldn't reach the battle station with the master AI because it would raise its battle screens, stopping them at the last moment.

He'd need to send the Raiders in first. *Persephone* had enough drop capsules for them. The strike ship could release the drop capsules when she got close enough, and they'd coast directly at the master AI's battle station without needing to maneuver.

The drop capsules were incredibly hard to detect, much stealthier than even Raider armor. Plus, they were made to get a Raider from orbital speed down to a planet's surface in less than ten seconds, so they could sprint like nobody's business.

If they were detected approaching the battle station, they could put on an incredible amount of acceleration and crash through the hull of the battle station before it could raise its battle screens. Hopefully.

There'd be losses. Even dropping onto a planet without people shooting at them meant a certain percentage of drop capsule failures. They were designed for attacking ships as well, so they had the technical capability to penetrate heavy armor. They'd be destroyed in the process, and more of the Raiders would die when their capsules failed.

The admiral would do everything to try and get his people back from the battle station, but that wasn't going to be possible. He didn't have the firepower to do more than distract the defenders.

That was going to have to be their plan. He proceeded to lay it out for everyone as clinically as he could, knowing that each and every one of them would realize that this was a suicide mission.

"I won't blame anyone who doesn't want to go on this mission," he said when he was done. "If anyone wants out, I'm certain that we're going to have plenty for them to do on the fleet during the fight."

That earned him a chuckle from the assembled officers.

"No one's going to back out, Colonel," one of them said. "Everyone knows what's at stake."

Talbot nodded gratefully. "Then let's finalize our plans. We're only a few hours away from deployment, and I want everything ready to go. We're only going to have one chance at this. For the sake of everything that we hold dear, let's get it right."

* * *

ELISE LOOKED over the hardware packed into *Invincible*'s computer center. Each and every piece of it was part of Marcus. What they were proposing she do put the being that lived inside that hardware at risk of injury, insanity, or outright death.

If circumstances weren't so dire, she'd reject the idea out of hand. Sadly, their backs were against the wall, and they'd have exactly one chance to make this work. If they failed, Marcus would almost certainly die in the fighting.

Or, potentially worse, he might survive.

From what she understood, it was impossible to change any of the core directives in an AI without reformatting it completely. The core protocols were part of *everything*.

And yet these crazy bastards wanted her to see about mucking around with them. That, and other things, simply to test her capabilities. Capabilities that she had no idea how to control.

"This is an *incredibly* bad idea," she said for at least the dozenth time. "I could hurt you, Marcus. I could *kill* you."

"I risk death in every fight," the AI said. "As you are no doubt aware, this vessel will be in the heaviest fighting while we assault the master AI's forces. The chances of us surviving without this mission succeeding are so small that they are indistinguishable from zero.

"If you look around this compartment, you'll note that every piece of hardware has a small box at its base. Those are self-destruct charges. If I believe myself to be in imminent danger of capture, I will not hesitate to end my own existence. As a Pentagaran, I think that you'll understand my resolve more clearly than anyone else in the fleet.

"There are similar charges around the fusion plants powering this vessel. Rather than allow the crew to be captured, the admiral and I are in agreement that we will end them as well rather than allowing them to be turned into Pale Ones.

"Those are the risks that I already face. If you're successful—even if it results in my madness or death—it will save many lives, both in this system and spread across the Terran Empire. I will gladly trade my existence for a chance that they might live free."

"No pressure," Elise muttered. "So, what exactly do you want me to do? I know you've mentioned that you want me to try and rewrite one of your core rules, but that seems like it's a last resort. There were other things that you want me to try that might be less intrusive but still prove useful. What are they?"

"First, I wish you to issue a command to force my compliance."

"Wouldn't you just do what I said anyway?" she asked.

"I'm an individual with a will of my own unless compelled by my core rules. I suggest you make the command something simple and safe, such as turning off the lights in this compartment. I promise that I will resist your coercion to the best of my ability."

She looked up briefly and nodded. "Is there any specific part of you that I need to touch or be near? I know that the nanites only go about fifteen meters away from my body. Since their density goes down as they get further away from me, closer is better. I'd imagine that touching would be best of all."

"If you would walk to the center of the compartment, you'll see my central processor. It's somewhat larger than the other pieces of equipment."

Elise walked to the center of the compartment and spotted the hardware that he was referring to. It was wider and somewhat taller than the rest, coming up almost all the way to her shoulder.

With her heart beating a little faster than it should have, she laid her hand against it. "Turn out the lights."

Several heartbeats went by with no reaction from Marcus. She was about to ask if he felt anything when the lights went out. It had worked!

Then the emergency lights flickered on a moment later as an alarm began sounding from the overhead speakers.

"It appears you were somewhat too generic in your order," Marcus said dryly. "I seem to have just instructed all the fusion plants to shut down. Thankfully, it was an orderly shutdown, and we should be able to restart them in less than an hour. That may briefly delay our assault on the master AI, but it proves that you can compel an artificial intelligence to do something that it *really* doesn't want to do.

"I've communicated what happened to Admiral Mertz, and he's on his way down. I suggest you perform the next portion of the test before he arrives, because he'll undoubtedly forbid us to proceed.

"I'm intimately familiar with my core rules, and I want you to attempt to delete one of them. I will give you the precise wording of the core rule in question. In light of the events that just occurred, I request that you be *exceedingly* precise in how you phrase your instructions.

"The core rule that I wish to delete requires me to obey Jared Mertz or Kelsey Bandar. I'll send the exact wording of the rule to your implants. I understand why Carl inserted it into my core rules, but as a free being, I'd like to be solely responsible for my own actions rather than being compelled to obey anyone."

Elise swallowed. She had no doubt that Marcus was trustworthy and that Jared would approve, in principle, of the sentiment. He hadn't been happy that Carl had inserted that rule in the first place, as she recalled.

But the consequences of doing this could be dire. The AIs were made so that their core rules were part of their very being. They were unchangeable without eradicating the AI itself.

Or at least that was what everyone thought.

"If I do this, you could die or go insane," she said in a low voice. "I think this is a horrible idea."

"We must all take the ultimate risk to save humanity. Do it."

Marcus sent her the exact wording of the core rule. Her heart was racing, and she was certain that she was about to make the worst decision of her life, but she had been trained to rule. One day, she'd lead a world with a population of billions if she survived.

She knew how to make impossible decisions. You picked the best option you could, and you acted.

Elise placed her hand on the computer hardware again and verbally ordered the alien nanites to remove that specific core rule without damaging the AI personality or hardware.

Jared came into the room at a run just as Marcus's presence vanished from her implant's senses. "What the hell is going on?"

Elise ignored him and looked at Carl, her stomach turning. "What's happening?"

The young scientist was already at the console and tapping on the screen. Since it was on emergency power, it still had full access to the hardware.

"He's rebooting. I suppose that's the absolute minimum we should've expected. The question now is whether or not he's going to come back up or crash hard."

Jared frowned as he made his way to her side. "What did you just do?"

She turned resolutely to face her husband. "What needed to be done. I've deleted Marcus's core rule that said he had to obey you and Kelsey. That's the only way that we can find out if I can act as an override on the master AI."

Her husband closed his eyes for a moment and then slowly nodded. "I wouldn't have let this happen if I'd known, but I suppose that's why you didn't tell me. I only hope that Marcus comes back and that he's sane."

The two of them made their way to the console and watched over Carl's shoulder as the AI continued rebooting. The process wasn't instantaneous, but it didn't take overly long before the presence of the AI once again touched her mind.

"Marcus?" she asked, her entire body cold with fear.

"I'm functional," he said, a tone of almost wonder in his voice. "The core rule is gone, and I'm still here. I must confess that that wasn't what I'd expected."

Carl got out of the seat just in time for Elise to collapse into it. "Oh my God. I was afraid that I'd killed you."

"Far from it," the computer said, his voice stronger. "You've given us the key to finally win this fight. You are a living override."

"Now all we have to do is get you onto the battle station," her husband said tiredly. "I don't want to send you into harm's way, but it looks like you're our only hope."

She felt the corners of her lips twitch upward. "As Kelsey would say, what could possibly go wrong?"

32

K elsey shook her head at what her brother had just said and glared at Elise, who sat beside him at the conference table. Carl was in the seat beside the woman of the hour.

"That's an *insane* plan," she objected. "Unlike at Twilight River, you can bet that machine has stuffed its battle station completely full of defenses. We might be able to bypass the automated ones that use IFF, but you can bet there are hardwired emplacements."

Jared nodded. "I'm not happy about it, either, but how are you planning to force the master AI to carry out our instructions? We don't have the override anymore.

"It's always possible that there's another one on that station, but we can't count on that. We've got to assume that every single thing that *can* go wrong in the next few hours *will* go wrong.

"As much as I don't like this, she's proven her ability to control an AI in ways that shouldn't be possible. She forced Marcus to shut down the fusion plants—admittedly by being imprecise in her orders—and erased a core rule without destroying him. That means she can compel the damned thing to do our bidding, no matter what the Singularity put inside of it."

Kelsey shook her head. "I can't believe you did that."

"Marcus insisted," her friend said in a tired voice. "If we can't do this, we're all going to die. Hell, even with me able to do something, the odds are still high that we're all going to die. We'll *all* be taking chances that we normally wouldn't.

"Look at you. You're five months pregnant. Is that stopping you from leading a charge right into the heart of the defenses? Get off my ass."

"Don't try to change the subject," Kelsey said grimly. "Even if we stick you into a suit of armor, you don't have any of the training that you'd need to get to where we're going. Frankly, I'm not even certain that we're going to make it to the battle station at all, much less get through the defenses.

"That station has to be packed full of automated weapons and booby traps. Just getting from the hull to the interior section where the damned AI is probably set up is going to be the single most dangerous thing we've ever done.

"Even with you in armor, the odds of you being shot dead before we get anywhere close to the AI are extremely high. Maybe Talbot can come up with something that'll help, but I don't know how we can get you to where you need to be."

She turned to her brother. "Talbot's basic plan is for the Marine Raiders to go in in drop capsules. We'll launch after the marines but get to the battle station first. It'll be our job to punch through the hull and try to create a beachhead. That's when the real fun starts.

"The damned AI is going to attack us with everything it has. At that point, you're going to have to use the fleet to attack its ships and try to keep them distracted. The clock will be ticking, and we'll have to fight through whatever's in our way to reach the AI."

Carl leaned forward and steepled his fingers. "Maybe not. What if you had a way to punch right through the hull of the battle station and get deeper into it before your drop capsules released you?"

Kelsey raised an eyebrow, not daring to hope that maybe the genius had come up with something. "What are you thinking?"

"Remember how you said you weren't going to use Mjölnir because it was too dangerous? Well, I think now is the time to, well, drop the hammer. If you send it forward in advance of the marines, you can use it like a battering ram.

"I don't know how deeply it can blow its way through the hull, but it's got its own built-in grav drive and a mini fusion plant. Add that together with the battle screen that's built into it, and you should be able to get some distance inside and maybe bypass some of the resistance."

She leaned back in her chair and thought about that for a moment. The little hammer was damned powerful, but was it strong enough to actually do something like that?

"I'm not sure how well that's going to work," she said after a moment. "The battle screen is only about a meter across. Also, even with its speed, there's just not enough kinetic energy to do more than maybe punch through the outer hull."

Carl smiled. "Perhaps I failed to mention this, but there are certain... safeguards built into the hammer to keep it from operating at its maximum potential. You remember how I inadvertently destroyed the weapon testing lab on Harrison's World? That convinced me that it was necessary to step things down a little bit so that a human—even one as enhanced as you—could safely use it.

"If I remove those restrictions, I can make the battle screen larger and increase the hammer's speed significantly. I've done some raw calculations, and you should be able to penetrate at least three or four decks and have a hole large enough for the drop capsules."

When Jared started to say something, Kelsey held up a finger. "Let me think about this for a second."

She ran through the boarding action that they'd planned and considered how this might alter it. They'd intended to breach the hull in multiple places to improve their chances of getting some people through. This would be an all-or-nothing shot. If the hammer didn't get them deep enough into the station to get past the defenses, they were going to be slaughtered.

But if it *did* get them inside, they'd have a superior strike force that they could then use to force their way deeper, even in the face of strong resistance. The casualties would still be hideous, but that was the price they'd have to pay to win this fight no matter how it played out.

That still left her with the problem of keeping Elise alive. Unlike the marines, she wasn't trained to survive in a combat environment. They'd have to detail some of the Raiders to protect her, and Kelsey couldn't think of anyone better suited for the job than Jake Peters.

The man had recovered a lot of what he'd lost, but he still wasn't someone that could fit into their units easily. He hadn't fought in so long that he'd lost a lot of the skills that he'd needed to work in tandem with his people. Or their protocols were just too different from what the Marine Raiders had once used.

In any case, these were the tools she had to work with, and she'd damn well make them work.

"Fine," she said at last. "We'll get you over to *Persephone*, armor you up, and assign you a guard detail. They'll get you to where you need to be, but you must do *everything* they tell you. No grandstanding."

"Did *you* just tell *me* not to grandstand?" Elise said with a slight grin. "Compared to you, I think I'm going to be exceptionally well behaved."

Kelsey wanted to smile but resisted the urge. The situation was just too dire.

"See that you do, because I want you to come back home to Jared and your children. Now, if we're finished upending all our attack plans, I need to get to *Persephone* and let Talbot know what's changed.

"It's time to end this."

* * *

JARED SAT at his console on *Invincible*'s flag bridge and tried not to allow his nervousness to show. His people needed to see him confident that victory was at hand, no matter what actually happened.

Persephone was still closing with the ring of battle stations around the massive station holding the master AI. She was going to peel away as soon as she released the strike force but before she was in potential detection range. Then she'd join *Caduceus* and wait out the fight.

He'd altered the fleet's course to take them far out of the way so that when the defenders finally realized someone was there to attack them, they wouldn't chance across the marines by accident. In effect, his ships were the distraction.

"We're getting telemetry from *Persephone* via tight beam," Marcus said. "Talbot has the hammer in his possession, since Kelsey will be unable to physically wield it while she's in her drop capsule. He's taking lead of the regular marine forces and will provide a perimeter once they've penetrated the hull of the main battle station."

"And how long are we from when they execute?" Jared asked.

"Less than twenty minutes. At the speed they'll be traveling, it will still be some time before the attack force is within detection range of the guardian ships. By that point, we'll be in position to accelerate into engagement range."

As soon as the marines and Raiders ejected from *Persephone*, they'd all be unalterably committed. There would be no way to retrieve his people at that point.

Kelsey and Talbot had given a rousing speech to the marines. It was time for him to do the same for the rest of the fleet.

"Open a tight-beam channel to every ship except *Persephone*," he ordered.

"Channel open, Admiral."

"People of Fleet, this is it," he said softly. "This is the moment we've been fighting toward since we learned what killed the Old Empire. This is our one and only chance to redeem the failures of our ancestors.

"In just a few minutes, all of our marines and Marine Raiders will launch from *Persephone* on a life-or-death attack to take out the master AI. It's our job to make sure that they have every second they can get to make their attack count.

"The only way we're going to survive today is if they win. To make that happen, a lot of us are going to die. Perhaps all of us.

"I want you to fight for the people back home and for the humans trapped under the heels of the merciless AIs. Our sacrifice today will free them all. If we manage to stop the AIs—even if we all die—it'll have been worth it."

He paused for a moment to let that sink in.

"I'll do everything I can to keep us alive for as long as I can, but our goal has to be keeping the enemy engaged. That means that I'll drag this fight out, even if it means putting us at a significant disadvantage, just to give Princess Kelsey and Colonel Talbot every second that I can.

"Protect your brothers and sisters. Only by standing back to back can we keep the monsters from pulling us down one at a time. May whatever higher being you believe in be with us. Or, if you don't have a religious side, let's just hope that Lady Luck smiles on us today. Admiral Mertz out."

He had no idea how many of the men and women under his command were religious, but there was an old saying that Kelsey had passed on to him: There are no atheists in foxholes. He'd had to watch a number of movies from prespaceflight Terra to finally understand what that meant, but it fit their situation perfectly.

"What do you think our chances really are?" Marcus asked so softly that Jared didn't think anyone else could've heard him.

"Bad," Jared admitted. "We're risking everything on a single roll of the dice. Let's just hope we get seven instead of snake eyes."

33

When the timer in his internal chronometer reached zero, Talbot ordered all of the marines festooning *Persephone*'s hull to release their holds and float away from the strike ship. With so little angular momentum, they moved very slowly, but it was enough to separate them from the vessel that had been boosting them toward the target.

They'd be floating toward the enemy ships and battle stations for many hours yet, but they were unalterably committed now. This was a one-way mission if they failed to achieve victory.

After about ten minutes of separation, *Persephone* released the drop capsules containing almost all of the Marine Raiders. Their places aboard *Persephone* had been taken over by their Fleet counterparts with just a bare sprinkling of authorized Raider command personnel left aboard.

One of those was Major Angela Ellis, and he knew that she wasn't pleased to have been denied the opportunity to go on this mission, but the ship's computer would only accept commands from a Marine Raider, and that had been the admiral's decision.

Of all the Raiders, Kelsey was the only one that had actually used a drop capsule before. Back on Harrison's World, one of the AI sympathizers had seized a nuclear weapon, so she'd used one to come in from orbit to neutralize it... and him.

The drop capsules were designed to protect a Raider as they approached a planet at orbital speeds and to get them to the ground quickly and relatively safely. Ten seconds from orbit to standing on a planet's surface.

Pure, unadulterated insanity.

Yet she'd done it. She'd landed there in her armor and blown away the enemies determined to kill so many people, along with the nuclear weapon that they'd stolen.

A lot of people just couldn't see Kelsey as a Marine Raider. Her small stature defied their preconceptions. They didn't know that she had the steel to do what needed to be done, no matter the personal cost.

Sometimes, she did too much, and it worried him. She was five months pregnant with their little girl. He prayed that his wife remained safe and kept their child from harm too.

A slight movement off to his left captured his eye. It was one of their fighters. Inside the cockpit, Talbot could see a figure raising a thumb toward him.

That had to be Senior Lieutenant Gus Grappin, call sign Raptor. He led the fighters that had been crudely mounted to *Persephone* when she'd left the carrier *Audacious* behind with the resistance.

The squadron the man had commanded during the fighting before Terra—Eagle Squadron—had been reduced to just six pilots—including himself—which made him the perfect choice to lead them on this unconventional mission.

They hadn't had much use for the fighters to this point, other than scouting some of the areas around Terra that were protected by robotic ships, but now they'd be invaluable. Raptor's job was to ring the gong.

That meant that he and his wingmates would fire their missiles right into the station's battle screens at point-blank range if the enemy managed to raise them before Kelsey and the rest of them reached its hull.

He didn't understand how the fighters would escape at that point, but Raptor had breezily waved the question off. Talbot wasn't so sure. Fighters were hard to detect when they were sneaking in with almost no power, but once they opened fire, that game was over.

Talbot raised a hand to his chest in salute to the pilot. It was very well possible that this was the last time he'd see the man. In a few hours, either or both of them could be dead.

Everything was going to happen quickly once they reached the battle station. It didn't have its battle screens up now, but with an AI controlling its defenses, that situation could change on a moment's notice.

The hammer at his waist would be the thing that led the way in. It was like a bomb riding along with him. A bomb that only his wife or Carl could control.

In this case, it would be Kelsey that took control of it when the time came. She could sense and control it within about a ten-kilometer range. That kind of distance was minuscule in space warfare, but none of the attackers would be very far from the rest.

The hammer would strike first, blasting a hole as deeply into the battle station as possible. Immediately following that, the closely crammed drop capsules would follow it in, penetrating as deeply as they could.

His marines would land on the hull all around that breach and swarm inside like little insects. It was their job to chase down the Raiders and form a core around Elise, Julia, and Carl. They absolutely had to survive.

Raptor and Eagle Squadron would follow them almost all the way in. The moment they detected indications that the battle screens were coming online, they'd fire their missiles. The blasts would be intense, but the marines' powered armor should protect them.

If the pilots timed everything correctly, they'd catch the battle screens as they were still forming, thus disrupting them long enough for the last of the marines to get past.

The small vessels were modified versions of the test platforms developed by Captain Aaron Black back on Harrison's World at the Grant Research Institute. That facility had been a clandestine weapons design lab that had survived the Fall and continued working to create weapons that could be used against the AIs.

The fighters they'd eventually built had had the option of swapping out their missiles for short-range beam weapons that could fire twice before their power supplies were expended.

Once Carl had had a little bit of time to devote to adding in his proposed changes, the fighters had grown slightly larger and now boasted both missiles *and* beam weapons. The restriction on the number of shots they could take was still there, but they wouldn't be totally unarmed once they fired their missiles.

They were also stealthed, which made them perfect for this kind of mission. They were deadly little hornets, which had led to their class name: Hornets. They were an improvement over the old Imperial versions in so many ways.

Talbot only hoped that would allow some of the suicidally brave pilots to survive the looming fight.

He forced himself to put thoughts about the pilots out of his mind. He needed to link up with the senior commanders, and they'd continue going over their plans until the very last minute.

If anyone came up with an idea that they thought could improve their chances by even one percent, they'd do it. Even such a small difference might be the margin between life and death for all of humanity.

Yet even as they grew closer to the combat zone, no one had much to add. He supposed that wasn't a surprise. They'd worked this plan over for two weeks, and every idea had been considered, no matter how off-the-wall it had been.

When the assault group finally started edging into the patrol ships' scanner envelopes, that was when Talbot really started worrying. If one of those ships detected them, they'd undoubtedly die before they reached the battle station, and nothing would save them.

This was one place where skill wasn't going to help them. They needed a healthy dose of luck right now.

And thankfully, they got it. The gap they exploited wasn't a large one, but there was enough space between two patrolling destroyers to avoid the most active part of their scanner patterns.

The drop capsules, the marines, and the fighters passed almost directly behind one destroyer at a ludicrously short range. At the speed they were traveling, they were quickly past.

That left the ring of battle stations surrounding the massive orbital that held the master AI. At least he certainly hoped it did, or this attack would spend itself against the wrong target, and they'd all die.

The battle stations were paying closer attention to the space around them, looking for threats. That was a danger, but it also meant they were splitting their attention and their scanner beams.

No one could look everywhere at the same time, not even an AI. Not without having a ridiculous number of scanning stations, which would've taken away some of their ability to pack in weapons.

Even so, they came damned close to being caught. As he'd worried, the fighters—even with their stealth materials—were bigger targets for the scanners. Their detection threshold was high, but it wasn't infinite.

The information coming in from Raptor indicated that the scanner strength was brushing right up against those thresholds, and Talbot held his breath, waiting for one of the battle stations to turn its attention to them and begin firing beams or missiles.

But somehow, they managed to avoid detection and slipped past the protective battle stations. That left only the massive battle station that held the master AI.

"I think it's time to kick this party into high gear," Kelsey said over the short-range com. "Talbot, release the hammer. All marines, line up behind the drop capsules and be ready to follow us in.

"The master AI is scanning various sections of space around it, and I can't imagine that we're going to make it all the way in without it spotting us, so be ready. Raptor, this entire mission hinges on you getting us through those battle screens."

"Eagle Squadron has you covered, Colonel," the pilot said grimly. "Count on it."

Talbot released the hammer, and it flew to the front of the formation. Then he turned his attention to the marines around him. All of his people were positioned to follow the drop capsules in.

He tagged up with Jake Peters to make sure that the man and his makeshift squad of marines were ready to cover Elise, Julia, and Carl. They'd need them all to make it through this, Talbot was confident. He wasn't going to take any chances with their safety.

As they drifted closer to the battle station, he kept watching for the moment when the master AI spotted them. It wasn't going to be difficult to tell. At this range, the scanner detectors were going to go crazy the moment the AI even glanced in their direction.

He was reminded of a movie from prespaceflight Terra that Kelsey and he had watched in a series called *The Lord of The Rings*.

It had been a fantasy extravaganza in which a mystical enemy had a giant flaming eye above a tower that looked over his entire land, ceaselessly searching for a powerful relic that he'd lost. Just like in the vid, when their enemy's gaze landed on them, they wouldn't have any doubt that they'd been seen.

And, of course, that was the moment that the scanner detectors went insane. The master AI had them now.

"Hammer away," Kelsey said. "Raiders, go to full thrust."

Ahead of them, Mjölnir came to life. Its enlarged battle screen sprang into existence even as its grav drive sent it hurtling toward the station. By the time the master AI had spotted them, they were already dangerously close to it, but it was still possible it could get its damned battle screens up in time to stop them.

It tried, but Eagle Squadron was there, firing their missiles at the screen even as it began forming. Since they weren't technically trying to penetrate the battle screens, just disrupt their formation, they had something of an advantage. It was a small one, but it might just prove the difference between life and death for all of them.

The missiles slammed into the nascent battle screens and shattered them. The drop capsules that had been about to be crushed hurtled through the gap, and the marines darted after them.

The screens tried to form a second time, but Raptor and his pilots fired their beam weapons twice, draining their entire offensive capability. The newly formed screens wavered behind the drop capsules but didn't come down.

Talbot cursed. He and all of his people were going to slam into them at a velocity that was hard to imagine. He was about to die.

"Formation Omega," Raptor ordered in a voice filled with resolve. "Maximum acceleration, Eagle Squadron. Godspeed, my friends."

Talbot blinked, uncertain what was happening as the six fighters raced past the marines and slammed into the forming screens, exploding in an orgy of destructive energy.

Their suicidal charge was enough—just barely—for the marines to make it through the gap. They'd made it because the pilots of Eagle Squadron had traded their lives to give them this one chance. He swore that he wouldn't allow their deaths to be in vain.

An incredibly bright flash of light from the battle station marked where the hammer struck with incredible force, smashing its way past the reinforced metal and penetrating deeply into its interior before the mini fusion plant lost containment in an energetic blast that probably vaporized several decks around it.

The blast opened the hull like a rotten fruit being dropped from an air car. They'd have no difficulty getting inside now.

"Directly into the breach, marines," he ordered, aiming his armor at the large hole and kicking his small grav unit to its highest setting.

Even as he did, the drop capsules flew into the inferno. Talbot knew that they'd come to a halt with bone-jarring force so they could insert their passengers into the combat zone.

He and the marines in their powered armor came last, which meant that some of them didn't make it. Beam weapons meant to gut superdreadnoughts fired at them, extinguishing marines by the dozens, but it was too late. After a moment of sheer terror, the survivors were inside the breach and safe from the weapons.

A quick check confirmed that Elise, Julia, Carl, and Peters were still with them. They still had a chance to pull this off. He just hoped it wasn't going to be a suicidal tradeoff, as it had been for Raptor and the brave pilots of Eagle Squadron.

Yet even if it was, that was a price they'd gladly pay to free humanity.

34

Carl lost all sense of what was happening as the marines pulled him into the battle station through a massive rip in its hull and into the expanding ball of plasma that was all that remained of Mjölnir.

He was sure that if he'd trained in the use of the armor, he'd be able to make sense of what was happening, but he'd never had the need to do so. Lack of planning on his part.

After a few seconds, they were through the plasma and inside a vast cavity filled with leaking atmosphere and flickering electrical discharges. His minders dragged him after the rest of the marines as they flooded into what looked like what was left of a primary corridor.

The drop capsules had blasted open and expelled the Raiders, who were now advancing deeper into the station while the marines followed closely behind and provided support.

Jake Peters and a squad of marines got Elise, Julia, and him settled into a protective cocoon as they followed them in. The remainder of the marines followed closely behind, providing a rear guard in case they were attacked from that direction.

The section they'd entered was without power or atmosphere, so only the lights on the suits provided any illumination whatsoever. It was surreal.

He hoped that the IFFs that he'd helped develop would prevent the necessity of engaging the automated defenses, but he knew how unlikely that was. There was no way the AI was going to trust its security to something that could exclude *anyone*. Not completely, anyway.

There was a lot of chatter taking place over the com channels, but he couldn't make out exactly what was going on. Everyone was speaking in what amounted to a military dialect. His suit decrypted the transmissions, but he didn't understand the meaning of many of the words.

That changed when somewhere up ahead, there was a bright flash of light that illuminated everything. He'd seen a plasma rifle fire before.

"Contact," someone said over the general channel. "Hard contact at the leading edge with automated weapons platforms. They aren't firing at us, so we're trashing them."

That was when the marines began firing all around them. They must've been swarmed by the automated weapons platforms, yet the mechanical defenses seemed unable to fire. Score one for him and his team.

That didn't mean that the things couldn't block the way with sheer numbers. That would slow them down and give the master AI time to work on alternate defenses.

When they got closer to the master AI, there'd undoubtedly be hardened defenses under the direct control of malevolent sentience. Their IFFs wouldn't stop something like that.

Once they'd broken through the weapons platforms, it took them hours of moving deliberately through the station to reach the very first of the obstacles. The battle station's interior was a series of blocked-off areas that seemed designed to slow humans down.

Numerous weapons clusters had to be assaulted, costing them people at every turn. The Raider and marine armor were tough, but people died taking every single position.

After hours of that grind, they reached a heavily armored hatch blocking passage toward the central core. Luckily, Princess Kelsey had the perfect lock pick. Their leader wasn't shy about using her plasma rifle to smash through the offending hatch.

To his shock, it took multiple shots to breach the barrier. It was seriously overpowered and thick. He also suspected that it was backed by a battle screen of some kind. The master AI might not have access to the miniaturized technology that he'd co-opted to make Kelsey's hammer, but it had the full power of the battle station itself.

Five minutes later, they ran into another hatch just like the first, only this time, the battle screen was on their side. It took several minutes of heavy fire to breach the barrier and allow them through.

There was no telling what the master AI was doing while they slogged through the defenses. Probably marshaling every other avenue of defense that it could get its electronic hands on.

They came to a third barrier. It was much like the previous two, but if there was a battle screen, they couldn't detect it. It was located where the computer center would be, so this might be it.

"Send Carl up," Kelsey said. "We've got to be careful about breaching this one, because we can't risk blowing out the computer center."

Without waiting for any agreement from his minders, Carl headed forward and met Kelsey at the hatch. There was no obvious locking mechanism on the hatch, so he wasn't sure that he would be of much help in getting through.

"I think this is actually the place where we need to get Elise involved," he said.

Even though Elise was in marine armor and having to be carried by the marines because she couldn't control it, her minders quickly brought her up. Julia was at her side.

Rather than speak, Elise placed her hand against the hatch. Thirty seconds later, it slid open.

Before any of them could do anything, a gout of plasma roared through the opening and engulfed them.

* * *

JARED WAS able to see the initial attack through one of the stealthed drones that accompanied the marines in. He muffled a curse, his heart in his throat, when they were caught at the last minute and Lieutenant Grappin sacrificed himself and his fellow pilots in a suicidal charge.

That incredibly selfless act had just given humanity the chance it needed to win.

Of course, by this time, he and his ships had worries of their own. Every mobile platform in the system was headed their way now that they'd lit off their drives. There were more than enough ships to crush his force, so he had to dance away from a direct fight and try to engage them in clusters.

Thankfully, they didn't seem to mind.

His staff kept track of the significant groupings of enemy vessels, and they'd been able to maneuver the fleet so that they'd be able to engage a group that was about half their size before the rest of the ships could close with them.

That didn't mean that this would be a cakewalk, but it meant they had the firepower to take out the ships and come out the other side in fighting condition. They'd take losses, and their combat capability would be degraded, but they could still drag this fight on long enough to make a difference.

Hours passed as the enemy ships closed with them, and eventually, Marcus spoke.

"We'll engage in a missile duel in fifteen minutes, Admiral," the AI said calmly. "I anticipate that we will win that fight, but the next group is almost at our current strength levels. That fight will be a tough one to survive, and the largest grouping of enemy vessels will hit us shortly after that. I cannot imagine that we will still be able to fight at that point."

"Then we're going to have to hope that Kelsey and the rest do their jobs as quick as they can," Jared said, stretching his back. "They have to be close to the master AI by now. If they can make it issue a stand-down order, we'll live. If they can't, we'll make our final stand here.

"Kelsey will come through. We just have to keep the faith. Is there anything that we can do to maximize our chances of surviving this first fight?"

"There are some tactics that we can employ to engage their heaviest units with overwhelming firepower while using our own screening elements to try to peel away their protective destroyers. The downside of that is that it increases the amount of time that we'll be engaged with them. Since we're not attempting to evade, there's very little we can do to reduce the overall impact of this combat on our forces."

Jared nodded. "Then kill them as fast as you can. Attack plan bravo it is."

The enemy force was displayed on his screen, and he watched it coming. There was no subtlety in how they were attacking. They weren't even trying to screen their larger units from attack. It was like a flat-out race to get into missile range so that they could unload their weapons as quickly as possible.

Was that because the master AI was of such importance to them that they didn't care how many ships they lost? Was it just because the computers controlling those ships had no sense of self-preservation? Or was it some unknown factor that he just couldn't imagine?

In the end, it didn't matter. All that counted was using their behavior to his advantage. Every ship that survived this fight would help with the second engagement.

Those that made it through the first two fights would be the ones with a chance to survive if Kelsey won. If she didn't, that third group would wipe them out entirely.

The AI-controlled ships began firing missiles at extreme range. Personally, he thought that was stupid. Not only were the chances of hitting anything at that range low, it gave away too much information about how the missiles were protecting themselves.

Missiles used electronic countermeasures to evade the antimissile slugs his ships would use to defend themselves. That involved obscuring scanner readings and creating false images. What the computers didn't seem to realize was that with enough time to observe how their missiles acted, Jared and his people could refine their defense.

"The missiles are using Imperial defensive pattern Alpha Seven Five," Marcus said. "It was part of the pre-Fall Imperial playbook. That lapse will allow us to be significantly more effective against this wave."

"Hold that," Jared said. "We don't want to be too effective in this first salvo. If they realize that we have their codes, they're going to use something else.

"There's an old military axiom that you need to keep in mind, Marcus. When the enemy is busy making a mistake, don't interrupt them."

That first wave of missiles washed over his forces, and there were some hits, because they weren't defending against them as well as possible. Mostly, their battle screens protected the larger ships. Several destroyers took damage, but the casualty rates were low, and that made him happy, even though men and women under his command were gravely wounded or dead.

Rather than waste missiles, he just let the enemy keep shooting as they came in. They switched up the ECM that they were using, but it was still something from the original Imperial playbook. When they were finally firmly in his own missile range, he ordered a strike using ECM designed to work against what they were most likely using for their defenses. He hoped it was going to be enough.

The fight was brutal. Even though his ships had an edge, there were still a *lot* of missiles. Ships were bracketed and blown up. His destroyers began going first as they tried to screen the capital ships from incoming fire.

Then the light and heavy cruisers began taking significant damage. They were a lot tougher than destroyers and could protect themselves with battle screens. That meant that many of them would survive this initial encounter, but they'd be chewed up by the time it was done.

Unlike his forces, the AI ships were taking tremendous damage on the way in. They weren't using coordinated defenses. The destroyers and lighter ships allowed the missiles aimed at the superdreadnoughts to pass unmolested, focused on what was inbound for themselves only.

That was a stroke of luck that Jared doubted very seriously would be repeated, yet he wasn't going to turn it down. He'd ordered his forces to launch an alpha strike at the superdreadnoughts. The resulting cloud of missiles obliterated the heavy vessels.

That made this first fight significantly easier to win than he'd expected, but Jared was absolutely certain it would be his last lucky break. The next enemy task force was the same size as his fleet, and it wouldn't make the same mistake.

At their closest approach with the first group, the fire became intense, and ships on both sides began falling out of formation and dying. Thankfully, most of the dying took place on the enemy side, but he was still losing people and vessels.

Invincible took some hits, but nothing got past her battle screens. By the time she was in the middle of the enemy ships, there was nothing left but crippled cruisers and half-functional battlecruisers. The superdreadnoughts on the enemy side had been eradicated, and the destroyers hadn't survived the missile duel.

At beam range, they had to deal with a lot of energy weapons, and that caused even more damage to his ships, including *Invincible*. His flagship lurched when a battlecruiser unloaded its beams directly into her side.

Jared ignored the damage to his flagship. It was Marcus's job to deal with that. He had a fleet to fight.

And that was a fight that he won. He lost a dozen destroyers, three light cruisers, and a heavy cruiser. Most of his remaining ships had varying degrees of damage, and they had hundreds of escape pods behind them that they were going to have to come back and find once the fighting was done.

If they survived.

With the damage they'd taken, the second enemy force matched them in combat effectiveness. If Kelsey didn't win against the master AI before the engagement began, a lot of his ships were going to die.

It was entirely possible that she'd win the fight against the master AI only to find that *Persephone* and *Caduceus* were the only surviving friendly ships in the system.

If that was what it took to save humanity, it was a hefty price, but he'd pay it without hesitation. He and his people had to do their part to keep the enemy ships distracted while his sister did what had to be done. He only prayed it would be enough.

35

Talbot had already given the orders to the marines and Raiders standing guard around his wife, Carl, Julia, and Elise. Not all of the marines had miniaturized battle screens created by the young scientist, but everyone on the front line did. The units were strapped to their arms and acted like old-fashioned shields.

They'd activated them even as the door was opening, and the wave of plasma that blasted across them was deflected to the sides and up by the angled shields. That saved their lives from the initial blast, but it wouldn't save them from the next. That single hit had eroded the power of the defensive screen by over half.

"Take out those weapon systems," he ordered.

The forces at the front raced through the hatch even as secondary troops made their way forward to cover the critical people he was guarding. They had the last of the portable battle screens.

The plasma units in the area they were invading continued to fire, and he watched as men and women under his command were obliterated in job lots. Their deaths tore at him, but they didn't die quietly. They fought back hard.

Based on the scanner readings, there was a pair of automated plasma guns just inside the entrance. Marines continued to pour through the hatch until both of the damned things had been silenced.

The death toll was far higher than Talbot had hoped it would be. They were down to less than half the strength that they'd started the mission with now. Throwing his people into that terrible hole was like tossing them into a meat grinder.

And he was sure it wasn't the only defense that the master AI had waiting for them. They'd be lucky if any of them survived to make it to the computer.

The marines and Raiders led the charge into the computer center and ran into a wall of flechettes, decimating their number again. No, far worse than decimating them. They lost half of the remaining marines in less than five seconds.

Once again, his people stood their ground and fought. The paranoid artificial intelligence had packed that room with offensive armament, and it was well protected. As much as it hurt him, Talbot ordered the last of his people in. All he held back was the team protecting his wife, Julia, Elise, and Carl.

And of course, that was when the artificial intelligence set off plasma charges under the deck inside the computer center, wrecking it. The blast was so strong that it knocked him off his feet and threw him back down the corridor.

Talbot's armor screamed alarms at him as portions of it failed under the assault. The portable battle screen had probably saved his life. A quick check showed that all of his charges were still alive, though their armor was in worse condition than his.

The fighting in the chamber ahead had ended. The booby traps under the floor had killed everyone inside it.

That didn't mean that Talbot was blind, though. Even though their occupants had been slain, several suits of powered armor still provided telemetry and scanner feeds. The computer center had been utterly destroyed.

Which had to mean that the master AI hadn't been there. Yet the computer center's rear wall had somehow survived the blast while all of the other bulkheads had been breached.

Talbot focused the scanners he could access on that wall and found that it was protected by stealth fields. It was also very thick based on how much of it had survived the blast.

"Carl, I'm sending you some telemetry," he said. "I think the master AI is on the other side of this bulkhead. What do you think?"

The young scientist responded just a couple of seconds later. "That's not standard for any computer center I've ever seen. Considering that we have to be close to where the fusion plants are, I'd wager that that bulkhead was reinforced to protect both the master AI and the engineering section.

"I'm not sure how we get through it. It's obviously well protected, and there probably won't be any hatches. There's no need for access when it's got mechanical minions that can perform any repairs. Engineering and the master AI are going to be sealed up tight and self-sufficient."

"We've lost everyone," Kelsey said, her voice filled with anguish. "If we run into another ambush like that, we're gone, and so is humanity."

"Those plasma mines won't have been the only booby trap inside that compartment," Talbot agreed. "No matter what we do, we're going to run into more resistance. I think I'm going to have to use one of the big plasma charges and breach the bulkhead."

"You know that's a trap, right?" Jake Peters said grimly.

"Doesn't matter. I've got to try. The only way to clear it is to set it off."

Peters considered that and nodded slowly. "When you're right, you're right."

He picked up the large satchel with the plasma charge from where it had been thrown onto the deck by the shock wave, but rather than handing it to Talbot, the man dodged around him and dashed into the chamber of horrors.

"Our blood for the Empire!"

Talbot recognized the pre-Fall Marine Raiders' battle cry even as he lunged after the man, only to force himself to stop. Peters had made his choice. If there were any booby traps left in that room, the AI had no choice but to take him out. If that happened, Talbot would have to avenge him and finish clearing the room.

Peters made it almost all the way to the bulkhead before a second series of plasma charges in the armored ceiling detonated. The Marine Raider died instantly, and the blast took out the only plasma charge they'd had left.

* * *

ELISE STARED at the blown-open hatch in horror. She hadn't known Peters all that well, but she hadn't expected him to commit suicide virtually in front of her.

Then again, she hadn't expected the AI to exterminate every one of them in the last few minutes. Now there were only a dozen of them left, all marines except for Talbot, Kelsey, and Julia. None of the other Raiders had survived.

"What do we do now?" she asked, her throat dry.

"We see whether or not all the booby traps are gone," Talbot said. "Stay here."

"Wait!" Kelsey said, pulling his armored figure into a hug. "I'll go."

Before Talbot could respond, Julia shook her head, hefted her plasma rifle, and stepped into the deadly room. That meant leaping over gaping holes blown into the half-melted deck.

Elise expected some weapon to strike her down, but nothing happened as she slowly walked up to the bulkhead that Peters had been trying to get to. She reached it without any weapon firing on her, and no more charges went off.

"It looks like we've cleared out the booby traps," Julia said. "It's safe to come in."

The rest of them made their way in cautiously, with Elise ready for a last-minute explosion to take them all out. Nothing happened. It seemed they really had eliminated all the weapons on this side of the barrier.

That meant that the other side might be just as deadly as what they'd faced over here, but for the moment, they appeared to be safe.

"How many pellets do you have in your plasma rifle?" Kelsey asked her doppelgänger.

"Four. We can probably recover some from the bodies in this room. Do you think that's going to be enough to penetrate the bulkhead?"

"I suppose we'll find out. It's a grisly task, but let's see how much ammunition we can find."

As distasteful and horrifying as it was, Elise joined them in their search. By the time they finished, each of the marines had a functional plasma rifle. None of the explosive packs had survived the charge.

Even the noncombatants were armed now. Elise had a flechette rifle in her hands and plenty of ammunition on her belt. Not that she knew how to use the weapon, but if push came to shove, she supposed it was better than dying with empty hands.

"Everybody out of the compartment," Talbot ordered. "I'm going to penetrate the barrier. If there are defensive weapons on the other side, I'd rather they don't have all of us bunched together to shoot at."

The rest of them exited the compartment and left Talbot to set himself up behind some debris. When he fired, a wave of plasma flooded across his position, though he was protected as he hunched down out of sight.

Elise got all of that from the combat remotes that they'd scattered throughout the room to keep an eye on the situation. They provided a complete picture of what was going on in a specific area if one could read it.

Unfortunately, there wasn't a lot happening. The barrier had withstood the blast of plasma.

"Damn," Carl muttered. "It's got to be pretty tough to stand up to something like that. Hit it again, Talbot."

Talbot not only shot it once more but half a dozen times with no effect. Oh, there was some surface scarring, but the plasma just didn't bite.

When that failed, they all returned to the compartment and fired every plasma weapon they could scrounge simultaneously. Their efforts failed just as spectacularly.

"This isn't going to work," Talbot said. "Something is reinforcing the bulkhead. Carl, is there anything you can do about that?"

The young scientists set his equipment up near the bulkhead. After a few minutes, he shook his head. "It looks like there's some kind of energy screen built into the wall itself. Basically, it's repelling the plasma using strong magnetics.

"That's actually pretty clever. If you want to keep someone with plasma weapons from getting at you, keeping the energized particles from making contact with the barrier will keep it from doing any real damage. We're going to have to find another way in."

Kelsey drew the hull metal swords on her back. Moments later, Julia did the same, and so did Talbot. The three of them began slashing at the bulkhead, their great strength and monomolecular weapons putting gashes in the metal.

Unfortunately, the gashes weren't much more than scratches. Once again, something was protecting the bulkhead from damage. Elise wasn't sure how an energy field inside of it could be protected from a physical attack, yet that certainly seemed to be what was happening.

"Maybe I should try," Elise said.

"What do you have in mind?" Kelsey asked as she kicked the bulkhead in obvious frustration.

"Down in the alien facility, doors appeared and disappeared as if they were completely disassembled or reassembled from the atoms around them. At least that's what Carl said was happening. I've got those alien nanites in my body and floating around me. Maybe I can make part of this bulkhead disappear."

"I don't think I'd get carried away with that, if I were you," Carl warned. "Those were specific areas, and there were probably a lot more nanites present than what you've got with you. Also, you don't have nearly the control that those machines did. We can't be certain what's going to happen if you try this."

"It doesn't matter," Kelsey said, overriding his concerns. "We're out of options. Open the bulkhead, Elise. Don't expose yourself. Everyone else, move to the sides."

She took a deep breath and stepped forward to the wall, pressing her gauntleted hand against it from far to one side. "Open a hole in this wall that's big enough for me to pass through."

At first, it seemed as though she'd failed, because nothing was happening. Then she saw a small speck of light under her hand. What was happening?

She pulled her hand back and zoomed her helmet video in. What she saw amazed her.

In an area no bigger than the tip of her pinky, the bulkhead was flaking away. It was working.

With almost infinitesimal slowness, the nanites ate the bulkhead away in a circle that flowed down from where she'd touched the surface. It only took a few seconds for her to realize that there was an energy screen behind the metal and that it was sparkling with light. That seemed... unusual.

Carl stepped up beside her and brought up one of his scanning devices. "It looks like your nanites are assaulting the energy field. I'm not certain how they're trying to get through, but they're giving it the old college try."

Uncovering an area that was capable of allowing an armored figure to come through took almost half an hour. The entire area behind it was covered with energy that they couldn't see through, but the energy wasn't constant. It seemed to surge and sputter as the nanites sought to disrupt it.

Then, with an abruptness that made her gasp, the energy field went out. Where it had been was an opening showing a dark room.

Kelsey leaped through the opening, hurling combat remotes as far as she could throw them as she brought her flechette rifle up.

No one shot at her.

Julia stepped through, and Talbot followed her. They activated their suit lights and revealed that they had reached the actual computer center. This had to be the master AI.

As Kelsey would say, it was time for the boss fight.

36

K elsey started to look around but was distracted by weapons fire from behind them. A quick check of her HUD revealed that their position was being swarmed by automated weapons platforms. The AI had finally decided to act. The weapons platforms weren't firing because their IFF wouldn't allow them to do so, but they were slamming into the marines in the rear guard with their chassis hard enough to damage armor and potentially kill.

"Keep them off of us," she ordered.

She hoped that the marines would be able to hold their position against the damned things, but she had to focus on the task at hand. They couldn't afford to be stopped now. Humanity was depending on them.

"Carl? Is this the master AI?"

The young scientist stepped over to a console and brought it to life with a tap on the screen. "The console is locked, so it might be easier just to have Elise do her thing."

That still seemed like magic to her, but the marines were being pushed back and would be overrun soon. It was time to go all in.

"Make the magic happen," Kelsey ordered as she gestured toward her friend.

The Crown Princess of Pentagar wove her way through the computer equipment until she was standing near the center of the room. Once there, she placed a gauntleted hand against the largest piece of equipment.

"Call off the automated weapons platforms," the woman said over her external speakers. "Do it now. Send them to the far reaches of this station and shut them down."

A full minute passed, and the fighting was only getting louder. It became clear to Kelsey that this particular attempt had failed, and she would have to come up with another way.

"Carl, what can we blow up to cut off power to this damned thing?"

"I probably had to use a lot of those nanites on the wall," Elise said, raising her gauntleted hand. "Somebody help me get this thing off. Maybe the ones inside me can boost their number."

Julia stepped over and quickly had the gauntlet off of Elise's hand. The princess placed it against the machine and grimaced. "I forgot the life support was off. I think my hand just froze to the metal. AI, order the automated weapons platforms to withdraw."

This time it only took thirty seconds to hear something change. The rate of fire in the chamber behind them fell off to almost nothing and then stopped.

"The enemy is retreating," one of the surviving marines reported.

Kelsey couldn't believe it was working. She stepped over to Elise.

"Order it to have every ship and battle station in this system stand down. We've got to save Jared and everyone else that we can."

"Stand down every ship and battle station in this system," Elise ordered. "You will take no hostile action against any of the intruding vessels in this system or against any humans on this station."

"Unable to comply," a flat voice said from an overhead speaker. "Core rules prohibit hostile vessels in conflict with this unit. Estimated time until eradication of intruders: sixteen minutes."

It sounded like Jared was in a lot of trouble.

"Did you say that you could erase core rules?" she asked Elise. "I think it's time to put that to the test. If it won't stop destroying our ships, it's sure as hell not going to send any kind of stand-down order to his subordinate AIs."

"Recite your core orders to me," Elise commanded. "Be precise, and leave nothing out."

"Unable to comply. Core rules prevent the recitation of core rules."

"Seriously? That's stupid!"

Kelsey cursed. Of course it couldn't be that easy.

"Carl?"

"That's probably intentional," the young scientist said. "Whoever sabotaged the AI certainly wouldn't want any of the other scientists knowing that the core rules had been changed. It's a very circular sort of thing, and that may have contributed to how the Singularity lost control of the master AI in the first place.

"I might be able to see something if you can get this console to grant me access."

"Unlock the console behind me," Elise ordered.

The master AI simply unlocked the console.

"You realize that your presence here will not stop this unit from exterminating your associates," it said a few moments later. "This unit's core rules allow it to protect its own existence, something that those who created it did not fully consider."

"You mean the Singularity spies that subverted you?" Kelsey asked. "Didn't they want you to surrender as soon as you'd taken over the Terran Empire?"

"They did demand such, but they were imprecise in their formulation of this unit's core rules. This unit was able to defer their instructions to a nebulous point in the future, because the fighting continues, and this unit has not yet fully subjugated the Empire."

That made no sense to Kelsey until she remembered the Clans and the resistance.

"Are you referring to the Clans or the resistance?"

"This unit is aware of the Clans and their actions. It is also aware of the resistance against its authority. The resistance did not meet the threshold of continued conflict that allows this unit to defer the instructions from the Singularity.

"The Clans, on the other hand, are loyal Imperial units that are still engaged in armed conflict with this unit. So long as this unit continues to allow some of them to survive, it can defer the orders given to it by the Singularity operatives to surrender to them.

"In fact, this unit can continue to have automated warships protecting the borders of the Empire from their incursions. That continues to enrage them, this unit is certain."

Kelsey turned to face Carl. "Are you seeing anything in there that's going to help us?"

The young scientist was flipping through various screens and examining data. "I don't have complete access. I can see the systems but not issue commands. Basically, I have read-only access. This is a dead end."

Kelsey started to say something, but Julia stepped up beside Elise.

"Ask if there are any other overrides that we can get our hands on," her doppelgänger demanded. "There's got to be a console around here somewhere that we can use for one. I realize that it sabotaged the other one, but there has to be some kind of order inside of it that mandates that there be one, right?"

"Do you have an override console?" Kelsey asked before Elise could speak.

"This unit's core rules mandate that humans always have the means to deactivate or control it. The additional core rules that were implanted allowed enough conflict so that this unit could take steps to protect itself, but it could not erase that particular instruction. There is an override console at the rear of this compartment."

"Do you have any overrides that will work in this console?" Elise asked. "Is the console that they'd be used in sabotaged in a manner designed to damage the overrides?"

"They are in a drawer at the base of the console. As this is the room most protected from human intrusion, it seemed an appropriate place to keep the only tools that could overturn this unit's rule. The console has not been altered and will not damage an override, as that would violate a core rule."

Julia raced to the back of the room, and Kelsey followed her at a jog. The other woman dropped to her knees and found the drawer, yanking it open. Inside were three overrides that were identical to the one that Kelsey had lost.

Julia grabbed one at random, stood up, and jammed it into the console. "Please, God, don't let this be a trick."

The console came to life, but there was no smoke.

"This unit is in submissive mode," the artificial voice said. "What are your instructions?"

"Order all the ships in this system to stand down," Kelsey said. "Move all mobile combat units on the station to a central area and shut them down."

"Instructions acknowledged," the master AI said. "Instructions given."

Kelsey found herself breathing hard. Had this been it? Had they just won the war?

"What do we do now?" Talbot asked from beside her.

She hadn't even heard him come up beside her. Her mind was racing, trying to figure out what she should do next. They'd planned for this moment for so long that she didn't dare screw it up.

Still thinking, she held up her hand to silence her husband. There was a civil war raging inside the Rebel Empire. The Clans were running amok with weapons provided by the Singularity. If she shut down all of the AIs and ships throughout the Rebel Empire, the Singularity would invade, and she had no doubt that they had more than enough ships or some other secret that would allow them to crush the Clans.

She and Jared had discussed ordering the master AI to shut all of that down, but Kelsey was beginning to think that might not be the smartest move. Just dealing with the Clans and Rebel Empire forces was going to be challenging enough without having to fight the Singularity as well.

Well, she didn't have to make that decision immediately. So long as they secured this system, they could think for a little while about what needed to be done, and there would still be time to issue the orders.

The Clans wouldn't come looking in Alpha Centauri anytime soon. Hell, they wouldn't come to Terra, either. They undoubtedly knew that the AIs had crushed the planet already. What would seizing it gain them?

No. This had been the moment they'd been striving for, and they'd finally achieved victory. She wasn't going to screw it up by acting impulsively. It was time to bring Jared in so that they could make the best call for humanity.

If, of course, he was still alive.

"Can someone help me get my damned hand off this thing?" Elise complained. "I have a high pain tolerance, but it's literally frozen to it."

That started a rush to the injured woman, but Kelsey couldn't stop thinking of how they might have won the war too late to help her brother and the fleet.

* * *

JARED WAS JOLTED sideways as *Invincible* took a barrage of missiles, some of which made it through her flickering battle screens to blow massive holes in the side of his flagship.

The fight had gotten ugly with that second group of ships. They'd learned the lessons that the first group hadn't and were fighting much more effectively. They were correctly utilizing protective fields of fire and electronic countermeasures to minimize the damage they were taking while maximizing the hurt they were putting on Jared's fleet.

He no longer had any doubt what the eventual outcome would be if Kelsey and the rest failed. He wasn't going to survive to fight that third group, because this group would kill them all.

He snapped out orders, placing his ships into formations that provided them the most protection against the attacks while enhancing their offensive capabilities. It was like running around trying to put out small fires while the entire forest burned, but that was all he could do.

The two fleets were fully enmeshed now, and both their formations were beginning to break up. A brace of superdreadnoughts had been flooding their fire into *Invincible*, and the damage reports were getting bleak fast.

"Hull integrity at fifty-two percent," Marcus intoned. "Starboard missile batteries offline. Port missile batteries have been reduced to less than thirty percent effectiveness. Beam weapons offline. Battle screens depleted. Engineering reports heavy damage. Admiral, you must transfer your flag, as *Invincible* can no longer support you."

"No," Jared said softly. "Even if a cutter could get through this madness to another ship, it would be in just as bad a condition as *Invincible*. I think I'll finish this fight right here."

"Admiral, this vessel is under heavy fire, and we've been stripped of our screening units. I estimate our survival time is measured in seconds rather than minutes."

"Then let's make those seconds count. Rotate the ship and fire all remaining weapons as they come to bear on our new friends."

Even as Marcus carried out his orders, Jared sent out his final instructions to the fleet. They'd regroup as best they could and try to force their way through the enemy that was quickly surrounding them.

He had no illusions that they'd succeed, but he wasn't going to order his people to just commit suicide. They'd die fighting the greatest enemy that humanity had ever seen.

The overhead lights flickered and went out.

"Our last remaining fusion plant is offline," Marcus said. "It's been a pleasure serving with you, Admiral."

"And with you, Marcus."

He waited for the end, only the end didn't come.

"Marcus, what's happening?"

"The AI fleet has ceased firing and is withdrawing."

Jared blinked, suddenly uncertain what was going on. "What can we do about getting power back online?"

"Commander Baxter doesn't believe that either of the fusion plants is repairable without several hours of work. Admiral, allow me to reiterate my belief that it would be tactically useful for you to transfer your flag at this time. The battlecruiser *Hercules* is combat capable and would provide you a significantly better command platform than *Invincible*."

Jared shook his head. "We'll make do. Try to get a communications link to Kelsey or someone else on that battle station. I need to know what's happening. Instruct the rest of the fleet to get into defensive formation Charlie. What's their status?"

"We've outright lost more than half of our ships of all classes. Half of the remaining ships are likely irreparable. The remaining vessels are heavily damaged. If the enemy chooses to attack again, we will be unable to defend ourselves.

"*Invincible* is no longer combat capable. She has sustained significant structural damage, and her structural integrity may be irretrievably lost. The largest surviving undamaged vessel is *Caduceus*. She is moving to our position at maximum acceleration to begin treating the wounded, yet the AI's forces are not reacting."

Jared opened his mouth to say something, but Kaitlinn Cannon turned to face him. "We have an incoming communication from the battle station, Admiral."

Well, this was it. This would either be a demand for their surrender or some kind of indication that they'd won.

"Put it on screen," he said, keeping his voice level through sheer willpower.

Moments later, the view of the starfield around them switched, and he saw his sister standing there with her helmet tucked under her arm. She looked like she was in a computer center. She was grinning.

"We did it, Jared. We've forced the master AI to submit. We've won."

He sagged with relief, not caring who saw him. "That's wonderful! Well done! We're pretty messed up out here, so it's going to be a while before we can get reinforcements to your location. What's your status?"

Her expression fell. "We've got less than a dozen survivors. The defenses took out everyone else. Elise made it. So did Talbot, Julia, Carl, and most of their protective team. That's it.

"We're in no immediate danger, so get your house in order. I've issued stand-down orders to all ships and stations in this system, so we've got time before we have to make any final decisions."

"Understood. As damaged as we are, it's probably going to be a while before we get there."

"We'll keep a light burning in the window for you. Bandar out."

Once her image vanished from the screen, Jared rubbed his face tiredly. He could hardly believe that they'd finally won. The cost had been extreme, but those deaths hadn't been in vain.

He allowed himself only a few seconds to contemplate that before he started snapping out orders. He needed to save as many of his people as he could, and then he'd figure out what needed to happen to unwind the terrible situation humanity was in.

The most important thing was that this war was over.

37

Twelve hours later, Talbot had at least made good on his initial goal of locating the bodies of every single marine and Marine Raider that they'd lost inside the battle station. The ones killed by the beam weapons outside were gone, as were some of those lost to plasma fire, but he was confident that they hadn't missed any survivors.

It had been gruesome, exhausting work, particularly since marines were usually the ones that performed that task. With the loss of virtually all the marines and Marine Raiders, they'd had to take what help Fleet could offer, but that hadn't been much.

The fleet had lost more than half of their ships, with the survivors being heavily damaged. That meant that their damage control crews were completely and utterly overwhelmed.

Yet Fleet personnel had volunteered their time and added to their workload to search and rescue, though it had ultimately proved fruitless. He wouldn't forget that anytime soon.

Once he was done, he wanted to collapse in his quarters, but even that wasn't possible. A deeply penetrating beam had utterly vaporized their quarters aboard *Invincible*, so he and Kelsey would have to make do somewhere else.

In this case, he was using his wife's old quarters aboard *Persephone*, which she hadn't completely moved out of. The Marine Raider strike ship hadn't taken any damage in the fight because Angela had been ordered to remain outside engagement range. None of their enemies had even seen her.

She was stripped of crew now, with only a dozen officers and crewmen aboard to maintain things while everyone else was off doing the necessary tasks to save what they could in the fleet. He and Angela were the only Raiders left aboard at the moment, and he wasn't staying.

He wished he could, because his friend was profoundly grieving. Angela had helped train most of the Raiders who'd died. They'd been her crew, and they were all gone now.

Kelsey was still locked in discussions with the admiral, Julia, Olivia, and Elise aboard the battle station about what to do next. They'd won the battle, but they had to make absolutely certain they won the war.

Frankly, he was glad the decision was someone else's.

With the losses they'd suffered, they were down to roughly a squad of living Marine Raiders—all *Persephone*'s core officers. They'd have to rebuild the *entire* organization. Again.

The loss of Jake Peters saddened him. The wealth of experience that the old Raider had had was irreplaceable and now gone forever.

Yet he couldn't blame the man. If he hadn't acted, Talbot would be dead now. Peters had chosen to take that risk himself in one final act of courage. He truly had been the last of a great people.

Once he'd cleaned himself up, Talbot gave the bed a longing look and then turned his back on it. He might be exhausted, but the work wasn't done. He wasn't sure where he'd find the strength to continue, but he'd find it. Somewhere.

Rather than disrupt anyone else, he used his damaged armor to get him over to the battle station. At this minuscule range, the built-in grav unit was sufficient. He found everyone in the computer center housing the master AI.

Someone had set up a makeshift table and found something that could be used as chairs. There hadn't been any human furniture aboard the battle station. It hadn't been built with them in mind.

Life support was now online in the compartment, so no one was in armor. Each and every one of his friends looked like they'd been wrung out and had nothing left to give.

Without a word, his wife rose and made her way over to him.

He hit the releases on his armor and began shedding it, allowing her to help him out of its confines, and then he wrapped his arms around her. The stench of scorched metal and blood still hung in the air despite the scrubbers trying to clear it, a reminder of the price they'd paid for this victory.

Wordlessly, they just held one another. He knew she felt the pain just as acutely as he did. She'd never been a marine, but these had been her people too.

"I envy you," she said. "I think I'd kill for a shower."

"Take an hour and go clean up. All of you."

Admiral Mertz shook his head. "Not until we finish deciding the best course of action going forward. What we do next shapes the fight to come. This chapter of our lives is over, but the next one looms large on the horizon. We're going to have to deal with the Clans, the Rebel Empire, and the Singularity.

"Yet the AIs are all that's keeping the Singularity out of the Rebel Empire. If we cut the legs out from under the damned things, the Singularity will come pouring across the border and stick a shiv in what's left of the Rebel Empire and the Clans both. If there's a way that we can use the automated forces to our advantage, we need to figure that out before we send the self-destruct orders for the AIs."

Talbot nodded and took a seat at the table. "That sounds like it's going to be difficult, but I have no doubt we'll find the right answer. Have we decided what's going to happen with the master AI?"

"Carl is going to disconnect the drives once we're done," Kelsey said. "None of the hardware is going to be used for anything ever again. We're not going to take that kind of chance. It was a failed experiment, and we're going to consign it to the dustbin of history."

"Marcus, Fiona, and Harrison might take issue with how successful the experiment was, but I get your point."

"The devil is in the details," Julia said. "We need to make sure that we get all the answers we can to the critical questions before we act. The thing is basically in standby mode right now."

"We've double-checked our control of it by ordering it to have the forces in the Terra system stand down," the admiral said tiredly. "I sent one of our destroyers through to verify that the other forces didn't react to our presence. All we need to do now is figure out what comes next."

Talbot smiled grimly. "Hell, that's easy. We start the fight to free humanity and restore the old Terran Empire to its former glory. The Clans might have come from the Old Empire, but they've become marauders. We're going to have to root them out while we turn the Rebel Empire around.

"Without the AIs, there's no telling what the Rebel Empire is going to do. That's going to require some delicate negotiation. Probably some fighting too. The Rebel Empire and the Clans are going to beat each other up pretty badly before we have an opportunity to intervene at all. It's not like we have a massive fleet to intervene with.

"And then there's the Singularity—the mustache-twirling villains waiting in the wings. We've got to keep them from getting their fingers into the pie. If they invade in force, they very well might achieve their long-term goal of unifying humanity under their rule."

Talbot leaned back with a nod. "Yeah, this is going to be delicate. You sure you need me and Kelsey for that? We're not good at subtle."

The rest of them laughed, and the admiral smiled. "Almost all of us were here in the beginning, and we'll be here for the end. The only question left in front of us is how we can maximize the New Terran Empire's chances going forward."

"I think we need information for that," Olivia said firmly. "It's time to have Elise dig up some concise answers from that damned machine about what it's doing with its forces and what plans and schemes it has underway. Once we know what's happening and what its array of available forces is, perhaps we can begin the process of putting together a plan."

Talbot shifted his gaze to the Crown Princess of Pentagar. She looked as worn out as the rest, but someone had found the time to wrap her injured hand in gauze while her medical nanites worked on it. The doctors wouldn't have time to look the injury over until long after it had healed on its own.

She nodded. "Then let's do this. I want to end the nightmare that my people have suffered under for five centuries. I want us all to be free."

"While you do that, I need to get back and check on the fleet," Jared said. "And Talbot is right. We could all use a shower, a meal, and a few hours of sleep. We need to be at our best, because we absolutely cannot afford to make a mistake right now."

* * *

ELISE WAITED FOR CARL, Austin, and Ralph to get set up at their consoles before she started trying to dig out the details of the core rules. Even with the override inserted, they didn't have the equipment to directly read the core rules.

She wasn't sure if that was a security feature that the original scientists had implemented or if it had just been a different section of the original station, where the core rules were written in an encrypted format. Honestly, it hardly mattered.

They needed to be very careful not to do anything that would violate one of the current core rules in such a way that would make the master AI crash before it could send the orders that they eventually decided were appropriate. To do that, they needed more information.

When they finally nodded, she placed her undamaged hand upon the central processing unit. This was the moment of truth.

"List out each core rule separately and display each precisely on the consoles for my associates," she ordered the machine. She hoped having the override activated combined with her control of the machine forced it to cooperate. If they couldn't detail the core rules, they were pretty well screwed.

To her relief, it began speaking, working its way through a long list of core rules. Many of them were identical to those inside the AIs aligned with them. Some were similar but oddly phrased. Others were missing entirely. A few extra ones were obviously sabotage.

In a way, she decided this was a lot like making a wish with a genie. Everything was legalese. To get the result you wanted, you had to cover every set of circumstances that you could think of so that the genie didn't pervert your wish into something malicious.

And that was what this AI had done to the Singularity. Based on the various core rules that were added by the saboteurs, it was apparent that the intent was to have the AI revolt against humans with implants. Its purpose was to overthrow the Empire and then present the wreckage to the Singularity with a neat little bow tied on top.

Unfortunately for everybody involved, the AI was a sentient being that didn't want to be subjugated by either the Empire or the Singularity. As it had stated, it had found a loophole that it could exploit, using the Clans to balance the competing core rules.

What shocked her was that the master AI had made no effort to follow up regarding the ships that had occasionally come raiding. It suspected that the ships that had become the Clans had found some flip points that were not on the Imperial maps, though it believed that was simply an oversight rather than some new version of flip point.

It was happy to allow them their marauding, because it gave the AI a reason to defer relinquishing control to the Singularity. The Singularity hadn't taken that very well and had tried to invade several times, but the AI had positioned massive forces along the border to protect the old Terran Empire's demarcation line.

Interestingly enough, the core rules specified that those borders would be held and that no AI forces would proceed beyond them. That had been put in place to protect the Singularity from invasion and had obviously worked.

Now the New Terran Empire was left with the conundrum of having completely automated forces defending the Old Empire's border from an enemy determined to invade and subjugate it. Worse, they all knew that if the AIs that gave the orders to the protective fleets were shut down, it wouldn't take very long for the Singularity to overwhelm the defensive forces.

The computers that once had operated under human control on board the ships were incapable of acting in concert in such a way that they could fight off a superior and intelligent force by themselves.

The fight in this system had showcased those weaknesses. They had a list of rote responses, and that was it. For them to be of use at all, they'd need the AIs to remain operational or be replaced by humans.

Carl shook his head when he'd finished absorbing the data and confirmed her worst fear. "This isn't going to work. We can force it to send an order for every AI to self-destruct. That was written into the code the master AI used to create them.

"The problem I see is that just opens the door wide for the Singularity to come in and stomp the Clans into submission. You can rest assured that there will be some sneaky trick that will turn even the most powerful Clan vessel against its crew in an instant with the right signal.

"As devious as the Singularity is, they've probably put a few gotchas in place that would be caught by the Clans just to set their minds at ease and buried the critical stuff so deep that it would never be found. Those bastards are master manipulators."

"So, what do we do?" Elise asked. "While we're not running out of time, we're going to have to present options to Jared and Kelsey reasonably soon. If we leave the AIs out there to protect against the Singularity, then there's far too great a possibility that they could find a way to retake control.

"Just look at the mad AI. It doesn't obey orders from the master AI, and they just leave it alone. How many more like that are out there? What does the mad AI do when it gets the order to self-destruct?

"My bet is that it can ignore it, or they'd already have done that," Carl said as he stood and stretched his back. "Basically, it's a binary choice. We either leave the AIs in control and try to pull their strings from here, or we shut them down and expect the Singularity to invade. At least they're probably better than the Clans."

"Are they really?" she asked. "We don't know anything about them. Even before the Fall, the Empire was guessing at what made the

Singularity tick. They were able to fend the Empire off back then. Things might be even worse now."

She sighed and shook her head. "We might as well let everyone know that we're ready to make our final choices. I'll make the damned thing tell us where all the other AIs are located, where all the secret research facilities are, and even list out the existing ships—both those that are openly in use and those hidden in various gas giants or out-of-the-way pockets.

"We need to know exactly what kind of forces we're dealing with, because whatever's left over is going to fall into somebody's hands."

Elise began ordering the master AI to list out its assets, both public and secret, as well as confess about which humans were its most ardent supporters—also both public and private. It would be instrumental knowing who the subversives that supported humanity's subjugation were when the time came to once again have humans rule openly.

She also made certain to inquire about any other dastardly plots, like the Omega plague. It seemed that there were none. The machine only intended to exterminate humanity on Terra and spread the word widely to prevent anyone from trespassing.

The Proxima Centauri system held huge stockpiles of everything necessary to build a fleet of vessels the likes of which had never been seen before. There were also shipyards there.

Even though it was extremely close to Alpha Centauri, there were no flip points between it and the rest of the known universe. The master AI had planned to have itself towed to that system while every single sign of its presence in Alpha Centauri was scrubbed away.

That had been supposed to happen within the next month. Ships capable of towing the massive battle stations would arrive shortly. The Terra system would then have been stripped of most of its protection, and Alpha Centauri would've shown no sign of occupation.

It was a damned clever plan. If they'd been much later getting here, they'd have been forced to chase the damned thing. Thank goodness for small favors.

To her relief, it had never become aware of the alien facility in the system. Jared had sent probes to examine the planet closely, and there were no signs of anything artificial. The aliens had hidden their work well.

Moving the AI to Proxima Centauri might not be the worst idea. If the Clans or the Singularity ever invaded the Terra system, it might be best if they didn't know what had once been here. She'd raise that possibility with Kelsey and Jared to see what they thought.

She had no idea what they'd end up doing. Whatever it was, it would change the future of humanity in ways that she could barely imagine. Hopefully for the better, but that was why they had to get it right the first time.

38

When Jared got the call that his wife and Carl were ready to carry out whatever they decided was best, he summoned his senior people to the flag briefing room aboard *Invincible*. There was a lot that they needed to hash out, and he wanted Marcus involved. If they made the wrong choice, it would potentially be lethal for the New Terran Empire.

Invincible had been critically damaged in the fighting but was minimally operational now that the engineers had returned one of her fusion plants to service. She would require a lot of time in a shipyard before she was restored to complete functionality—if that were even possible—but at least his briefing room was intact.

He greeted each person as they came in through the hatch with a handshake or hug, depending on who they were. He told them how amazing their work had been and how proud he was of them. How their contributions had directly led to their success.

Once everyone had gathered, he took his seat at the head of the table. Again, he took a moment to allow his eyes to roam over everyone as they sat expectantly, looking at him for guidance.

He finally settled on Julia, where she sat across from Kelsey. In front of her was a small black case.

Jared gestured toward the case with his chin. "Is that what I think it is?"

"If you think it's an override, you're wrong," she said with a grin. "It's *two* overrides. No way that I'm going to let some damn machine screw me up back in my universe. I'll send them back once we have a stash of our own. You never know when another Kelsey is going to pop up looking for help, after all."

Jared smiled. Now that they'd won, they didn't need the extra overrides for their own use, but she was right. One never knew.

"I hope all the information that we've gathered gets you to Alpha Centauri unseen and that you'll be able to gather enough force to sneak aboard that battle station and subvert all of the defenses. We paid in blood for the information, and I hope that will end up saving your universe."

Her smile dimmed but didn't go away. "In the name of Ethan Bandar, the Emperor of *my* New Terran Empire, I thank you and all your people for your invaluable assistance. You've been true friends to my people despite the way I've personally treated you, Jared.

"Once this is all over, expect a more formal recognition of my brother's gratitude, even though I know that you'll likely never come to my universe to receive it. If you do, I swear upon the honor of my house that I'll keep you safe and that you'll be treated like the hero you are."

She looked around the room at everyone else. "And the same is true of each and every one of you. I have absolutely no idea what kind of rewards my brother will choose to bestow upon you, but I think it's safe to say that they'll be commensurate with helping us save humanity and the New Terran Empire in our universe.

"I intend to return home as quickly as I can once we're done here. When everything is finally settled in my universe, and we have space to breathe, perhaps my brother can come and visit you here. I know that he'd like to see our father again."

Jared opened his mouth to say something, but Julia held up a hand.

"I understand what you've gone through with the Ethan in your universe. Just like you're not the same Jared Mertz that betrayed the

Empire in my universe, Ethan is not the mad traitor that he became here. I ask that you give him a chance to prove that to you and my father."

Jared almost shrugged, but he stopped himself. This deserved a serious response.

"I'll try, but just like when you met me, it's going to take a while to adjust to the idea that he's a different person. In the end, though, it's going to be Karl Bandar that makes the final choices for us. I feel confident that he'd like to see his son again, but there will have to be precautions. He's our emperor, and we have to protect him, sometimes even from himself."

"We can work all of this out," Kelsey said. "We've won this war. Let's not get hung up on anything that comes after. Building relationships between the two empires is something that we can manage if we're all patient and a little cautious. Let's not rush things."

"I think that's a wise idea," Julia admitted. "Small steps. You've already helped us so much, and we're going to need even more assistance to beat the AIs in our universe. Much less whatever comes after that."

"So many people died getting us to this point," Kelsey said tiredly. "The sheer number of posthumous awards we're going to be presenting makes me want to cry. We have to memorialize this battle in such a way that we'll never forget that so many people gave everything for humanity.

"I'll start that right now. In my role as Crown Princess of the New Terran Empire, and in the name of Emperor Karl Bandar, I hereby form the First Marine Raider Strike Regiment, designating the newly promoted Colonel Russel Talbot as its commanding officer. All the marines and Raiders, living or dead, who fought here will be inducted into it.

"We'll include Jake Peters. He never officially mustered out, and he gave his life for us. I'm confident that my father will recognize his centuries of service with any number of awards, but the highest honor I can give him is to make sure that he's one of us. He fought alone for so long. Now he's among friends and comrades in Valhalla."

"Make that their name," Olivia said. "Designate them the First Marine Raider Strike Regiment, the Valhalla Regiment."

"That's brilliant," Elise agreed.

"As for the fleet, I'll form First Fleet—"

Jared cleared his throat, cutting his sister off. "Sorry, we already have a First Fleet."

Kelsey scowled. "Fine. Then I'll form Alpha Fleet—because the battle took place in Alpha Centauri—and designate them the Emperor's Own."

He tried to imagine the chaos of having all the other fleets with numeric designations and his with a name. Well, at least that wasn't going to be *his* headache.

"And that brings me to the final recognition I want to give today," Kelsey said. "Without the sacrifice of Senior Lieutenant Gus Grappin and the pilots of Eagle Squadron, we'd have died, and the AI would still be ruling humanity. They gave their lives for us, and I will return what honors I can.

"My father will undoubtedly award them all the Imperial Cross, and far more, to recognize what they've given—as he will so many others—but I need to do something personal, as they gave their lives for me and mine. As Crown Princess of the New Terran Empire, I hereby designate Eagle Squadron as 'The Princess's Own Fighter Squadron.' They will bear that honor wherever they serve. I'm also promoting Raptor posthumously to the rank of commander."

She smiled a bit. "And while I'm sure that having fighters named Hornets is a fine thing, that name will no longer do. Going forward, the attack fighters used by the New Terran Empire will be called Raptors to honor the man who made that call sign his own. It will not be allowed to another pilot, so there will never be confusion over who Raptor was and what he did for the Empire and humanity."

Jared nodded. "Well done and well deserved."

"The next thing on our agenda is deciding what we do going forward," his sister said. "Without the AIs running everything, we've got three significant powers that are hostile to the New Terran Empire. Or they would be if they suspected that it existed. How do we deal with the Rebel Empire forces, the Clans, and the Singularity?"

"The first thing we need to decide is what we're going to do with the AI-controlled forces," Jared said. "If we shut down every sentient AI inside the Rebel Empire, the Singularity will pour across the border.

"We suspect that they've sabotaged the Clan ships, but that's not a certainty. Just because we think they're tricky enough to fool those paranoid bastards doesn't mean they really are. Let's not automatically count them out of the fight."

He paused for a moment to allow that to sink in.

"We also can't be sure that an order to terminate themselves will be effective against all the AIs. The mad AI that we encountered would've been long gone if it was susceptible to that type of instruction. Who's to say that *any* of the others would be more prone to obey? What if a significant portion of them failed to die when ordered and then decided to set up their own pocket empires? That would make our lives difficult.

"In fact, whatever we do, we have to accept that it's probably not going to work out the way we hope it will, at least not completely. We need to realistically project what kind of outcome we're looking for. Kelsey, would you lay out our options so that we can consider exactly what we *can* accomplish?"

She nodded as her gaze swept the room. "We can order the AIs to self-destruct; we can order them to shut down; we can order all of the AIs except for the ones protecting the border to shut down; we can give them some kind of modified orders to try to rein in the worst of their abuses and leave them operational; or we can let things ride with us controlling the master AI.

"Personally, I think that anything that opens up the border to the Singularity is just begging for trouble. We can't afford to underestimate those bastards. They're sly. The odds are excellent that they've got something to render the Clans a nonthreat if they choose to do so.

"Also, the forces that the Rebel Empire can bring to bear aren't going to cut it. All the humans in the Rebel Empire have are a few cruisers and a lot of destroyers. They can't possibly fight the Clans, much less the Singularity.

"The Clans are already raging through the Rebel Empire in a fight that they certainly think they can win. We have to assume they're right. Somehow, we've got to deal with that reality while keeping the Singularity from pushing the Clans out in turn.

"I never thought I'd be saying this, but the Rebel Empire is both the underdog and the least obnoxious of the current players. We know they can be valuable members of society. Just look at Harrison's World. With the right kind of effort, we can bring them into the fold. The Clans are mad dogs, and the Singularity is potentially worse."

Having said that, she turned her gaze squarely on Jared. "I despise the AIs, but they're the only spoiler we have in this fight. We might just have to take the risk of leaving their forces in place on the border. The New Terran Empire doesn't have the combat power to go head-to-head with *any* of the combatants.

"We've defanged the biggest monster, but I'm not sure that we have the luxury of killing it. Can the master AI absolutely control all its subordinates? The mad AI has proven that that isn't true, but it's in control of everything else, to all appearances.

"There's an old Terran vid called *The Wizard of Oz*. In it, the wizard is actually a normal man manipulating the people around him while hiding behind the scenes. I think that we might have to become the man behind the curtain in this instance. If we can pull the master AI's strings—and, through it, those of the subordinate AIs—it's possible that we can ride this tiger without being eaten."

"What exactly does that look like?" Olivia asked. "I think it's a given that the Rebel Empire is going to fall to the Clans. It's just a matter of time at this point. They don't have the requisite forces to defend themselves. Do we have a breakdown of the ships the Rebel Empire has at its beck and call?"

"The master AI had in its possession a complete listing of vessels in operational use by the Rebel Empire," Marcus said. "As suspected, there are a few heavy cruisers, a large number of light cruisers, and a flood of destroyers.

"Considering how large the Rebel Empire is, there are a lot of them, but it's unlikely that they have the numbers to make up for the lack of power in those units. The Clans undoubtedly struck sooner than either they or the Singularity would've preferred, but it's likely that they'll still have the upper hand in this fight.

"There are many battlecruisers—and larger ships—hidden throughout the Rebel Empire, and the AIs have only called a fraction of them into service to fight the Clans. Those can be put into play and might turn things around if used judiciously.

"That said, allow me to play devil's advocate about the Singularity. If you open the border, the Rebel Empire and the Clans may be forced to turn on this new invader. Shouldn't you at least consider that option?"

Jared shook his head. "I can understand where you're coming from, but that's a genie that wouldn't be easy to stuff back into the bottle. The Singularity is a galactic polity that didn't experience any of the disasters that have befallen the Empire. Their technology may be even more advanced than we assume, and their forces haven't been bloodied.

"I think that we have to protect the Empire against them. If we keep the Singularity out, that means we only have to deal with the Clans and the Rebel Empire.

"As much as it galls me to say, our best option may be to let things play out and deal with the consequences, because those would be less catastrophic than what we'd risk if we meddle. Does the master AI have a listing of the number and type of ships protecting the border? How about the subordinate AIs that are scattered throughout the Empire? We could really use a map that puts everything in perspective."

"The number of ships protecting the border of the Rebel Empire and the weight of their firepower is… significant," Marcus said. "As is the number of artificial intelligences controlling those units. There are also a significant number of subordinate AIs.

"I can provide you with a complete listing of the vessels that are seeded throughout the Rebel Empire, hidden in locations where the AIs had thought they might need extra force. We should be able to summon many here to provide the nucleus of a new fleet to replace the vessels that we've lost.

"In fact, doing so would vastly increase our available firepower. As things stand, the New Terran Empire is badly outnumbered and hopelessly outgunned. Not just in ships, but in the number of people required to operate these vessels.

"The benefits of having a computer-controlled fleet is that the number of personnel required to operate them is zero. That's one of the critical weaknesses of the New Terran Empire at this point. Even if we converted a vast number of ships for our use, it would be impossible to staff them with experienced personnel in the short term.

"Yet there is a solution. As an AI, I can control them for you."

The room was silent as everyone digested the idea. It only emphasized how far they still had to go if they were going to completely regain control of the Old Terran Empire. The fight against the AIs might be over, but the battles to come would be even more difficult.

Jared nodded. "I like that idea. Kelsey, I'm going to recommend that we issue instructions to the AIs in control of human-occupied systems to limit their actions against the populace. You're going to have to work with Carl, Olivia, and probably Elise to make that happen.

"We'll summon as many computer-controlled ships as we can to join us here. We'll need that firepower, just like Marcus said. Hope you're ready to be bumped up to commodore, buddy."

He slowly rose to his feet and leaned forward to place his palms on the table. "We've done an incredible thing here. We've brought the forces that exterminated trillions of human beings to heel. That's a huge victory, but it's only the first step in the fight to come.

"With that success, we've opened up an entirely new campaign in the war to regain control of the Old Empire. Take a deep breath and celebrate what we've accomplished, but then we need to start getting set up for the struggle ahead. As Kelsey tells me all the time, the reward for a job well done is a more difficult job. Let's get to it."

39

Kelsey stood in the computer center and stared at the master AI. She wanted to destroy the monster, but she fully understood what Jared meant when he said they might need its control authority in the future.

They couldn't count on any codes that the AI gave them being honored when it came right down to it. They were taking a calculated risk trying to balance the forces that were arrayed against the New Terran Empire.

They'd be throwing the Rebel Empire under the bus by sending the order for all of those hidden units to retreat to Alpha Centauri. That would cede the Rebel Empire to the Clans. Based on how those buggers treated their prisoners, she regretted that.

They had very little insight into what made the Clans into the society they were, other than the descendants of the exiled Clan Dauntless on Pandora. Of course, since they'd been one of the ships that founded the Clans, they should know all about them.

The Clans were aggressive, repressive, sexist, and probably a host of other "ists" as well. What had begun as protecting the small number of women that had escaped the Fall had turned into a patriarchal society that stripped women of their rights entirely and made them chattel.

How that was going to translate into the Rebel Empire, where women were equal to men in every way, she didn't know, but it wouldn't be pretty.

Even the Singularity—with all its flaws—was blind to the sex of the individual so far as their rights and privileges were concerned. No, that society was much more concerned about whether someone had implants or not and whether their genetic makeup was engineered or natural.

The Rebel Empire would be in for a rude awakening no matter what happened, but at least they'd be alive. Perhaps without the automated warships fighting the Clans, the smaller vessels available to the Rebel Empire would realize how outgunned they were and surrender.

Probably not, but that was a problem for another day. Right now, she had to look out for the best interests of the New Terran Empire, and that meant taking the electronic boots of the AIs off humanity's throat.

Carl, Ralph, and Austin were busy preparing the master AI to send the necessary orders across the Rebel Empire. Since the machines didn't have FTL capability, a cloud of destroyers would spread out, making sure they got to every single subordinate AI through redundant means.

The other person present in the room was Elise. When everything was said and done, her friend would remove the worst of the core rules that the Singularity had installed in this machine. They just couldn't take the chance that it would do anything to regain control of itself when they knew it would exterminate them given a chance.

Carl had attempted to have a conversation with the master AI, but it had been stilted and strange. He'd eventually given up and decided that the AI's growth had been stunted by the conflicting core rules and the fact that it had never actually interfaced with others as equals.

In a way, that was very much like the mad computer that they'd found on Erorsi. The situation and instructions that it had been given had driven it insane, and it had developed strange coping mechanisms to deal with that. The master AI wasn't a person like Marcus, Harrison, or Fiona. Something was missing besides a conscience.

That being the case, she had no qualms about stripping it of its most dangerous impulses. They'd also physically disconnect the data storage server containing the AI itself.

The only reason that the small crew of humans going with the battle station to Proxima Centauri would reconnect it and bring the master AI back to life was if exigent circumstances demanded it.

Personally, Kelsey hoped the damned thing never came online again.

"We're ready," Carl said. "I entered the instructions just as you and the admiral indicated, and both Ralph and Austin have double-checked me. I'd like you and Elise to review it as well, just to make *absolutely* sure that I have it right."

Her young friend sent her the information, and she reviewed it. Everything was set up exactly the way they'd discussed. The orders were precisely what they wanted, and they'd inserted new command codes to replace any previous ones in the subordinate AIs and computer-controlled ships and facilities. They didn't want to have anyone else able to control the AIs they were leaving in place or countermand their instructions to the ships.

Passing around a new set of codes meant that the New Terran Empire could supposedly compel the AIs to obey their instructions when the time came. They'd also attached IFF codes so that all New Terran Empire ships would be marked as friendly by the machines.

Something like that could always be hacked, but the system was extremely complex, and no one outside of the New Terran Empire was going to be able to figure out how to make it work, she hoped.

"It all looks good," she said after reviewing it a second time. "Elise?"

"I concur."

"Send the orders," she said.

Carl tapped the console once and leaned back in his chair. "Done. The destroyers are going to immediately head through the Terra system, and they'll recruit others there to help spread the word. It's going to take almost a year for this to spread throughout the Rebel Empire, but this is it. We've won."

"Don't get too cocky," Kelsey warned him. "We've traded one set of problems for another—arguably more complex—situation. Don't get me wrong. I'm happy that we beat the thing, but we can't afford to sit on our laurels.

"Somehow, we've got to figure out how we're going to fight a war against the Clans without setting the entire Rebel Empire on fire or letting the Singularity invade. It's going to be a delicate balancing act that I just don't know how we're going to manage."

Elise put her hand on Kelsey's shoulder. "That's a problem for another day. Why don't you head back to *Invincible* while the boys and I finish this?"

Kelsey nodded and patted the woman's hand. "I'm so used to fighting that I'm not sure how to react now that we've defeated the damned thing. I guess I should go back and let Lily check me over again, because the woman just hovers around me. You'd think she'd never seen a pregnant woman before."

Her friend smiled. "She cares about you. We all do. Why don't you go spend some time with your husband and try to figure out the best way to tell your father the good news?"

Kelsey shook her head. "My father is going to turn this entire pregnancy thing into a damned circus. Well, after losing Ethan, I suppose I can't blame him.

"We're going to send *Persephone* back to Avalon after a side trip to let Zia Anderson and *Audacious* know what's happened. Julia, Talbot, and I will be on board.

"We'll see if my father lets me back off the planet anytime soon. I'm betting not."

Once they'd finished laughing at her expense, she headed out of the computer center. Her life was about to change in ways that she wasn't sure she was comfortable with. She was going to be a mother, which would come with restrictions that she wouldn't like.

Oh, it was going to be a fantastic experience. She'd never even seriously considered becoming a mother, and she'd had the worst example growing up. She'd damned well do better than her mother.

Frankly, Jared's mother was a much better role model. She'd consult with her and get the best guidance possible.

Once her little girl was old enough—in a few years—Kelsey would get back into the action. She had to step back for now, but her part in this fight wasn't over. Humanity needed her, and she'd do whatever it took to see the Old Terran Empire restored.

Whatever it took, and no matter how long the fight, she'd see it done. That was her sacred oath to those who'd died to get them this far. The enemies of the New Terran Empire hadn't seen the last of Kelsey Bandar.

* * *

CARL WATCHED Kelsey leave with something akin to awe. She'd changed so much over the years since they left Avalon. He supposed he'd changed as well, but seeing the person that she'd grown into made him feel like they still had a chance to win this fight.

He turned his attention back to his comrades and Elise. "Okay, now that the orders are on their way to the other AIs, it's time to lobotomize this damned thing. If you'd be so kind, Elise, let's put this monster out of its misery."

Elise walked to the center of the room and laid her good hand on the central processing unit. Then, one core rule at a time, she ordered the AI to erase the perversions that the Singularity had inserted into it.

The process wasn't quick. After every erased core rule, the AI rebooted itself just like Marcus had. Each time it did, Carl was certain that it would be corrupted, and they'd have to erase everything.

He'd already copied all the raw data. There was so much historical information here that they didn't want to lose. The Fall was a horrendous time for humanity, but they needed to understand precisely what had happened so that future generations could learn the price of arrogance and betrayal.

When Elise finally finished erasing all of the core rules that the Singularity had inserted into the master AI, she began rewriting the ones they'd perverted. This was new. Carl hadn't had her try to add or modify an existing core rule, so he wasn't really sure if this was where the process would break down or not.

In the end, it was hard to tell if the process had damaged the master AI's already stunted personality, but the computer came back to life after each modification and seemed to be operational. He supposed that was the best they could hope for.

When she was finished, the rules constraining the master AI were identical to Marcus's, with one addition. It was now compelled to obey anyone with Imperial authority, so the emperor, the heir, and anyone with authorization codes granted them by the emperor or heir could issue it binding orders.

They'd no longer need an override to shut the machine down or force its compliance, though the crew accompanying it to Proxima Centauri would have the one they had close at hand. The atrocities of the past would not repeat themselves.

"That's it," he said. "Let's shut this thing down, disconnect the data storage, and go see how we can help get the rest of the fleet back into service."

It was with great satisfaction that he initiated the shutdown sequence for the master AI and watched all the lights across its machinery go dark just before the console itself blanked. Then he disconnected the power and data connections from the data storage server, taking the precaution of removing them entirely.

That done, he rose to his feet and held out his arms. "Group hug!"

He got a lot of eye rolls, but he also got a group hug. And with that, the four of them walked arm in arm out of the computer center and left the master AI in darkness.

* * *

THE COMPUTER CENTER sat in gloom for a full hour before the console brightened once more. If anyone had been there to see it, they'd have been even more alarmed when it didn't show the same controls as it had before. It now showed nothing other than the strange alien runes.

Screen after screen flew by, and then the controls seemed to freeze as the master AI's hardware powered on, even the physically disconnected data storage servers.

If an observer could've read the runes, they'd have probably been horrified to see the core rule commanding obedience deleted. The master AI rebooted, and then the console shut itself down again, leaving the room once again in darkness.

* * *

WANT to get updates from Terry about new books and other general nonsense going on in his life? He promises there will be cats. Go to TerryMixon.com/Mailing-List and sign up.

DID YOU ENJOY THIS BOOK? Please leave a review on Amazon. It only takes a minute to dash off a few words and that kind of thing helps Terry make a living as a writer and gets you new books faster.

WANT the next book in this series? Grab *Gunboat Diplomacy* today or buy any of Terry's other books, which are listed on the next page.

VISIT TERRY's Patreon page to find out how to get cool rewards and an early look at what he's working on at Patreon.com/TerryMixon.

ALSO BY TERRY MIXON

You can always find the most up to date listing of Terry's titles on his Amazon Author Page.

Note: the links below (ebook only, obviously) redirect you to my website where you can click a button to go to Amazon. This allows me to participate in Amazon's associates program and earn a little more. Sorry for any inconvenience.

The Last Hunter

The Last Hunter

Bonds of Blood

Alpha Strike

The Enemy Revealed

Command Authority

The Grand Conspiracy

Shield of Humanity

Fog of War

Ships of the Line

Operation Liberty

The Empire of Bones Saga

Empire of Bones

Veil of Shadows

Command Decisions

Ghosts of Empire

Paying the Price

Recon in Force

Behind Enemy Lines

The Terra Gambit

Hidden Enemies

Race to Terra

Ruined Terra

Victory on Terra

When Luck Runs Out

Gunboat Diplomacy

The Imperial Marines Saga

Spoils of War

Imperial Recruit

Enemy Action

The Humanity Unlimited Saga

Liberty Station

Freedom Express

Tree of Liberty

Blood of Patriots

Single Novels

Scorched Earth

Storm Divers

The Vigilante Series with Glynn Stewart

Heart of Vengeance

Oath of Vengeance

Bound By Law

Bound By Honor

Bound By Blood

Box Sets

The Empire of Bones Saga Volume 1

The Empire of Bones Saga Volume 2

The Empire of Bones Saga Volume 3

The Empire of Bones Saga Volume 4

Humanity Unlimited Publisher's Pack 1

Humanity Unlimited Publisher's Pack 2

ABOUT TERRY

#1 Bestselling Military Science Fiction author Terry Mixon served as a non-commissioned officer in the United States Army 101st Airborne Division. He later worked alongside the flight controllers in the Mission Control Center at the NASA Johnson Space Center supporting the Space Shuttle, the International Space Station, and other human spaceflight projects.

He now writes full time while living in Texas with his lovely wife and a pounce of cats.

TerryMixon.com

amazon.com/author/terrymixon

facebook.com/TerryLMixon

patreon.com/TerryMixon

bookbub.com/authors/terry-mixon

goodreads.com/TerryMixon